About the Author

John Steinberg was born in 1952 and spent many years in business before becoming a writer in 2007. Since then, he has co-written and produced comedies for the stage and has created a series of books for children. Nadine is his third novel. He is married with three children and lives in North London.

NADINE

John Steinberg

2QT Limited (Publishing)

First edition published 2019
2QT Limited (Publishing)
Settle, North Yorkshire BD 24 9BZ
www.2qt.co.uk

Cover concept & illustration by Balcony Art & Design Studio

Printed in Great Britain by IngramSparks UK

All characters in this book other than those clearly in the public domain
are fictitious, and any resemblance to real persons, living or dead,
is purely coincidental.

A CIP catalogue record for this book will be available
from the British Library
ISBN 978-1-912014-28-6

A spark remains in those we leave behind.

A Monday Morning in August…

London, 2012

Greenberg, biting into a smoked salmon bagel, stared aimlessly down on the rush-hour traffic from his office high above the Duke's Theatre in London's Soho. He always ate when he was stressed. Down below, a traffic warden had appeared from nowhere and was placing a parking ticket on his 1985 Bentley Continental, which he'd inadvertently left in a loading bay outside Sammy's Sandwich Bar.

'Bravo!' he cheered. 'Tow it away. You'd be doing me a favour. It's on its last legs anyway.' At least he could see the funny side of it. Stuffing the rest of the bagel into his mouth, he wiped his lips on a napkin. If things weren't bad enough, he'd now have indigestion to add to his worries.

The August heat was overpowering. Greenberg passed a stubby hand through his head of curly grey hair.

Despite his current financial problems, it was a relief to come to work. He had tried talking to his wife about the dire state of their affairs, but knew he was wasting his breath. It was years since Suzanne had taken any interest in his business. So long as she still had her expense account and her personal trainer three times a week, she appeared happy enough. How was she to know another show had closed early and left him practically bankrupt, with the very real possibility that their house would be repossessed? Thank goodness the villa in Spain was in her name.

Turning around, Greenberg caught sight of himself in the mirror, and saw the dark shadows under his eyes and puffy complexion. He stuck out his tongue – not a pretty sight – and hardly reassuring for someone who worried constantly about their health.

Moving over to his desk, Greenberg slumped into his chair and glanced at the pile of unread scripts in front of him. Maybe there was a winner in there somewhere. That's the way he'd always thought and, up to recently, it usually paid off. The trouble now was that he'd run out of money.

The first six weeks of his musical adaptation of *The Scarlet Pimpernel* had been fine. The house had been two thirds full for most performances and he'd broken even. Then two spanking new shows had opened in theatreland the same week. Audiences at the Duke's immediately dwindled and Peter Greenberg began to lose money hand over fist. It was as if someone had it in for him, he thought woefully.

Four weeks later, just halfway through its designated four-month run, they were forced to close and he was facing losses to the tune of half a million quid.

Greenberg cringed at the memory of that night.

Thirty years at the top of his profession, starting when he was a boy wonder of twenty-one, a decade of the longest-running musicals in the West End... It all counted for nothing. His theatre had gone dark.

He gazed at the line of awards adorning the walls of his

office. How had it gone so wrong?

Although it galled him to admit it, he might have lost his touch.

There was only one way out of his predicament.

He needed a hit and he needed it now.

Greenberg felt his innate optimism starting to return. Taking a Romeo y Julieta cigar out of his breast pocket, he nipped off its end and lit up.

Through a cloud of fragrant smoke, he heard the gurgling sound of the percolator coming from the kitchenette. Heavy footsteps approached as a young woman with a long horsey face and wearing baggy shorts and Converse sneakers entered the office. He stopped what he was doing and looked up at Issy Williams, his new PA. She was carrying a selection of the morning papers under one arm and holding a small china cup in her other hand. The aroma of strong coffee stirred Greenberg's senses.

'Morning, Issy. How was your weekend?' he said, sounding upbeat for the benefit of his sole employee.

'It was really good, thanks, Mr Greenberg. My brother Ryan was home on leave from his unit in Afghanistan. We had a bit of a celebration,' the young woman divulged, overcoming her usual shyness. She let the papers slide on to the desk, knocking an iPad out of its holder. Then she placed the espresso cup in front of her employer.

'Sorry. I should have been more careful,' she said, blushing with embarrassment.

'It's nothing. Forget about it,' Greenberg replied, trying not to let his own nerves show. Issy was willing enough, and the way business was going at the moment he couldn't afford anything better than someone fresh out of university.

Issy Williams said timidly, 'Were the roses OK you asked me to arrange for your wedding anniversary?'

'Fabulous. My wife adored them,' Greenberg lied, glancing at the framed photo of a tanned, thin-faced woman with a mass of red hair. He had no intention of mentioning the row Suzanne had initiated because he hadn't bought her a suitably expensive gift.

'Is there anything else bothering you?' he enquired, wondering why Issy was continuing to hover over him.

'Well, actually there is something. I hope you don't mind me bringing it up, and I know things have been quite difficult recently, but it's just that my mother wants to know if everything's all right with my job. You see, I've still got my student loan to pay off, and—'

'What? Just because of one or two minor setbacks? No need to worry about *that*.' Greenberg laughed dismissively, slamming the cup down on the desk harder than he intended to and spattering his clean white shirt. 'Now, I've been summoned to the accountants this afternoon, so don't let me delay you any further if you've got work to do. I imagine the landlord's rent is due and the actors are still owed their holiday pay, so you can be getting on with that.' Even as he spoke, Greenberg knew he was perilously near the limit of his overdraft.

Sensing that she might have overstepped the mark, the PA mumbled something then turned around and scuttled back to her office.

'And please do find out when the engineer's coming to fix the air conditioning. Feels like this week is going to be another scorcher,' Greenberg called out after her, confident that he'd allayed her fears.

Issy Williams had made up her mind, however, to

continue looking for a new job. Her first interview was that same afternoon – with a man she had borrowed a smart new dress for.

Greenberg picked up one of the newspapers and began browsing through the arts section. His attention was immediately drawn to a headline.

Celebrated Broadway Director Considering Permanent Move to the US

The article continued:

Dominic Langley, with several Broadway hits to his credit, appears intent on following his latest success by relocating to America. Speaking at the Tony Awards ceremony last night in New York, where his show Brooklyn Brawl *picked up seven accolades, including Best Director, Dominic said, 'I've worked on and off Broadway for the last five years. The action is here, the best writers are here – so why would I want to be anywhere else?'*

Greenberg tried, as he had done on so many previous occasions, to put the young man's name out of his mind. This time, however, creeping slowly into his overburdened heart, the past came to life once again, reminding him of his unfulfilled obligation to the only woman he had ever truly loved.

Nadine.

Greenberg recalled the last entry in her diary. She wrote that she hadn't deserved the love he had given her, and asked for his forgiveness. Her final wish, so far denied to her, was that her son Dominic should know the truth about his mother.

Putting down his cigar, Greenberg sat back in his chair and closed his eyes. Several lifetimes had gone by since he had last thought about Nadine. But nothing would make him forget her, nor the first time he saw her onstage, all those years ago…

PART ONE

The Girl in Blue

1

London, 1974

Greenberg bustled his way to his seat in the packed Victorian theatre. Being in the business had its uses. Even the fact that his enemy Ken Brookman was the producer hadn't stopped Greenberg from getting a couple of complimentary tickets for Brookman's musical, *Me and My Girl*.

Ken, the vindictive sod, had never forgiven him for stealing the limelight with *One Step Up*, Greenberg's play about factory girls turning around the fortunes of a sinking fashion business. In Ken's opinion the West End was *his* domain where musicals were concerned, and he didn't want anyone – especially a precocious kid of twenty-four – moving in on his territory.

Greenberg looked at the empty seat next to him. Melissa, his fiancée, had cried off at the last moment. He wasn't that surprised, as theatre was not really her thing. They had been going out for a year and, with her being the eldest daughter, Melissa's parents, Costas and Maria, were pressurising them to get married. All his friends were tying the knot, so it seemed the right thing to do. It wasn't as though he couldn't afford it. He had his own flat in the smart area of Marylebone and money in the bank. He could certainly support a family. And he did quite fancy the dark-haired girl with the curvaceous figure and bubbly personality. It was just that he was more in love with the idea of getting married than he was with Melissa herself.

At that moment the orchestra came to life. The curtain went up and the chorus broke into their opening routine.

Greenberg's attention was immediately focused on one particular dancer, a stunning girl with short blonde hair, wearing a pretty 1930s-style blue dress with a wide skirt. The lightness in the way she moved onstage made her stand out from the rest of the cast. And there was something else. The other dancers all seemed to be following her lead.

Right then, Greenberg was glad that Melissa wasn't with him. He had to find a way of being introduced to this girl. He couldn't keep his eyes off her. Fortunately, Ken wasn't in the audience that evening, which gave Greenberg the opportunity that he needed. He checked in his wallet for his business cards, and after the show ended, he made his way backstage.

'Evening, Vince. Congratulations ... great show,' Greenberg said, going up to shake the stage manager's limp hand.

'If it's Ken you're after, he's not here, thank the Lord,' replied the effeminate man with a heavily pockmarked face. Vincent Coates had the same low opinion of the producer as Greenberg had. Experienced stage managers like Vince were rare – and you had to treat them properly, Greenberg thought, not bully and humiliate them as Ken did.

'Don't suppose there's any chance of an introduction to

a certain member of your cast, is there?' Greenberg asked.

'The girl in blue – with the legs?' Vince said intuitively.

'How did you know?' Greenberg asked, trying to retain his poise.

'You and a thousand others,' the stage manager grunted.

'Who is she? What do you know about her?'

'Listen, ducky, take my advice. You're wasting your time.'

'Can't you at least tell me her name?'

'Nadine, and she's French. But that's all you're getting, unless you want to get me sacked,' the lanky man said, waving his hands frantically in the air.

Realising that he wasn't going to be allowed backstage, Greenberg handed Vince a business card, saying, 'There are auditions for a new play of mine starting in a few weeks. I will need a stage manager too. Don't suppose you know someone who might be available?'

'What's it paying?' Vince Coates enquired, his interest suddenly aroused.

'Normal Equity rates plus a bit more on top. Say fifty pounds a week. Anyway, do let me know if you can think of someone.' Greenberg turned to leave.

'Yes, I will. You never know, it might suit *me*,' Vince told him.

'Why doesn't that surprise me?' Greenberg muttered under his breath as he left the building.

Greenberg didn't have to wait long. A fortnight later, he found Vincent Coates waiting in the reception of his plush suite of offices above the Aquascutum shop in Regent Street. The rumour he had heard circulating round the West End was that Coates had been caught with his head buried in the crotch of a young male member of the cast during the interval of his show and had been dismissed on the spot.

Greenberg didn't care. He didn't hesitate to offer the out-of-work stage manager his new musical at a higher wage. In return, as he expected, Vince had no qualms about supplying his new employer with the personal details of the French dancer. However, the fellow took a perverse pleasure in telling him that the chap she was with was married and had the dancer well ensconced in a flat in Chelsea. It came as a blow.

Despite knowing what he was up against, Greenberg refused to be deterred. He had already ended it with Melissa. Unable to get the dancer with the fascinating looks out of his head, he decided it was unfair to prolong a relationship that had no future.

It was a rainy December morning when Greenberg arranged to meet Nadine for lunch in the Kings Road, Chelsea.

Nadine was installed at a corner table of the fashionable Don Paolino Italian restaurant when he arrived. She was dressed in a baggy woollen cardigan, tight blue jeans and a pair of brown suede knee-length boots. Even without make-up, Greenberg was taken aback by her exceptional beauty. Her flawless complexion and the way her huge almond-shaped eyes lit up when she smiled simply took his breath away. For a moment, he was staring at the film star Mia Farrow.

He introduced himself and extended his hand to his guest.

'I'm Peter Greenberg. I hope you haven't been waiting

long. It was impossible to get a taxi.'

'Hello, I'm Nadine Bertrand. Please don't worry. I've only been here a few minutes,' the girl replied in a soft French accent. 'Paris is the same when it rains.'

'Congratulations, by the way. I hear the show is a great success,' Greenberg said, sitting down opposite her.

'Our director is happy, I think, with our performances. I hope Monsieur Brookman is also.'

'Well, from what I saw, he certainly should be. Packed houses and the hottest show in town. He's probably raking it in.'

When the waiter came to take their orders, Nadine said, 'A mixed salad is enough. I have rehearsals this afternoon.'

Greenberg had no intention of eating a salad.

'Mario,' he said, 'I'll have my usual.'

'Would you like some fried zucchini with the escalope milanese, Signor Greenberg?'

'How can I resist?' the producer grinned.

'And some wine? We have a new Barolo.'

'Just coffee,' Nadine interjected swiftly.

'I'll have a glass of the Barolo,' Greenberg said, disappointed not to be sharing a whole bottle of his favourite wine with this woman he so wanted to impress.

Suddenly the colour drained from the dancer's face. Without any explanation, she clapped a hand to her mouth and dashed to the ladies. When she returned, five minutes later, their food had arrived and was on the table.

'Nadine, are you all right?' Greenberg asked with genuine concern. 'The restaurant will call you a taxi if you are feeling unwell.'

'It's nothing, really. Just a stomach bug. A few of the other girls have it also,' she said, brushing the matter aside and beginning to pick at her salad.

'Well, so long as you're sure,' he stressed, taking a large mouthful of veal.

'You mentioned on the phone that you were starting auditions for a new show,' the dancer said, becoming pragmatic.

Greenberg chuckled to himself. Actors and dancers dreaded the prospect of being out of work.

'It's a new musical. Actually, it was a play that I tried out in a small venue, and I'm currently adapting it for the West End. It's about a group of policewomen who work nights in a strip club to earn extra money.'

Nadine's eyes opened wide.

'It sounds fantastic – so original. And the auditions, when do they begin?'

'Soon. I'll be in touch.' Greenberg knew full well that her production was in the last fortnight of its run. The timing was perfect.

'And the show will be for how long?' Nadine was naturally curious about the length of her employment.

'Four months for sure, but it could be for longer if it does as well as I anticipate.'

Greenberg was quite used to having to manage the expectations of the artistes he employed. It was part of their inherent insecurity caused by an unstable profession.

'Yes, I can say that I would be most interested,' Nadine responded, nodding her head.

'Great. I'm sure I can sort something out with your agent. It's Lesley Stanton, isn't it?'

Nadine's face broke into a broad smile.

'Monsieur Greenberg, you are very well informed.'

'It's my job to be. And please, call me Peter.'

'Actually, I prefer Greenberg. It suits you better.' Nadine then glanced anxiously at her watch. 'I'm sorry, Greenberg, but I really do need to go.'

'Yes, of course.' Disappointed that the lunch date had been so brief, Greenberg asked for the bill.

Collecting their things, the pair left the restaurant together, and walked out into the teeming rain, which had not eased off.

When their shared taxi turned into the Haymarket and pulled up outside the theatre, Nadine grabbed hold of the wicker basket containing her costume. Aware that he only had a few seconds to stake his claim on the dancer, Greenberg panicked.

'I'll call you about the auditions,' was all he could think of saying.

Nadine returned a fleeting smile as she jumped out gracefully.

'Goodbye, Greenberg,' she called back. They were her only words as she disappeared through the stage door.

Greenberg paid the driver and, despite the rain, returned on foot to his office, a quarter of a mile away. He felt disconsolate. Beyond showing the usual interest in a new role, Nadine had not given him any encouragement on a personal level.

Patience had never been his greatest attribute. But, if he had to take things slowly in order to gain her trust and then her affection, that was what he would do. He would leave it a few days, then call Lesley Stanton to ask the old harridan to provide him with some recommendations for the auditions of his new musical. That way, Nadine's name was bound to be on the list. It would put things on a professional level and give him another opportunity to

15

get to know the Parisian girl better.

2

Later that afternoon, Nadine left the doctor's surgery in Flood Street, Chelsea, her test results in her hand. Her worst suspicions had been confirmed. After being cajoled into having unprotected sex, she was three months' pregnant. Returning to the theatre in a daze, she tried to think clearly.

There was only one solution. To have an abortion. The show was in the last two weeks of its run, so there would still be time if she acted quickly. She wondered whether she should even tell Charles. After all, he was married.

So much had happened in the two years since she'd been in London. At first, she'd been working nights as a waitress in Keats, an exclusive French restaurant in Hampstead, north-west London, close to where she lived at that time. She spent her days auditioning for any dance roles that her agent could find for her.

The evening she met Charles was still so vivid in her mind. Nadine had been waiting on a table reserved in the name of Langley, and found herself being chatted up by a good-looking man dining with a couple of friends, who he was obviously trying to impress. Dressed in a tie and navy-blue blazer, she put him in his early thirties. His air of superiority was consistent with a British public school education. Charles flattered her, said he could tell by the way she moved that she was a dancer, and boasted in front of his friends that he knew several producers who might give her a chance to audition.

When he paid the bill, Charles left Nadine a generous tip, along with his telephone number on a piece of paper.

Nadine hadn't given the matter any further thought until a few weeks later, when she came across the piece of paper tucked away in her shoulder bag. Out of curiosity, she decided to make the call. She and Charles arranged to meet for drinks in a wine bar opposite Harrods in Knightsbridge.

Over a bottle of champagne, Charles owned up immediately. He confessed he had absolutely no knowledge of the theatre and was just using it as an excuse to see her again. Rather than feel upset for having been misled, Nadine was merely disarmed by his easy manner. Charles confided in her that he was heir to a large estate in the north of England and that he didn't really need to work. The fact that he had trained as a City stockbroker in his uncle's firm was just to give him some sort of occupation to keep his father happy, he said. Personally, he preferred the ski slopes of Gstaad or cruising around the Med on the family's hundred-foot yacht to the world of business, which he found incredibly dull.

Charles then disclosed that he was married, which didn't come as any great surprise to her. He had met his wife, Clare, he said, at a debutante ball when she was nineteen. Being a distant cousin to Queen Elizabeth, she was considered by his family to be suitable marriage material.

'It was a loveless union from the start,' Charles told her. 'Why, we even had separate bedrooms on our honeymoon in Rome.'

Later, when they proved unable to start a family, it was expected that they should stay together. In the meantime, the marriage had broken down. Clare had moved back to her parents' place in Suffolk and Charles stayed on in the family house in London.

'It's awfully lonely, living on my own,' he said to her, and she reached out to take his hand.

A romantic relationship followed that Nadine was powerless to prevent, even if she'd wanted to. Needing little persuasion, she moved into a flat Charles owned in Chelsea, and soon they were living together.

As Nadine left the theatre that evening, she felt exhausted. There was no doubt that the earlier revelation had affected her performance. All she wanted now was a hot bath and to be in bed before Charles got home. Tonight she couldn't face telling him that she was pregnant. She'd had enough drama for one day.

Nadine was just about to hail a taxi when she saw his grey Aston Martin parked on the other side of the street. Charles was sitting behind the wheel, a dour expression on his face. Unnerved, she got into the passenger seat and they drove off in silence. His usual good humour was missing, and Nadine wondered if there were difficulties at work or whether he had had another argument with his wife. Whatever it was, it must be something serious. Charles had never waited for her outside the theatre before.

When the car pulled up outside the block of flats in Chelsea, Nadine turned to him and asked, 'What is wrong, Charles?' Her lover sighed.

'I had a meeting with my father today, and I'm afraid

there's a problem,' he said glumly. 'He made it clear that unless I make a go of it with Clare, I'll be disinherited.'

'But you said that you were getting a divorce.'

'Clare's entitled to half of everything. It's out of the question.'

'Are you saying that we can't see each other any more?'

'My wife came back to London this evening. We've talked it over and agreed to give our marriage a second chance.'

Nadine searched for something to say, but the words wouldn't come.

'Look, Nadine, I'm not throwing you out, and I promise I'll help you find somewhere else.'

'I just didn't expect… I mean, it's all so sudden.' Tears began welling up in her eyes.

'And when things settle down, we can still meet up,' Charles continued unconvincingly.

For the second time that day, Nadine was in shock. It seemed like a bad dream, and the day had begun so optimistically too, with the prospect of a new musical at the end of her current run.

Charles let her out of the car and drove off at great speed. Despondently, Nadine entered the 1930s block of flats, walked past the night porter's desk and, after giving the man a brief nod, took the lift to the seventh floor. Too tired to eat, she curled up in bed, still fully dressed, and immediately fell into a deep slumber.

Nadine dreamt she was on the podium during her graduation ceremony at the Conservatoire de Paris, receiving her professional dance diploma. She was looking desperately around for her mother, but Irène Bertrand was missing. Nadine rushed out, running as fast as she could, the applause still ringing in her ears. Suddenly she saw a large cardboard box blowing away in the wind, leaving a trail of grubby clothes in its wake. Nadine managed to catch hold of it. She badly wanted to read the writing on the box.

The name of Soeur Jeanne le Croix, Couvent de Saint Dominic, appeared in bold letters.

'Who is she?' Nadine heard herself asking.

'A special person has passed away,' answered a subdued voice. Nadine turned around to find it was her mother who had spoken. She stood staring at a letter, her eyes swollen from crying.

'But I don't know her,' Nadine protested.

'Sister Jeanne helped me escape from a dreadful place called Drancy, a hellhole on the outskirts of Paris. It was many years ago.' Irène had a haunted look on her face as she spoke.

'I don't understand what you mean,' Nadine said.

'It was an internment camp. We were herded together, thousands of men, women and young children, thrown into barracks by guards and forced to live like pigs in filthy, overcrowded conditions.'

'But what were *you* doing there?' Nadine asked her mother.

'I wore the yellow star … as did the others. Like you, *ma fille*, I am a Jew – *une juive*. Come, I shall explain everything to you.'

With the slow steps of a dream, they entered a pretty garden that surrounded a magnificent white arched building. Small groups of young women, veils covering their faces, were going about their daily chores. Nadine sat down on a bench next to a kindly-looking nun in a grey habit, with a large silver cross hanging around her neck. Nadine's anxiety dissipated and she felt herself change. Unwittingly, she had become her mother, Irène.

'Who are you?' she asked in her mother's voice.

'I'm Sister Jeanne.'

'Where have you taken me?'

'To this convent, where you will be safe. Irène, you've been through a terrible ordeal. But, thank the Lord, you will soon be well.'

'And … my baby?' Irène held her breath.

The nun took hold of the young woman's hand.

'You were bleeding heavily. Do you not remember?' she said compassionately. 'You were too weak to ride the bicycle on your own without holding on to me. It was a miracle that the guards allowed us through the camp gate.'

'I just recall being in great pain,' Irène replied slowly, her eyes filling with tears as she understood that her escape had led to a miscarriage.

'You're still young, my dear. God willing, when all this madness is over, you will have other children. Until then, you will be safe at St Dominic's.'

'You mean I can stay here?' Irène breathed.

'Fortunately, you look most convincing in your novice's vestments,' replied Sister Jeanne, gazing at the long white garment that covered her protégée's slight frame. Then she added, 'We have two other Jewish girls arriving today. I'm afraid that's all we can take. My brother is in charge of new arrivals at the camp, and he says that it's becoming too risky to get any more young women to us. He's already under suspicion from the Germans.'

'What will happen to the rest?' Irène asked.

There was a moment of silence. Irène could see that Sister Jeanne's eyes were closed. Her hands were clasped together and she was mumbling through quivering lips. Irène followed her example and began to pray for the thousands of unfortunate souls who had been left behind to await their fate.

Nadine woke up feeling unsettled. The images of her mother had been so vivid it was as if she and Irène were in the same room. What did it all mean? Of course, she had known about Gérard, her mother's Moroccan first husband, and she'd heard about La Jolie Vagabonde, the nightclub they ran in the Place du Tertre in Montmartre before the war, and how Gérard had been killed in a backstreet off the Boulevard de Clichy over an argument about a gambling debt. But she hadn't known, till recently, that her mother had been arrested by the Gestapo five months later, nor that she had been pregnant at the time with Nadine's tiny half-brother or sister, who died before he or she had a chance to draw breath. *Pauvre maman.*

The fact that her mother had felt the need to reveal these hidden aspects of her past on the very day that Nadine left for London – as if she was somehow preparing to give a final account of herself – was totally unexpected. At the time, Nadine didn't pay too much attention, focused as she was on establishing a career in musical theatre and looking to the future, not the past. Subconsciously, however, those words must have stayed in her mind.

Nadine placed her hand on her stomach. She knew then that she was going to keep this baby. If only for her mother.

After breakfast, she'd packed up all her things, then rang her friend Sophie and, without giving a reason, asked whether she could move back into the tiny flat they had shared when Nadine first came to London. It would just be for a short while, she promised.

She was in luck. Sophie was at home, pleased to hear from her and happy to go back to their previous arrangement.

'You can have the place to yourself for the next ten days,' Sophie told her, 'as I will be on a catering course in Geneva. I'll hide the key in the usual place.'

'That's great. Thanks, Sophie.' Nadine was relieved. That would give her just enough time to finish the current show before quitting England for good and going back to France to have the baby.

She had tidied up the best she could, left the keys on the table, and was just about to leave the flat in Chelsea when Charles himself suddenly opened the front door and strode inside.

'I'm sorry about last night,' he blurted out. There was a horrified look on his face at the sight of the two suitcases in front of him. 'It's just I'm under a lot of pressure at the moment. I don't know which way to turn.'

'You should have told me the truth instead of saying you were getting divorced,' Nadine said flatly. She felt drained of any emotion.

'I know, I'm sorry,' Charles muttered. 'That was very stupid of me. But, the thing is, I've grown rather fond of you and the thought of not seeing you again—'

He walked up close to Nadine. She could feel his warm breath on her neck as he drew her towards him. Slowly, she felt her resistance begin to wane. Then, summoning her inner strength, she pulled away.

'Charles, when the show finishes, I've decided to go back to France,' she announced, still not divulging that she was pregnant. 'I haven't seen my parents in almost a year. It will give you time to decide what you really want.'

'But what about your career?' he asked, a pained expression on his handsome face.

'So long as I keep in shape, it shouldn't affect my prospects,' she shrugged, fobbing him off. Without warning, her mind turned to Greenberg, the producer who had taken her to lunch the previous day and who had witnessed her embarrassing dash to the ladies' loo, where she had vomited.

He was such a warm man that she had taken to him immediately, and had more or less told him that she would be available for his new show. Now she would have to bow out and tell her agent the reason why she wouldn't be working for the next few months. Lesley Stanton would, she hoped, be sympathetic to her predicament, as one woman to another.

'How long will you go for?' Charles asked.

'If I can find work, I might decide to stay. There's nothing to keep me in London,' Nadine replied with uncharacteristic aloofness, and went to pick up her cases.

'At least tell me where you're going,' Charles pleaded.

Nadine went up and kissed him on each cheek, a formal farewell. Then, without saying another word, she walked out of the flat for the last time.

Outside in the street, she hailed a taxi to Belsize Park, feeling more resilient than she had expected. Perhaps it had something to do with the life that was already growing inside her.

Settling immediately into her former home, as though she'd never left, Nadine walked down to the travel agents in the parade of shops next to Belsize Park Tube station and booked a flight to Paris for the following week. Her next act was to telephone her mother to say she would be arriving home on the Saturday before Christmas.

3

As the taxi pulled up outside the imposing block of flats, an elegant lady, her gleaming blonde hair pulled back in a chignon, stood waiting on the street in anticipation of her daughter's arrival.

'*Bonjour, maman,*' Nadine called out, going up to greet her mother. The two women embraced each other with genuine affection.

A porter in grey uniform was immediately on hand to take the luggage up to the top-floor apartment.

'You must be tired from your journey,' Irène said, once they were inside the huge apartment, which offered the sort of luxury accommodation, Nadine thought, recalling her dream, that might once have been requisitioned for his personal use by the head of the German occupying forces in June 1940. 'I've prepared dinner for the two of us as your father is away again on business. When you've rested, it will give us a chance to talk – and then you can tell me what's wrong,' she added perceptively.

Nadine looked around her bedroom, where nothing had changed. The posters of Josephine Baker and the Harlem dancers of the 1920s were still on the wall. As a child, she had spent hours practising and trying to emulate their routines, hoping that her father might just once poke his head around the door so she could impress him. But he never did. There was also a poster from Bob Fosse's

Cabaret, the film starring Liza Minnelli, about Berlin in the 1930s. It was still her favourite movie. Musicals had always provided an escape into a world of fantasy, where she could feel good about herself.

Now she sat down on her bed, feeling suddenly exhausted and wondering whether she had made the right decision. Putting her career on hold to have the baby was one thing, but wasn't she being presumptuous, taking her mother's support for granted?

It will only be for a few months, Nadine told herself. *Then I will take the baby back to London. Things will work out.*

Nadine found her mother seated in her usual place at the heavy oak dining-room table. She was grateful that she wouldn't have to break the news to her father herself. They had never been particularly close. It might have been different, had Jacques Bertrand had a son to follow him into the vast multinational oil company he presided over. Then he might have had time for his daughter. She often wondered why her mother put up with her hollow marriage. So long as he had an elegant wife by his side when he needed to entertain in Paris, Jacques was happy. And as far as Irène was concerned, if he remained discreet about his other women, she never complained.

'It was quite unexpected when you telephoned to say you were coming. How long do you intend to be at home?' Irène asked, as she poured a ladle of vichyssoise into each of two soup bowls.

'I know it must have come as something of a surprise.'

'Well, it has been over a year,' Irène admonished her daughter.

'I'm sorry to have left it so long,' Nadine replied, starting on her first course. She was very hungry.

'Nadine, you forget that when you were at the Conservatoire, you were always so busy helping out this friend or the other with their problems, we never saw you from one month to the next.'

Reminded of the lame excuses she used in those days to fob her parents off with made Nadine feel nostalgic. For most of those four hedonistic years she had spent her time vying for the attention of Julien, the handsome Algerian dance tutor who had his pick of both male and female students. Julien it was who had introduced her to the pleasures of sex, and they would frequently slope off between their hectic schedules to his flat in the rue Cujas to get high on marijuana and make love.

'But now you're here you can make up for lost time, that's the main thing,' Irène said happily.

Nadine knew she had to tell her the truth immediately.

'*Maman*, I'm afraid it's not that simple. You see … I'm pregnant.' She divulged her news hesitantly.

The older woman's expression said it all.

'You don't seem surprised,' Nadine said.

'*Chérie*, you don't need two suitcases for just the weekend. And I know from the newspaper clippings you sent me that your last show was a big success. So, I just assumed—'

'You're not angry with me?' Nadine said as she burst into tears and reached for her mother.

'My first grandchild… How could I possibly be cross?'

'But what about Papa? What will he say?'

'With the number of offspring he's probably got scattered all over France, good Catholic that he is, I shouldn't think he's in any position to be too judgemental.'

'You knew?' Nadine gasped.

'*Bien sur, ma fille*. A wife knows everything.'

'No, I mean how did you know that I'm not with the father?' Nadine stressed.

'Things are different today. Believe it or not, I'm rather more broad-minded than you think. I actually expected you to say that you didn't want to keep it. Bringing up a child on your own … it's not going to be easy to have a career.'

'You could always move to London,' Nadine suggested shyly.

Her mother's eyes lit up.

'You mean that we could live together? Oh, that would be wonderful.'

'And Papa?'

'First of all, I have no intention of telling him, and in any case, it would take him at least six months to realise that I wasn't here.'

They both laughed.

'By the way, *maman*, do you remember when you told me what happened to you in the war?' Nadine asked, hungrily mopping up the remains of her soup with a piece of crusty fresh baguette.

'Yes,' Irène replied, a puzzled look on her face.

'Well, I dreamt that I was at that convent, and Sister Jeanne was comforting me because I had just lost my baby. She called me Irène. It was all so vivid.'

'Now I think I understand,' her mother replied, looking affectionately at her only child. 'You want to continue the bloodline, after what *they* did.'

The next day, Nadine went for what she thought would be a straightforward examination by Monsieur Gervais, the family doctor, who confirmed the earlier diagnosis. When, however, he warned that because of the smallness of her pelvis, it was likely that she would require a surgical delivery, she began to worry. She tried convincing herself that perhaps he was just being overcautious, but ever since she had nearly died from a burst appendix when she was twelve years old she had had a terror of going under the knife again.

For the next twenty weeks, hoping for a natural birth, Nadine tried to keep herself active. At first, attending the dance studio at the Conservatoire, she put herself through a rigorous routine of ballet exercises to maintain her muscle strength and the flexibility in her joints. Then when she became bigger with the baby, she enrolled in a gentler keep-fit class for expectant mothers at an exclusive health club a few streets from the apartments where the Bertrand family lived. Anxious about her career, she couldn't afford to be off work for a moment longer than was necessary.

Surprisingly, her father showed far more concern than she had expected. Nor did he express any of the adverse sentiments she suspected he was harbouring.

At thirty-eight weeks, on 15 June, three days before her twenty-third birthday, Nadine panicked because she couldn't feel the baby moving. The doctor was summoned and she was rushed to hospital. Six hours later, after an emergency caesarian, she gave birth to a boy.

After several days of deliberating about what to call her son, Nadine suddenly remembered the name of the convent where her mother had been hidden and protected by the nuns during the war: the Couvent de Saint Dominic. The name felt so right. She knew she had been prompted by her dreams. Tears came to her eyes when she made the decision and told her parents, both of whom were deeply moved.

Dominic's birth was registered at the local town hall. The father's name on the certificate was recorded as *Charles Edmund Langley* and the mother's as *Nadine Solange Bertrand*.

Nadine knew she should be feeling happy, but the circumstances of the birth had left her traumatised. More worryingly, as she recovered she found that she was devoid of any maternal instinct towards her baby son. Although the hospital maternity staff said that the feelings she was going through were not unusual after a forced procedure, it gave her little comfort.

To make matters worse, Nadine began experiencing the same sense of worthlessness and low self-esteem that had tormented her during the first throes of adolescence. Carted off against her will to numerous child psychiatrists, none of whom could offer any satisfactory explanation for her condition other than diagnosing a slight hormone imbalance (which she would eventually grow out of) left her feeling desperate. She knew the doctors were wrong because, as her adolescence progressed, the only respite from the violent mood swings that plagued her was the feeling of well-being that dancing offered. Only that, together with the diaries she was encouraged to express her deepest feelings in, brought her some solace.

Now, after the birth of Dominic, followed by several weeks of postnatal therapy and an ongoing course of medication, Nadine had become listless. While Irène slept with the baby in the spare bedroom, which had been turned into a nursery, Nadine slept alone, plagued with guilt because she felt resentment of her own child.

One morning, Nadine got out of bed with a new sense of purpose. Whether it was the higher dose of her medication or the early autumn sun breaking through her bedroom blinds, she suddenly felt re-energised. It was as if she had awoken from a nightmare. After bathing and dressing, she made her way to the nursery at the end of the corridor, next to the kitchen.

Nadine's mother sat in a rocking chair giving the baby his bottle.

'*Maman*, please let me,' Nadine said, picking up her son in her arms. Slowly at first, with tears in her eyes, she began feeding the child, who she had neglected for the first twelve weeks of his life. It was too late to give him her breast. Her milk had long since dried up and gone.

'This is what he's been waiting for,' Irène proclaimed, looking on joyfully.

'Do you think that he will forgive me?' Nadine wept, as she gently patted the baby's back.

'I believe the worst is behind us now. You'll have plenty of time to show him the love he needs,' the older woman said as she comforted her.

'*Maman*, you will still come to London with me?' Nadine fretted.

'But you're not well enough to go back yet, darling. You need more time to make a full recovery.'

'If I leave it much longer, it'll be impossible to find work.'

Nadine suddenly thought about that charming young producer with the curly hair who had taken her to lunch. But her mind was fuzzy and she couldn't recall his name. That must have been nearly a year ago. She had lost all track of time.

'You've always been in so much demand,' Irène continued. 'They will not find anyone to replace you that easily.'

'I've already left several messages with my agent, but she hasn't replied,' Nadine said, trying not to show her disappointment. 'Now that I'm feeling better, tomorrow I'll go to the dance studio.'

'But the doctor said to avoid any strenuous exercise for another four weeks. You will be careful, won't you?' her mother urged, taking baby Dominic from her daughter to change his nappy and then put him down in his cot.

'Yes, I promise. Please don't worry.'

Nadine went off to get her breakfast, silently vowing to give herself three weeks to get back into shape for the London stage.

One afternoon, Nadine had just arrived home after her class, when she overheard her mother talking to someone with a familiar-sounding voice. Peeping through an opening in the living room door, she saw the back of a man. The pair were drinking coffee and appeared to be deep in conversation.

'Hello,' the visitor called out, and stood up as she entered the room. He was smiling, and she saw a large brown envelope resting on the arm of his chair.

'Charles,' Nadine said breathlessly. 'Whatever are *you* doing here?'

4

Nadine stood transfixed, staring at the man who had caused so much turmoil in her life. There had been no contact between Charles and her for months, and for him to suddenly turn up at her parents' apartment without any advance warning was frankly surreal.

'*Maman*, this is—'

'We've already been introduced, my darling,' her mother said, a smile lighting up her face. Irène seemed to have been charmed by the visitor. 'Now I think it's best that I leave you two alone. I'm sure that you must have a great deal to talk about.'

Irène then patted her gleaming blonde hair and got up and left the room.

When Charles came towards her, Nadine was lost for words. She could still recall the feeling of numbness the night when his car had sped away, the night he'd said that their relationship was over. She glanced again at the armchair where he had been sitting and recognised the envelope containing the tests that had confirmed her pregnancy.

'What did you say to my mother?' she demanded, sounding agitated.

'Just that our son has a father,' Charles replied, with an uncharacteristic display of emotion. 'Why didn't you tell me about the baby, instead of rushing off to Paris like that?' he asked softly.

'What was I supposed to do? You finished with me before I had an opportunity to tell you. Anyway, if you remember, you're married. Why would you have wanted the complications of a child?'

'You don't understand. My life is a complete shambles,' he muttered, a petulant frown on his handsome face.

'Well, you can't just decide to reappear after all this time and expect nothing to have changed,' Nadine said bitterly.

'I want us to be together. I've missed you,' he tried, approaching her again.

'It's too late for that,' Nadine replied, retreating.

'I want you to come back to London,' Charles announced. 'You can stay with me until you're better.'

'My mother mentioned that I'd been unwell?' Nadine was shocked at how much had been said about her while she'd been absent.

'No. Actually it was Sophie. I rang to find out whether she knew when you were coming back. All she said was that you were going through a difficult period and she didn't know how long you would be staying in Paris.'

'How did you get hold of the tests?' Nadine asked.

'I found them recently when I was tidying up the flat,' Charles lied glibly.

'And so you knew that was the reason I came back to France?'

'I just wanted to make sure, that's all. So, I went to that doctor friend of mine, Tim – you remember him? We had dinner together a few times. I know it wasn't strictly ethical, going behind your back—'

'And *he* told you?' Nadine raised her voice, furious that

36

her medical condition was being discussed without her permission.

Charles nodded.

'Tim was at my wedding. We were at Eton together and I knew that I could trust him to be discreet.'

Nadine had trouble bringing her mind into some semblance of order. She had already decided to return to London. Her mother would come with her and look after the baby while she got herself fit and strong, ready to resume her dancing career. She needed to move forward with her life, but the truth was that Charles's appearance had unsettled her.

'I think it's best that you leave,' she said, confronting her former lover.

Just then, her mother came into the room carrying the baby, swathed in a white crocheted blanket.

'*Maman!*' Nadine exclaimed, showing the full extent of her anguish.

'It's time for Dominic's feed. I thought you might like to give him his bottle,' Irène suggested, addressing her comments both to the child's father and her daughter. She had a sly look on her face.

Nadine was livid. What the hell did her mother think she was doing? If this was an attempt to bring her and Charles together, it was completely out of order. Irène had no right to interfere in her daughter's private life when she didn't know all the facts.

Charles needed no further prompting. Gently taking the baby from Nadine's mother, he sat down on the sofa and, supporting the child's head, began giving his son his bottle.

'*Chérie*, are you feeling unwell?' Irène asked her daughter, completely oblivious to the upset she had caused.

'Charles was just leaving,' Nadine replied coldly. 'He won't want to miss his flight back to London.' She went over and grabbed the baby from the man she no longer wanted in her life.

'Yes, of course, Nadine's quite right. I should be going,' Charles said, getting up.

'At least allow me to call you a taxi to take you to the airport,' Irène offered, reaching for the phone.

'That would be most kind. So long as I'm not putting you to any trouble,' he replied, as suave and well-mannered as ever.

Before too long, the concierge rang to say that the car was outside.

'Well, it has been a pleasure meeting you, *madame*,' Charles said, extending his hand to Irène Bertrand. 'I know that I haven't behaved particularly well, but that's all in the past.' To Nadine, he said, 'I hope that you'll give me a chance to make it up to you, Nadine, when you return to London.'

Nadine offered no response and carried on feeding her son.

'Now we have a child, I have every intention of fulfilling my paternal responsibilities,' he added, turning to leave.

'I will see you out,' Irène said, escorting Charles to the front door.

The anger that had threatened to erupt inside Nadine just a short time ago had now magically been replaced with a feeling of tranquility from holding the baby, who had fallen fast asleep in her arms.

When Irène came back into the room, she said guiltily, 'My darling, I believe I owe you an apology.'

38

Nadine frowned, wondering what had caused her mother to change so suddenly.

'It was just that he seemed such a pleasant young man. All he talked about was how foolish he had been to let you go, and he did sound genuinely remorseful.' Irène paused. 'Something, however, something ... doesn't quite make sense.'

'I'm not sure what you mean,' Nadine said.

'Charles is clearly fond of you.'

'The problem is that he's married,' Nadine interjected.

'Yes, yes, that I already suspected,' her mother said, wanting to continue with her train of thought.

'If you knew, why did you try to throw us together?'

'I was simply curious.'

'About what?'

'Mainly his reaction towards you.'

'*Maman*, I don't understand what you're trying to say.'

'If he is as contrite as he appeared to be, why did he leave it so long to get back in touch? Then, as to the matter of him just suddenly coming across your pregnancy results out of the blue... Well, I'm afraid I don't believe it.'

'You mean there's another reason?'

'I'm certain that he has an agenda and it has something to do with our little Dominic. The problem is, I can't work out what it might be.'

'I didn't know you were that cynical,' Nadine remarked, laughing.

'In my experience, when it comes to men, there are very few surprises. When you return to London, just be careful.'

'But you will be there with me, remember?'

'Yes. Yes, of course,' her mother replied after a slight

hesitation, and she started walking away.

'Where are you going?' Nadine enquired.

'I've got a doctor's appointment. I don't how long I'll be, so let's eat out tonight. Your choice.'

'Is anything wrong?'

'I shouldn't think so. Just something that I want to check out with Monsieur Gervais,' Irène called from the hall.

The cleaner, Victoire, had arrived to babysit her adored 'Dom-Dom', and Nadine was getting changed for dinner when her mother came into her bedroom. Irène's face was pale, Nadine saw. She looked old and ill.

'Is there bad news?' Nadine was distressed by the change in her mother.

'Where did you reserve for dinner?' Irène asked, doing her best to be cheerful.

'Chinese. But I'm quite happy to stay in and cook. *Maman*, you look so tired.'

'Not at all.'

'Are you sure you feel up to going out?' Nadine reiterated.

'Give me ten minutes, and I'll be ready. We have a lot to talk about,' Irène said finally.

Late that night, Nadine lay sleepless in her bed, struggling to come to terms with her mother's revelation. The word 'cancer' kept going over and over in her mind. All of a sudden, she was terrified by the very real prospect that she was going to lose the person closest to her. Of course, Irène had agreed to commence treatment immediately after her emergency hysterectomy. The doctors would then be able

40

to determine whether the disease had spread. If only she hadn't ignored the symptoms she now admitted that she had started to experience some months earlier.

The last thought in Nadine's head before she finally fell asleep was that when she returned to London, it would just be Dominic and her. The little boy had brought such joy to his grandmother. She prayed with all her heart that Irène would live to see him grow up.

5

It was a cold foggy day at the end of November 1975 when Nadine carried her five-month-old son carefully down the steps of the Caravelle 737, having just completed the short flight to London. She was feeling relieved. Her mother's operation had gone well. Although the cancer appeared to have been contained, Irène's ovaries had also been removed as a matter of precaution.

Nadine had insisted on staying for the duration of the eight-week radiotherapy course. It was the least she could do. Ironically, being forced by Irène's incapacity into taking full responsibility for Dominic had enabled her to develop a bond with her tiny son.

The £3,000 that her father had given her afforded Nadine the breathing space she needed to get settled. Nadine was still surprised by how deeply Irène's illness had affected Jacques Bertrand. For the first time that she could remember, her father had taken time off work to be with his family. Ensuring that his wife had the best professional full-time care had allowed Nadine to return to London before her mother had fully recuperated.

With the new responsibility of a grandchild and a sick wife, Jacques had also seemingly forgotten about the other women in his life, who had been the reason for his prolonged absences.

Nadine's first priority was to get settled in a new flat

that would be big enough for the au pair she would need to employ. She had already established that there was plenty of accommodation available for about £900 a year. And au pairs were inexpensive, costing only their keep and around £10 per week pocket money. She'd start organising things once she was back with Sophie.

Equally importantly, she needed to get back on form and working again. Her one concern was that her agent Lesley continued to be vague about her prospects of finding a new show. It wasn't really surprising, Nadine allowed, since she hadn't worked for over a year.

The taxi pulled up outside the small parade of shops in Belsize Park and the driver helped Nadine, who was holding Dominic, with her luggage. She had telephoned Sophie to let her know when she would be arriving and had asked if her friend would order a cot and a pram from Mothercare, the big store near Bond Street that everyone used. However, Nadine had given no real consideration as to how they would all manage. A cramped studio flat overlooking a noisy main road was hardly suitable. It could barely accommodate an extra person, even if that person was a baby. Where would the cot and pram fit? She and Sophie would be sharing the sofa bed, which took up one side of the rectangular-shaped room, with just a single wardrobe on the opposite wall. There was nowhere to put Dominic's things.

On the way up to the apartment, Nadine's mind turned to Charles. Maybe she had been too harsh in dismissing him. Her mother could have been wrong about his motives in tracking her down. It was understandable that, with the worry about her health, Irène wasn't able to think clearly.

*

Three weeks went by and Nadine found herself tied to Dominic and unable to leave the flat. The truth was, she was completely unprepared for the constant demands of looking after the baby all on her own. More than once, she had to rely on Sophie to give Dominic his feed because she couldn't get out of bed in the morning.

Fortunately they were close friends and Sophie, who had become attuned to Nadine's delicate mental health, loved caring for the tiny boy and was prepared to accept the crowded living conditions until Nadine found a new home. In reality, Nadine was going downhill and urgently needed medical help for her clinical depression. However, she was in denial, unwilling to accept that she was slipping back into the darkness.

One evening a few days after her arrival, when Sophie had gone into the West End to see *The Man Who Would Be King*, Nadine had just managed to settle her son when the phone rang and woke him up again. He started to cry.

'Hello,' she said in a voice weighed down by exhaustion.

'Nadine, it's Charles.'

'How did you know I was back in London?' Charles hadn't been in touch since that surprise visit to Paris and she hadn't expected to hear from him.

'Sophie told me that your mother has been unwell.'

Nadine wished that Sophie would be more discreet.

'She's going to be fine. Charles, what do you want?' she asked irritably, still trying to settle the baby.

'Just wanted to see if you're getting by with Dominic,' he said cagily.

'Look, there's really no need for you to be concerned. As soon as we can find a larger apartment and I can get some help for him—'

'Which is what I wanted to talk to you about,' Charles butted in. 'Look, I don't suppose you'd consider moving back to Chelsea?'

There was a short pause. Nadine had difficulty taking in what she had just heard. Deprived of sleep, she was unable to think straight.

'It's a bit tight,' he went on, 'but the baby and Nanny could sleep in the spare bedroom.'

'Can we talk about this at another time? I'm really very tired.' Nadine felt as if she was going to burst into tears at any moment.

'Wait. Please don't hang up. I'm not suggesting we get back together. It'll only be until you feel more able to cope.'

'Charles, I know you're trying to help, but I just can't think about it at the moment, OK?' Nadine put down the phone and played the musical box chime that Dominic loved until he was calm again and fell asleep.

As she was getting ready for bed herself, the door opened quietly and Sophie crept in.

'Hi, Nadine, how's it going?' she whispered in the English that they insisted on speaking to each other. 'The film was great – I just love Sean Connery. He's so handsome, and that Scottish accent—'

'Charles rang,' Nadine said dully.

'What did he want?' Sophie asked.

'Something about wanting me to move back to Chelsea,' Nadine mumbled.

'If he's offering to help, in the circumstances it might be the best solution. You could pay someone to look after Dominic while you get back on your feet.' Sophie went over to the kitchen, whispering, 'I'm going to warm up the soup. Will you have some with me? It will do you good and you need to keep up your strength for the baby.'

'Thank you, but I'm not hungry. I just need to sleep. We'll talk tomorrow, I promise,' Nadine yawned. She felt overwhelmed by all the challenges. Living like this was not fair on any of them. Things needed to change.

Another month passed and Nadine decided to accept Charles's offer of moving back into the two-bedroom flat in Chelsea. Dominic was crawling now and she needed someone to keep an eye on him at every moment. Sophie contacted an au pair agency on her behalf and immediately secured the services of a young French girl called Anne-Marie, who had come to London to learn English.

One morning shortly after moving back to Chelsea, Nadine woke up after another disturbed night's sleep. It wasn't Dominic teething that had kept her up but another dream about her mother. In this case her mother had died and no one had told her.

She immediately reached for the telephone. It was more than three weeks since she had last been in contact with her parents, and she prayed that it wasn't a premonition. Happily, when her father answered the call, his voice sounded completely normal. He said that Irène was recovering, but that she was still sleeping. Jacques Bertrand then enquired about his grandson and asked when Nadine would be bringing the child to Paris. Not wanting to cause her mother any additional concern, Nadine avoided mentioning that she had moved back in with Charles.

When the call was over, she breathed a sigh of relief and got out of bed to check on her son.

Passing the dressing table under the window, she glanced

at herself in the mirror, noticing that her complexion had become pasty. The luminosity that always lit up a room had deserted her. What chance did she have of finding work, she asked herself, looking the way she did? She had let herself go, both mentally and physically.

It was then she decided to seek medical help.

Nadine decided to allow Charles to make an appointment for her with his friend Tim Merrick, who would now be her new local GP. She had no choice but to become reliant on Charles once more. At least this time it wasn't as a lover but as a trusted friend, who she believed had only her own and their son's interests at heart.

Dr Merrick immediately referred her to a psychiatrist who, after giving her a thorough examination, advised changing the medication that she had been taking intermittently since Dominic was born, to a psychoactive drug known as benzodiazepine, which was commonly used to treat a variety of mental disorders.

Gradually Nadine began to feel normal again. Fortunately for her, Charles continued to be supportive and paid regular visits to play with Dominic, to feed and look after him. In addition, he appeared in no hurry for her to find alternative accommodation, and this, combined with the fact that Dominic had taken to Anne-Marie, allowed Nadine to resume her search for work.

Her agent Lesley Stanton was always 'too busy' to see her, so Nadine made up her mind to seek new representation. Her efforts, however, proved fruitless. Her long absence from the West End stage had caused her to be written off, she soon discovered. She tried to console herself by spending time with her son. In the afternoons, while Anne-Marie was at her English class, she'd take the little boy, well wrapped up in his pram, to feed the ducks in Hyde Park, or else she'd take the number 74 bus to London Zoo. Even at his young age, she could tell that Dominic recognised the giraffes and the elephants, so much so that he wouldn't settle at night without the soft toy versions of his favourite animals next to him.

There was one last hope: the producer she had met briefly the year before. But she had forgotten his name and had no way of contacting him. Nadine was flipping through her address book, hoping for inspiration, when she came across the entry for Vincent Coates, the stage manager she had been working under at that time. Vince would be sure to have the details she required, since he had been the one to introduce them.

One rainy morning in May 1976, a young woman dressed in a chic raincoat and a beret entered the Regent Street offices of PG Productions. Passing the sleepy receptionist without stopping to introduce herself, she walked unannounced through the producer's open door and said,

'Hello, Greenberg. Remember me?'

Greenberg looked up and stared, amazed to see the woman who'd had such a profound effect upon him. He still remembered putting the phone down after speaking to her agent. Lesley Stanton's words had been unequivocal: Nadine had finished her show and gone away. She offered no explanation. The first thought that went through Greenberg's mind was that Nadine must have been taken ill. Top artistes didn't risk their career by disappearing for no good reason, especially not when they were approaching the top of their game, as Nadine had been.

'I do remember you, yes, of course,' he managed to say. 'But I can't have made a very good impression if it's taken all this time for you to recover from that lunch we had together,' he quipped, quick to regain his poise.

'I've been away from London,' Nadine told him, deliberately sounding vague. 'But now I'm back, I was wondering if you've a new show that might be suitable for me.' She undid her coat and sat down, facing the man she was relying upon to find her work. Then, opening her brown shoulder bag, she took out a pack of French cigarettes and offered him one. Greenberg refused but immediately found his lighter and lit her Gauloise Disque Bleu.

'I'm no longer with Madame Stanton,' she announced, producing a fine stream of smoke from her sensuous lips.

'I can't say that I'm surprised.' Greenberg knew that no reputable agent would keep a wayward artiste on their books, however talented he or she might be. There was something slightly disturbing about the enigmatic Nadine, which probably made her a nightmare to work with.

It occurred to him that if she hadn't worked in more than a year, then she was no doubt desperately short of money, and only a sense of pride was preventing her from revealing the true state of her predicament.

'It's not going to be easy to find new parts without an agent,' Greenberg remarked, attempting to have his suspicions confirmed.

'So, you are unable to offer me anything?' The young woman got up to leave. 'I'm sorry to have taken up your time,' and she began stubbing out her cigarette in the ashtray on the desk.

'There's no need to rush off!' Greenberg exclaimed,

surprised by her abrupt reaction. 'Look, there's a new musical that has just come over from Broadway. If you want, I'll have a word with the producer.'

'*Merci. Merci beaucoup.*' Nadine beamed. She went around the desk to Greenberg and, placing her slender hands on his shoulders, kissed him resoundingly on each cheek.

'Hold on a minute. I didn't say it was definite,' Greenberg tried to warn her. 'Just tell me where I can get hold of you.'

'I'm staying at a friend's flat in Chelsea.' Nadine rummaged in her bag for a pen. Then, tearing a corner off a page in her diary, she wrote down her telephone number and passed it to the man she was truly relying upon to help her.

'I do hope we shall be seeing more of each other,' she told him, a warm smile on her exquisite face. She then turned around and walked out of the office.

For a moment Greenberg just sat, clutching the small piece of paper, in a state of shock. Nadine's strolling into his office after more than a year of absence, as if it was the most natural thing in the world, had completely unnerved him.

It wasn't as if he'd been idle in the interim. *Girls in Between*, the musical that he had originally had in mind for Nadine, was still packing them in at the Shaftesbury Theatre, and there were also new shows in the pipeline.

And he hadn't been short of women. There'd been more than one occasion when he took advantage of actresses throwing themselves at him in the slim hope that they would be offered a part in one of his shows. He'd even got quite close to a girl named Josey with jet-black hair that flowed down to her waist. The only problem was that she wasn't able to reproduce her spectacular bedroom performances onstage.

In truth, he hadn't managed to get the beautiful French dancer out of his system.

Greenberg picked up the phone and dialled Ken Brookman's number. He still hated the bastard. But Ken had got his greedy hands on *Swing Dance*, the hottest show to come off Broadway in years, and he probably had a part that was ideal for Nadine.

'Hello, Ken, it's Peter Greenberg. Congratulations on your latest coup. I trust you'll put a few comps my way for the opening night?' There was a creaking sound as Greenberg's heavy frame reclined in his plush leather chair.

'Of course. And while it's most kind of you to call, I can't imagine that you're doing so just to offer me your good wishes,' a curt voice replied at the other end.

'All right, I'll get to the point,' Greenberg conceded. 'I was wondering, if you're not fully cast, there's a sensational dancer who would be just right for the show. You used her before on *Me and My Girl*. She stood out onstage – that blonde girl. French. Ken, I'm telling you, this girl's got the lot.'

'Sounds like what she's got is you – by the balls – or else you're fucking her,' Ken Brookman said crudely.

Greenberg grabbed hold of the bronze paperweight on his desk and was tempted to either throw it at the wall or tell the man on the other end of the line to get stuffed. He then took a deep breath, aware that he needed to bite his tongue.

'Have her agent contact Miles Bradbury. He's the director. It's up to him, not me,' Brookman continued impatiently.

'Come on, Ken, you can do better than that.'

'All right. Send her along to Drury Lane, Thursday morning – but I shall expect you to return the favour.' The line went dead.

Greenberg slammed down the phone. He had done what he could. The rest would be up to Nadine. He spent the remainder of the day fiddling around, unable to apply his mind to the full schedule of work that he had set himself. Instead, he kept thinking about hearing the sound of Nadine's voice when he called her that evening.

That there might be another man in her life didn't concern him. Greenberg had made up his mind. He had found the woman he was going to marry.

6

It was another sultry weekend of an exceptionally hot summer as the open-top E-type Jaguar pulled up outside the 1930s block of flats in Chelsea.

Before Greenberg had a chance to manoeuvre his stocky frame out of the driving seat, he saw Nadine walking confidently towards his car. It was the same routine every time he came to pick her up. She would always be there waiting for him. He wanted to believe that it was because she was looking forward to seeing him.

Although she was never prepared to elaborate on the friend in whose flat she was living, he suspected that it was the married City businessman who she'd been in a long-standing relationship with before they met. However, that wasn't going to deter him from claiming her for himself.

Nadine had got the part that she had auditioned for in Ken Brookman's show. Who could have foreseen that the production was going to bomb after just eight weeks? It could happen to the best of them, but unlike Ken, Greenberg did not get pleasure from other producers' flops.

Just as well he had found something else for her shortly afterwards in a new musical that he was intending to tour.

He noticed what a different person Nadine was when she was working. The rush of adrenalin filled her with such energy, he could barely keep up with her. And then when it ended, she would become listless and morose.

'Sorry for being a bit late,' Greenberg excused himself, opening the passenger door from the inside. 'The phone hasn't stopped all morning.'

'But it's Sunday,' Nadine objected, getting into the car. She reached across and kissed Greenberg, continental-style as usual, on both cheeks.

'Doesn't stop them from driving me mad. That director … bloody prima donna. I don't know who he thinks he is, upsetting the cast again. I wouldn't mind, but I'm the one paying for all this aggravation.' Then, looking around at the buildings, Greenberg whistled and said, 'Chelsea's definitely got something,' before driving off at great speed.

'Yes, I'm very lucky,' Nadine answered airily. She was in fact deeply embarrassed at constantly having to find excuses to keep Greenberg away from the flat, but she wasn't ready to tell him the truth about herself. And whenever she brought up the question about finding somewhere else to live, Charles actually got quite upset. He said he was happy with the arrangement that allowed him to be just a short distance away from his son. Hadn't he remembered Dominic's first birthday on 15 June and left the office early, armed with a handful of gifts, so that he could play with him before bedtime?

Moreover, Nadine was grateful to Charles for helping her get her life back on track. She'd even managed to make friends with the wife of a banker in the flat opposite who, having a young family of her own, had agreed to look after Dominic when Anne-Marie was off. Suspecting that Charles would disapprove, Nadine thought better of informing him of this ad hoc arrangement.

Vital for her peace of mind was the fact that she was

able to resume her career. From bitter experience, Nadine knew that she needed to feel better about herself before she could respond to the needs of her child.

'I hope you're feeling hungry,' Greenberg said, as the car approached the motorway. He was feeling particularly buoyant that afternoon. He and Nadine had seen quite a lot of each other since that morning when she had breezed into his office out of the blue. At first, he thought the only reason she had agreed to go out with him was from gratitude for getting her work. They had dinner a few times a week in Soho after the show. When the performance went well, she would still be on a high and they would go on to a club and dance until the early hours of the morning. Other times, she was too exhausted even to eat so he would just drive her back home. She was unpredictable and he never knew what to expect.

Then three weeks ago, they had spent the night together. It was the closing performance of the show and Nadine was feeling particularly down. He could only think that it was the effect of the several vodkas they had drunk during the evening that had left her almost comatose in his car on the way back to Chelsea. For a moment, he was convinced that she had stopped breathing and he was afraid to take her home.

Turning the wheel, he drove north to Marylebone. With his arm held tight around her narrow waist to prevent her from falling, he somehow managed to support her up to his mansion flat overlooking the high street. Still she didn't stir. He was in two minds whether he should take her to hospital but settled instead on placing her in his large double bed, where he could keep an eye on her.

The next morning, they woke together, neither

attempting to disengage from the surprising compatibility of two such disparate bodies moving in unison. No words passed between them. This was what he had been waiting for, all this long time.

Suddenly, the magical moment was broken. Nadine had become anxious and, without offering him any explanation, said that she needed to go home right away. He could only assume that it was because of the other chap she was involved with, who exercised some control over her.

The tension on the silent drive back to her flat was followed by several days when he was unable to contact her. Then, on the first day of rehearsals, she turned up as if nothing had happened. The feelings of exasperation that had been plaguing him immediately dissipated.

The fact was that he was hopelessly in love.

'Where are we going?' Nadine called out now, her voice drowned out by the rasping sound of the car's engine as Central London disappeared in the distance behind them.

'Somewhere romantic,' Greenberg shouted back, keeping his eyes on the road. 'We should be there in just under an hour. Have you been to the English countryside before?'

'No, I haven't,' she replied, forcing a smile, deciding to make a conscious effort to enjoy the afternoon. After all, it had been a long time since she had been invited out for the day. Greenberg had said that he wanted to surprise her and she didn't wish to disappoint him.

Nadine had liked Peter Greenberg from the very first time they met. There was a sensitivity about him that she found appealing and she felt safe in his company. She realised, of course, that he had a personal motive that went beyond their professional relationship. And while she was grateful to him for going out of his way to find her work, she didn't want to mislead him. The night she had spent in his flat was a huge mistake, but there was no way of telling him that without hurting him. However much she tried to deny it, she was in love with Charles. Since the arrival of the baby, she had seen another, more caring side to him, and deep down, Nadine still hoped that they might have a future together.

The car turned off at the Maidenhead roundabout. Passing through picturesque country lanes, they shortly arrived in Bray, a sleepy village on the banks of the Thames.

Together, they entered the Waterside Inn, a gourmet French restaurant run by the famous Roux brothers and occupied by smartly dressed couples taking their time over their Sunday lunch. The aroma of the wonderful food served there pervaded the riverfront establishment, and they could see some of the beautifully presented dishes and the expensive wines on offer being carried in by the waiters.

Greenberg knew that it wasn't him but his stunning female companion, dressed in skinny white jeans and an open black silk shirt, who turned the heads of the other diners, men and women alike, as they were escorted to their table on the terrace.

After they had ordered from the Menu Gastronomique and were enjoying their hors d'oeuvres and a bottle of Saint Emilion, Greenberg cleared his throat and asked, 'Do you think you could get used to this?' as he gazed at the ripples in the water below.

'It reminds me of Barbizon, outside of Paris. It is also

very romantic. My parents took me there quite often when I was a child,' Nadine remarked, sipping her white wine.

'Actually, I was referring to me,' Greenberg said.

'I'm sorry, I don't understand.'

There was a momentary pause, while Greenberg drummed up the courage to say what was on his mind.

'Nadine, darling, I'm asking you to marry me.' He came straight out with it, the words passing effortlessly through his lips, belying the palpitations within.

Nadine remained silent. He couldn't tell by her expression what she was feeling or whether she was even likely to offer a response.

'Well, at least it's not a no,' Greenberg joked after a short while, trying not to let his disappointment show. It was clear that the proposal had caught his companion by surprise. He began to feel foolish for taking her answer for granted.

As their plates were removed and the *plats du jour* they had ordered were neatly placed in front of them, he decided to make the best of it.

'I still think a celebration is in order,' he gabbled. Grabbing the bottle embedded in the ice bucket by the side of the table, he refilled their glasses.

The impromptu comment achieved the required result. Nadine burst out laughing.

'Greenberg, you are bizarre,' she said, reaching for his hand. 'We have only been together a short time. There are many things that you don't know about me.'

'Sorry to disagree, but you're wrong on both counts.' He shrugged. 'Firstly, you've obviously forgotten our lunch in the Kings Road.'

'But that was nearly two years ago,' she protested.

Greenberg just smiled. He had an overwhelming desire to reach across and take this woman in his arms. There was a vulnerability in her large brown eyes that he had never noticed before. It was as if she wanted to open up to him but was being prevented by an opposing force.

'And you made your mind up that quickly?' she teased.

'If you want to know the truth, it was when you were in *Me and My Girl*,' Greenberg revealed, beginning to tackle his grilled langoustines.

'I didn't know that you came to see my show,' Nadine replied, taking a mouthful of her salmon with Bois Boudran sauce and sighing with pleasure.

'It's quite normal in the theatre to see what the competition is up to,' Greenberg replied flippantly, beginning to feel a little more optimistic about his chances.

'So you regarded me as a commercial proposition. That's not very flattering,' Nadine remarked, pouting her sensuous lips.

'It would never take that long in business to find out you've got a deal,' Greenberg jested.

'You mean you're used to getting your own way?'

A moment of tension gripped the table.

'Let's not spoil such a beautiful setting,' Nadine said, gazing at a swan gliding across the lake.

Greenberg felt deflated. It wasn't even being turned down that was so bad, more the fact that he just couldn't fathom what was really going on in her mind. The small black jewellery box weighed heavily against the inside pocket of his open blazer. He knew that paying four thousand pounds for the two-carat diamond was a bit excessive, but he didn't care. He had wanted everything that day to be perfect.

'Don't look so disappointed,' Nadine said softly. She had obviously underestimated the strength of his feelings for her, she thought. He deserved to know the truth – that she was not the virtuous woman he imagined her to be. The fact that she was not able to explain this to him was proof that she was unworthy of such a decent man.

'Well, you can't blame me for trying,' Greenberg sighed.

The awful thought that this might be the last time he would see her crossed his mind. There had to be a way of salvaging their relationship. He had been far too keen and needed to start playing it cool. That was easier said than done, however, when all he could see was the woman he loved slipping through his fingers.

Greenberg took a deep breath.

'Of course, you do realise that this now presents a problem,' he said with a straight face.

'What do you mean?' Nadine asked, suddenly fearing for her job. Surely he wasn't insinuating that she wouldn't be included in his tour just because she hadn't agreed to marry him.

'The hotel booking will have to be changed for tonight.'

'Excuse me?'

'I'm well aware that I take up a lot of room, but a suite is rather extravagant for just one person.'

Nadine burst out laughing.

'I thought you were going to cancel my contract because—'

'Whatever gave you that idea?' Greenberg came back, feeling that all might not be lost.

'You're making fun of me.'

'You should know by now that I don't give up without a good fight.'

'I didn't know the English were so gallant.'

'You haven't answered my question,' Greenberg pressed.

Nadine wasn't sure whether it was the effects of the alcohol, but she felt herself being drawn to this man, who had gone to such lengths to win her over.

'Greenberg, it was only your proposal of marriage that I didn't agree to—'

'Well, that's good enough for me,' he exclaimed joyfully, emptying the last of the wine into their two glasses.

She and Greenberg were clearing the last morsels from their plates. Then Nadine suddenly announced without warning, 'I have to go to Paris. It will mean missing rehearsals. You see, my mother has become ill again.' Her voice was filled with emotion.

'But surely your father is there,' Greenberg said, unprepared for her sudden change in mood.

'No. He's away travelling on business,' Nadine said angrily, unable to hide her resentment. She should have known it would be only a matter of time before Jacques Bertrand got bored and reverted to his usual ways, and Irène would be left on her own again. Nadine had originally planned to go alone. But knowing that Dominic's presence would really benefit her mother, she had decided to take the child with her.

'And you're returning when?' Greenberg asked, wanting reassurance. He had visions of her disappearing again.

'I'll only be away a week,' Nadine told him. She couldn't disclose the other reason why she had decided to get away from London at such short notice.

Her thoughts turned to Desiree, the beautiful young Jamaican girl in the cast. She had created such a scene when their relationship ended. How was Nadine to know that she would become so emotionally attached to her? They had met in a discotheque in Soho, where Desiree was the resident exotic dancer. Rejected for every part she auditioned for, convinced it was because of the colour of her skin, this was the only work she could find. Nadine had persuaded their director to give the eighteen-year-old Desiree a chance to show him what she could do. Colin was so impressed with her that she was hired on the spot.

Nadine now acknowledged that she should never have agreed to those afternoons alone together after rehearsals. But Desiree had pleaded with her. She said that she wanted to know how to please her boyfriend. Coming from a strict Christian background, she was still a virgin, she claimed, and needed to be given guidance in matters of love. Thinking that nothing serious would come of it, Nadine threw herself wholeheartedly into the role of a love coach.

She didn't believe there was anything unnatural about being attracted to women. It was just the aesthetic part of her that needed fulfilling. And how could she have foreseen that the adolescent would fall in love with her?

'So, you'll definitely be back in time for the tour?' Greenberg asked now, still anxious.

'If you haven't found a replacement for me by then,' Nadine teased.

Suddenly, Greenberg stretched across the table and, in front of the whole restaurant, he kissed Nadine passionately on the lips. The few grunts of older patrons expressing their distaste were drowned out by those at tables of younger diners, who broke out in spontaneous applause.

Not at all embarrassed by his moment of fame, Greenberg bowed to the other tables. And then, grinning, he sat down again. After declining the waiter's offer of the selection of desserts, or a celebratory glass of champagne on the house, he called for the bill.

By the time the couple walked arm in arm out of the restaurant, the late afternoon sun was beating down on them. And with the sound of The O'Jays singing 'I Love Music' blaring through the car speakers, they drove back towards London.

Then, disturbing Nadine, who had dozed off next to him, Greenberg shouted out, 'Bollocks.'

'What's the matter?' she said groggily.

'It's my father's sixtieth birthday and I've forgotten all about it. Nadine, do you mind if we go in for a few minutes?'

'Perhaps it would be better if you took me home. I don't want to impose on your family celebrations,' she yawned.

'It'll be fine. Don't worry,' Greenberg said, feeling far from sure of himself.

The car eventually turned down a quiet suburban street in North London and drew up outside a small terrace of modern townhouses.

'Right, we're here,' Greenberg announced. Hurrying around to let Nadine out, he took her hand and they walked up the small paved front garden to the door, where he rang the bell.

Almost immediately a bear of a man appeared at the door in swimming trunks and an open-necked short-sleeved shirt. A taxi driver's leather identification tag was tied around his massive neck.

'Ah, the prodigal son has returned,' bellowed Clive, Greenberg's eldest brother. 'With a new lady, I see…'

7

The entire family, comprising three generations of Greenbergs, were sitting crammed together around an extended dining table. Platters stacked high with overfilled bridge rolls and silver cake stands supporting a variety of cream cakes covered the surface of the embroidered white tablecloth, which was only taken out for special occasions. The presence of the two late arrivals went largely unnoticed as the babble in the stifling room reached a crescendo.

'Peter, darling, you came!' exclaimed a woman in a deep voice. She was sitting perfectly upright at the near end of the table dressed all in white, a stylish turban held together with a diamanté clasp covering her oval-shaped head.

'Mother, this is Nadine. She's from Paris.'

'My, she *is* beautiful,' Valerie Greenberg remarked, peering above her sunglasses.

'Nadine's appearing in the West End.'

'You're an actress? How simply wonderful,' enthused the eccentric woman, twirling an extremely thin arm dramatically in the air.

'Just a dancer, *madame*,' Nadine replied modestly.

'I was on the stage. I could have been famous,' Greenberg's mother told Nadine, her eyes glazing over at the memory of happier times.

'So you decided to show your face, did you, Peter?' a

completely bald man bellowed from the top of the table, his huge mouth stuffed full of food.

'Happy birthday, Dad,' Greenberg said, going up to greet his father.

'Aren't you going to introduce me to your lady friend?'

'Nadine, this—'

Before Greenberg had a chance to finish, the older man, a paper napkin still tucked into his beach shirt, moved his vast carcass up from out of his seat.

'I'm Raymond Greenberg, *mademoiselle. Enchanté*,' he said, taking Nadine's hand. 'Peter, don't just stand there like a big dolt. Go and get a couple of chairs from the lounge, unless you don't intend on staying,' he added.

The younger Greenberg, his face showing his displeasure, quickly left the room. He hated these family get-togethers. Why he had chosen today of all days to expose Nadine to them all, he couldn't think. If his marriage proposal hadn't put her off, this would for sure.

He swiftly reappeared with a gold lattice-back chair under each arm.

'Come on, budge up,' the head of the family ordered, stirring those at the table to move even closer together so that they were practically sitting on each other's laps.

'You speak French?' Nadine said, flattering the older man when she found herself squashed up against him.

'*Mais oui.* Fought there during the war. Most beautiful women in the world, the French – with one exception, of course,' Raymond Greenberg said, gazing affectionately at his wife, who he remained deeply, if unrequitedly, in love with.

'I can see that you are quite a romantic,' Nadine said, liking him immediately.

'My wife was a real looker when she was younger. Wasn't easy getting her to go out with me, a boy from the East End. Her folks didn't take too kindly to that, I can tell you.'

'Where did you meet?' Nadine enquired, showing genuine interest.

'One day she just came into the shop. We were in leather goods, see. It was a decent living when we just had the markets. But when my sons joined the business, they had big ideas. They persuaded me, against my better judgement, to take this shop in the West End. I have to say it was a smashing place, right off Oxford Street.'

The big man paused to take another bite of his pastry. Spraying crumbs, he continued, 'So, one day, I happen to be serving, must have been shortly after we moved in, and in comes this gorgeous-looking woman and asks if we do repairs. She had this old tote bag and one of the handles had come off.' He grinned at Nadine. 'Anyone else, I would have told them to sod off. But I decided to put myself out – best decision I ever made. Had the bag back from the workshop the next day, good as new. Never charged her a penny. Told her she could let me buy her a coffee instead. And that was it. Believe it or not, I wasn't a bad-looking fella in those days.' He released a belch.

'You'll have to excuse my father,' Greenberg said, turning to Nadine, his face red with embarrassment. 'It's just that when he's got an audience…' And yet, by her relaxed expression, Nadine appeared to be thoroughly enjoying herself.

'Don't listen to him. Thinks he's too good for the rest of us because he mixes with all those toffee-nosed arty-farty theatre types,' the older man responded, using a fat forefinger to push his nose in the air. 'We had a bloke like him in the forces – Francis Edwards, known as "Fanny". He played the banjo on the stage. Queer as you come but he kept the boys entertained.' Ray Greenberg picked his teeth thoughtfully. 'Awarded the George Cross posthumously for single-handedly breaking through enemy lines. Just shows, you never can tell.' He snorted. 'I thought our Peter was that way inclined until he started bringing girls home.'

'Dad, let's not start that again,' Greenberg pleaded.

'Go on, love, don't be shy. Take a piece of chocolate cake. Michelle over there bakes them herself,' Raymond said cheerfully, grinning at his chubby daughter-in-law at the other end of the table. 'And that's my grandson, Luke,' Greenberg senior added, pointing to the fat little boy in denim dungarees on the next chair who was stuffing a cake into his mouth. 'He's only five but he likes his grub. Must take after me.'

Greenberg gazed at his oldest brother's wife. Today Michelle was dressed in an unflattering black and white check dress that made her look like an oversized chessboard.

'We're a bit short of plates,' Raymond added. 'Hope you don't mind using mine.' In a single movement, he had wiped the plate clean with his paper napkin and placed it in front of his youngest son's girlfriend.

Then he said, nudging his son, 'Peter. Go and get her a fork. Can't have your young lady thinking that we're uncouth.'

The comment provoked a ring of laughter, which broke out around the table.

Unable to hide his growing feeling of discomfort,

Greenberg went over to the cutlery canteen open on the mahogany sideboard and then returned to his seat to see his father leaning with some difficulty across the table.

'Here, let me serve you,' Raymond said, cutting a large wedge of cake, which he picked up in his hand and put on the plate in front of Nadine.

'She's watching her weight,' Greenberg started to say, then looked on in horror as Nadine began to eagerly devour the rich chocolate sponge. After all, lunch was a long time ago and they hadn't had any dessert.

'There's nothing of her,' Raymond bellowed, chewing another mouthful of food. 'I like women with something to hold on to. Isn't that right, Janine?' he said, leering at his other daughter-in-law.

Embarrassed that she had become the focus of attention, the rosy-faced woman laughed nervously, trying to hide behind her black frizzy hair, and carried on feeding the son resting against her generous bosom.

'Shame about her Barry not being well,' Ray Greenberg said, referring to his second son. 'Don't know who he takes after with his delicate stomach. Me, I've got a cast-iron constitution.' The big man patted his huge stomach with pride.

Greenberg couldn't take any more.

'We really should be going. Nadine's got rehearsals early tomorrow,' he said to his father and got up from the table.

'You can't go yet when we're just getting acquainted,' the bald man retorted, appearing aggrieved. 'It's my birthday, Peter. Besides, your lady friend hasn't finished her tea.'

Greenberg's face again showed his displeasure.

'Oh go on, bugger off then, you miserable sod. I was

only joking,' the older man said.

Unhappy about being rushed, Nadine finished the last piece of her cake, wiped her mouth and reluctantly got up from the table.

'It was delightful meeting you, young lady,' exclaimed the head of the household, taking hold of Nadine's hand. 'Although what you're doing with our Peter is beyond me,' he added and winked.

Nadine laughed and reached up to kiss Raymond Greenberg on each cheek.

'*Bon anniversaire,*' she said fondly. 'Congratulations on your special birthday.'

Greenberg couldn't wait to get away. It was the same the first time he introduced them to Melissa – after which he swore he'd never do it again. Why didn't he ever learn? Ignoring the looks of disapproval from the remaining members of his family, he walked briskly out of the room with Nadine following behind, smiling at those she passed on the way.

As they let themselves out of the house, they could detect they had already become the main topic of conversation.

Once in the car and heading back down to Chelsea, Greenberg cleared his throat and said sheepishly, 'I'm sorry that I had to put you through that.'

'I think your family is spectacular,' Nadine replied. 'Your father is so amusing.'

'*What?*' Greenberg nearly choked.

'And your mother, she is *très élégante*—'

'You're not telling me that you actually liked them?'

'I am an only child. It was very different in my home. I

never had the same closeness that you have in your family. It is perhaps because you're Jewish, *non*?'

'What's that got to do with it?' Greenberg wanted to know.

'I am *juive, aussi*,' Nadine announced.

But Greenberg didn't hear. He was het up and paying no heed.

'Anyway, we're not close,' he blustered. 'They all hate each other. My father was only nice to me because you were there. He's never forgiven me for not going into the business like my brothers. I wouldn't mind if I hadn't—'

Greenberg stopped himself from revealing that he had supported the whole family at one time or another. Fortunately, he was in a financial position where he could afford to. The fact that the rest of them resented him for it was something he had been forced to put up with. No good deed went unpunished, that was for sure.

'But it's clear that you've inherited your love of theatre from your mother,' Nadine said.

'She is the only one who gave me any encouragement,' Greenberg said dispassionately. He didn't think it worth mentioning how his first stage experience – of the musical *Oliver*, which his mother had taken him to as a teenager – had blown him away, nor that it was Valerie who had put up the money for his first play, *Shimon*, about a gladiator who became a famous biblical sage.

When they arrived back at her apartment, Nadine planted a kiss on Greenberg's cheek and climbed out of the car, saying politely, 'Thank you. I had a marvellous afternoon.'

'So you haven't been put off completely?' Greenberg said, trying to disguise his insecurity and feeling again unsure about his chances.

'I'll call you when I get back from Paris,' were her only words before hurrying into the block of flats.

Not for the first time, Greenberg drove home doubting whether there was any future in his relationship with this unpredictable woman.

When Nadine opened her front door, she was surprised to find Charles, perfectly at ease, playing with Dominic on a rug in the middle of the living room.

'We were starting to get worried,' he said, looking up.

'What are *you* doing here? Where's Anne-Marie?' Nadine asked, concerned that her au pair was nowhere to be seen.

'I'm afraid she's quit,' Charles informed her.

'*Ce n'est pas possible.* She never said that she was unhappy.' Nadine went to look in the nursery. The single bed had been stripped and the wardrobe was empty. She couldn't believe that Anne-Marie had just walked out without saying anything.

Feeling particularly despondent, she rejoined Charles and her son in the lounge.

'Perhaps she thought that you were taking advantage of her,' he speculated. 'To be fair, she was only supposed to be working twenty hours a week.'

'Charles, I'm sorry. I really had no idea,' Nadine said contritely.

'At least she had the common sense to call me. Just as well we were at home, really,' Charles responded.

Images of Dominic being left on his own flashed through her mind and Nadine felt herself sliding into a black abyss. It was then she realised that she had forgotten to take her medication.

Panicking, she rushed into her bedroom and began searching frantically for the packet of white capsules. They were always on the dressing table but they seemed to have disappeared. She checked the drawer of her bedside cabinet but there was no sign of them. Her head was throbbing. She was sure that she was beginning to lose her mind.

Charles appeared at the doorway with Dominic in his arms.

'Looking for these, by any chance?' he said, holding out her pills.

Nadine gasped.

'I found Dominic playing with them. But there's no harm done. He wasn't able to bite through the box.' He handed across the crumpled packet.

'But how did they get there?' Nadine asked, trying to come to terms with her shocking carelessness. 'I don't even remember seeing them this morning.'

'All I can think is that you must have been in such a hurry that you just left them out,' he said softly.

Nadine noticed that Charles had adopted the same compassionate expression as when he had visited her in Paris. But it was her fault. She had left Dominic with a young girl who was clearly irresponsible. Maybe she was a bad mother, just as she had always feared.

'I need to be off,' Charles said, passing his son to Nadine. 'I suggest you get on to the agency first thing in the morning.' Heading for the front door, he added, 'That reminds me. Didn't you mention something about going to see your mother?'

'Yes, yes. I'm leaving tomorrow,' Nadine replied,

sounding distracted. 'I'm taking Dominic with me.'

'Not sure that's a good idea,' Charles commented. 'It'll put him out of his routine. Look, why don't you leave him with us? It'll only be for a few days.'

'But what will you say to Clare?' Nadine asked, aghast at the suggestion. Charles had told her that his wife knew of their affair, and that she had been prepared to forgive his 'indiscretion', as he called it. But he had never mentioned that she knew about the child they had together.

'Clare has had several miscarriages,' Charles explained. 'The doctors doubt that she'll ever be able to carry a baby to full term. She's desperate for a child. Looking after Dominic, even for a short time, might actually help her conceive. Taking into account what she's been through, it's the least I can do.'

'If you're sure, then very well. You may take Dominic. I'll be back on Saturday.' Nadine was suddenly filled with admiration for the wife of her former lover. Even though they had never met, she doubted that she herself would have been as understanding and generous in the same circumstances.

'I'll pick Dominic up first thing in the morning, if that's OK. I suppose we should really get hold of a few baby things ourselves, if this is going to become a regular occurrence,' Charles said, letting himself out of the flat.

Nadine felt emotionally drained. Still berating herself for the earlier neglect of her son, that night she moved Dominic's cot into her bedroom. She would be away from him for nearly a week and wanted the little boy near her. The last thought before she went to bed was how lucky she was to have Charles to fall back upon.

*

The next morning, she woke early, gave Dominic his breakfast and got him ready.

All of a sudden, the phone rang. When Nadine picked up the receiver, it was a woman calling from the au pair agency that had found Anne-Marie. The woman began explaining that she was calling because Anne-Marie was so distraught at being dismissed. She was adamant that she had been falsely accused of allowing the baby in her care to put tablets in his mouth, when it was just an empty box that he had taken out of the wastepaper basket. Moreover, she had been told to leave immediately without being paid what was due to her.

Taken aback, Nadine replied that there had obviously been some kind of a misunderstanding. However, she agreed to put a cheque in the post and promised to supply Anne-Marie with a good reference. Something, however, just didn't feel quite right. Both she and Charles had liked her and trusted her with their son. So what had suddenly changed? she wondered.

For a moment, Nadine was tempted to ask Charles for some kind of clarification of the whole matter when he turned up to collect Dominic. But since she was due to leave for France in a few hours, she was busy packing and too preoccupied to address her mind to the matter. Also, aware that she would not be able to use the agency's services again, she had no choice but to rely upon Charles to find a replacement for Anne-Marie while she was away.

8

Nadine arrived back in London on the early evening flight from Paris and took a taxi straight to the flat in Chelsea. The week's stay with her mother had proved more traumatic than she had expected. The cancer had returned and spread to Irène's bones. The doctors' prognosis gave her no more than six months to live.

Despite Irène's insistence that she was being well looked after, and the fact that Jacques Bertrand's dressing room had been turned into a bedroom for the rotation of nurses who provided twenty-four-hour care, Nadine felt torn. Part of her wanted to stay with her mother, but she desperately missed Dominic. The episode with the pills had shaken her badly, and she vowed that she would never leave her son again under the supervision of someone who couldn't be trusted.

At least she didn't have to worry, with Charles always being on hand.

Charles was waiting at the door with Dominic to greet her when she arrived home from the airport.

'Good journey?' he enquired, helping her with her luggage.

'Yes, thank you, but I'm glad to be back,' Nadine said, going over to pick up her son.

'Our son has been no trouble, thanks to Miss Pinkham

here,' Charles remarked, pointing out a dour older woman in a navy-blue uniform who'd just appeared from the nursery.

'Young Dominic took to Mrs Langley immediately,' the woman said smugly.

'I am extremely grateful,' Nadine responded, taking an instant dislike to the woman who had obviously been installed as the new nanny while she was away. Charles had no right to employ someone without her meeting them first. She also found it strange and unsettling that his wife was willing to look after the child her husband had had with another woman.

'Right, it's high time Dominic was tucked up in bed,' Charles said, taking his son from Nadine and passing him to Miss Pinkham, who promptly carried the little boy off. His tone changed. 'Why don't you go and freshen up, Nadine? And then we'll go out for some dinner. You must be hungry after your journey.'

'But haven't you got to get back?' Nadine said, bewildered, seeing that he was in no rush to leave.

'Clare's gone to visit her parents, so we've got the evening to ourselves,' Charles replied with a knowing smile.

They had just ordered their meal at the Tandoori Indian restaurant in the nearby Fulham Road when Charles produced a shiny wallet from his jacket pocket.

'Dominic took his first steps while you were away,' he said. 'I shot these with my Polaroid,' he added, pushing the photographs Nadine's way. 'Clearly the young fellow enjoys being the centre of attention,' he added proudly.

Nadine forced a smile. She should have been pleased

that her son seemed so happy playing with the new toys that the Langleys had bought him. She also knew that however much her parents were looking forward to seeing their grandson, taking him with her to France would have been impossible in view of her mother's sudden deterioration.

Nevertheless, she couldn't help feeling slightly jealous of the bond Charles had forged with his son.

Later, feeling mellow from all the wine they had drunk over dinner, the couple crept stealthily back into the flat and went straight for the bedroom. In silence, so as not to wake their child or his nanny, they removed their clothes, assisted by the light of the full moon that shone outside their open window. They kissed softly and then more passionately. Nadine had existed for too long on dreams that left her body aching for Charles, and unsatisfied. Charles picked her up in his arms, wrapping her slender legs around his athletic waist. Nadine eased herself on to him. She just wanted to please him.

Her last thought before she fell asleep, weirdly, was of her father. How he had never shown her the love she craved. Was that the reason she constantly sought affection wherever she could find it? She looked over at Charles. He was sleeping peacefully. Cuddling up to him, she realised how much she had missed him.

In the morning he got up to leave and she watched him dress. As she lay there she felt sad. It was unrealistic, she knew, but she continued to harbour the wish that they could be together, even though in her heart she knew there was little prospect of Charles ever leaving Clare.

Nadine recalled her mother's doubts about him. What was it, she asked herself again, that he *really* wanted?

9

Nadine entered through the stage door and made her way to the dressing rooms amidst the sounds of rehearsal from the auditorium above. She thought about the eight-week tour. It was remiss of her not to have telephoned Greenberg to tell him she was back. The truth was, she'd had second thoughts about leaving Dominic if she joined the cast of this play. The one day off a week when she would be able to see him seemed totally insufficient.

Charles, however, had insisted that she go.

'Think of your career. You'd be crazy to pass up an opportunity like this,' he had protested. In the end she reluctantly agreed that Miss Pinkham would move in with the Langleys and look after Dominic for the whole two months. Although it put her mind at ease, Nadine once again had the feeling that she was being manipulated, and that the control of her own life was being taken away from her by some unseen sleight of hand.

As she changed into her costume, adrenalin coursed through her. She couldn't wait to get started. Several female members of the cast stopped in the middle of their routine to welcome her as she strutted confidently on to the stage. Nadine loved the attention she drew from her peers. It made her feel special. There were two new girls she had never seen before, but no sign of Desiree.

Suddenly, Greenberg strode into the theatre, a plaster

covering a wide cut above his eye. He couldn't remember when he'd last felt so annoyed. This time, that little shit of a director had gone too far. Playing around with his routines was one thing, but insisting on major changes to the script was purely destructive. Greenberg feared he was being paranoid, but the thought did occur to him that the competition was paying Colin Reeves to sabotage the show.

'I need your attention, everyone,' he shouted, clapping his hands. The music faded out. The cast froze. Looks of concern suddenly appeared on their sweat-covered faces as their employer marched up to the stage.

'There have been some changes,' Greenberg told them. 'As of this morning, Colin Reeves is no longer involved in the production.'

The announcement produced a mixed reaction, ranging from genuine surprise to unrestrained joy. None regretted the departure of the man who had taken a sadistic pleasure in making all their lives a misery.

'Your new director, Tony Vasey, will be here in the morning, so if you want to take the rest of the day off, I'll see you all at nine o'clock tomorrow,' Greenberg concluded.

Apart from the cost of delaying the show for two months, he was already reconciled to losing most of the cast, especially those who could find other jobs.

In the meantime, there was another reason for his unusually grim mood that drizzly October morning: the assault two days ago outside his office that still preoccupied his thoughts. At first, he was sure that the baby-faced youth in the tatty denim jacket must have confused him with someone else. The boy seemed upset and overwrought, and kept screaming abuse at him – something about losing his girlfriend. Apart from incurring a glancing blow to the side of his head, Greenberg soon overpowered him. One meaty knee in the groin was all it took to restrain his assailant. Then the lad just broke down in tears. By that time, a small crowd had gathered and were having a go at *him* for starting on the young man.

The police turned up and, highly embarrassed, Greenberg was marched off in broad daylight with his attacker to Vine Street police station a few hundred yards away.

The youth explained to the duty officer that his girlfriend, a dancer called Desiree, had gone off with another woman at the theatre. Greenberg still hadn't grasped what any of this had to do with him, so out of curiosity, he asked her name. Unexpectedly, he was lunged at again.

'It's your fault, you bloody pervert,' his attacker shrieked.

Greenberg thought that the kid was high on drugs or else terribly deluded, but he was in for an unpleasant surprise.

'It's that French dyke with the short blonde hair,' the youth hissed, his voice filled with venom.

Greenberg didn't realise for a few moments that the boy was referring to Nadine. At first it didn't register. In his experience, in the theatre it wasn't uncommon for the camaraderie amongst members of the cast to spill over into their private lives. As long as it didn't interfere with their performance, it wasn't really any of his business.

Then he remembered how James, his stage manager, had said something about the young black girl who had recently joined the cast. She had arrived at work badly bruised after an argument with her boyfriend. James had sent her home, and that was the last anyone had seen of her. However, she hadn't mentioned anything about Nadine.

Greenberg told the officer that he didn't wish to press charges. He bore no ill will towards the youth. Maybe it was because part of him believed that anything was possible about the mysterious woman he was in love with.

Disappointed that he wasn't going to hear any of the lurid details, the policeman let the two of them off with a warning about their future conduct.

Greenberg stopped at the doors and looked back at the arena. Nadine was still onstage, rehearsing a routine. Seeing him look over, she gave him a smile and a wave. Would he ever be party to what was going on in her head? he wondered. Or, more likely, would she always remain an enigma?

One thing was certain. He had changed his mind about confronting her about the Jamaican girl. He watched as Nadine pirouetted gracefully, before joining the rest of the cast making their way backstage.

10

Greenberg once again concentrated his attention on the entrance of the hotel bar. He should have felt ecstatic, since his show *All at Sea* had been a huge success. They had played at packed houses from Nottingham to Edinburgh and all eight venues along the way. The closing performance in Manchester's Theatre Royal had brought the house down. An extended run in the West End was practically assured. Instead, he had a dull feeling that Nadine wasn't going to appear. He had left the end-of-the-run party early. After showing his face and making the expected speech of thanks to the cast for all their hard work, he was glad to get back to the hotel and leave them to celebrate.

Glancing at his watch again, he wondered how much longer he was going to devote all his energies to what he had long ago resigned himself was a lost cause.

Greenberg had seen practically nothing of Nadine while they were on the road. On the rare occasions when they might have had a moment to themselves after the show, she had either vanished or else was too preoccupied holding centre stage with a group from the cast to pay him any attention. It was as if all traces of any intimacy that they might once have shared had been completely erased.

After the incident of the Jamaican dancer's boyfriend, Greenberg had promised himself to back off. He had a business to run and, quite frankly, he could no longer afford the distraction. But it was so hard. He was in love with the girl, who didn't love him in return: one of the great themes of classical Greek drama.

Greenberg drained his tumbler and then unwisely ordered another Johnnie Walker.

How differently my life would have turned out, he brooded, *if I hadn't gone to that show of Ken Brookman's. I'd still be with Melissa, for sure. We'd probably have a couple of kids by now and a safe suburban life in a North London street, just like my brothers.* He sighed and rattled the ice in his glass. For a few moments a safe life had sounded appealing. The trouble was, being safe wasn't for him.

He paid his bill and moved unsteadily across the hall to the lifts. At least he would now sleep well. The train to London wasn't until ten o'clock the next morning. There was a chance that Nadine might appear in the dining room at breakfast…

Greenberg put the key in the door of his suite and entered the darkened living room. As he did so, the lights came on and a thunderous sound of music boomed out from a large twin-speaker cassette player – the signal for the twenty-strong chorus, still in full costume, to break into the show's opening number.

Greenberg stood motionless, trying to control his emotions. That's what was unique about theatre. When a show was a success, no one wanted it to end.

As the music faded out, it was replaced by affectionate applause directed at their producer.

'Look, I just put the show together,' he yelled, trying to make himself heard. 'You're the ones who deserve all the credit – and Tony Vasey, of course.' He looked around the room but there was no sign of the director.

'We left him behind at the wine bar,' a rather bitchy male cast member called out, producing a roar of laughter from the others.

Greenberg just smiled. He had known that his fifty-year-old director had a drinking problem when he hired him. But Tony was the only one he could get hold of at such short notice. Being sober for the whole of the eight weeks had obviously been a terrible strain on his levels of endurance.

'Whose idea was this, may I ask? Or was it a team effort?' Greenberg wanted to know.

All eyes in the room were focused on Nadine.

'I should have guessed,' he sighed. 'I don't suppose there's any point in asking how you gained access to my room.'

Nadine, wide-eyed, stepped forward dangling a key. There was a mischievous look on her exquisite face.

With an outward show of affection towards each other, the cast filtered slowly out of Greenberg's top-floor suite. It was always the same at the end of a successful run: the expressions of camaraderie and the promises of keeping in touch that faded as soon as there was another job to audition for. He had seen it all before. The reality was that the show would have to be completely recast before going to a bigger venue. It would be a surprise if more than a few made it through the far more rigorous selection process instituted by a West End director.

'Nadine, I don't suppose you feel like joining me for a late supper?' Greenberg asked, seeing that she was the last to leave. 'After all, it is our last night.'

'I thought you were never going to ask me,' she replied, coming back into the room and beginning an impromptu inspection of the suite. 'It really is too big for one person,' she called out from the double bedroom.

Part of him wondered, despite her appearing not to care, whether Nadine had actually expected to share his room during the tour. Then he shook his head. Just more wishful thinking.

Greenberg glanced at the room service menu on the sideboard. Despite his heartache, he was hungry.

'Nadine, what would you like?'

She appeared barefoot from the bedroom wearing an oversized white towelling bathrobe bearing the hotel crest.

Greenberg's mouth fell open.

'You don't mind?' she asked.

'No. It's just I didn't expect—'

'Jeanette usually keeps me up,' she said, yawning. 'Don't worry. I'm happy to sleep in the other bedroom.'

'Yes, of course that's fine,' Greenberg replied, startled at what he had heard. He was sure that each member of the cast had been provided with a room of their own.

Unable to picture which one of the chorus it might be, he surmised that it was the new ginger-haired girl from Liverpool who Nadine had taken under her wing. Greenberg found himself thinking of the young Jamaican woman, aptly named Desiree. Perhaps he wasn't as open-minded as he imagined.

He picked up the phone and he ordered two steak sandwiches and a pot of coffee. Nadine, looking on, nodded her approval.

'Where did you go on your days off?' Greenberg asked as they sat down to eat, certain that it was to her long-standing lover.

'To my flat to get new clothes, see friends – you know, the usual things,' Nadine said casually. 'At the beginning of the tour I went to visit my mother, since she wasn't able to come to the phone. But now she's sleeping the whole time, she barely recognised me. It was terrible to see her that way.'

Nadine tried to keep to the truth as far as possible. She remembered the last time she had returned home, a few weeks ago. It had upset her so much that she came away crying. The nanny had brought Dominic over to see her. But when she tried to pick him up, he had a tantrum and started screaming. It was as if her own child didn't know her. Worse was the expression on the woman's face, as if to say, '*What do you expect?*'

The deep guilt she felt at that moment threatened to tear her apart. How could she have been so selfish as to think that she could be a mother just when it suited her? Although she was loath to admit it, she was no better than her father putting his career above his family. Nadine was convinced that she was now being paid back, after witnessing Dominic's reaction to her. Would her young son go on to develop the same complexes that had plagued her from her childhood – in his case because of a lack of maternal love and attention?

Thoughts of self-loathing began churning through her head. She took her medication when she remembered – and when she renewed her prescription. But the truth was that she only felt normal while she was performing, when she could escape into a world of fantasy.

Nadine was suddenly filled with dread. The show had ended. What was she going to do tomorrow?

'Nadine, your food is getting cold,' Greenberg announced, concerned about the melancholy that seemed to have gripped her.

'Yes, I'm sorry,' she replied, attempting to pull herself together. She wasn't feeling at all hungry but, not wanting to cause offence, she took a hasty bite out of her sandwich.

'What are your plans for Christmas?' Greenberg asked, his mouth full of food.

'I'm having a few friends over for lunch,' Nadine replied, more perkily. She had in fact arranged to spend the day with Charles and Dominic. He had apparently told Clare that he was obliged to be with his widowed mother in Kent and that he would join her at her parents' place in the evening.

Nadine thought about her mother being on her own during what was likely to be her last Christmas. Jacques Bertrand would put in an appearance, as he always did when Nadine was growing up. His pretence was that for those few hours they were a normal family. Then there would be the excuse that something important had arisen, which would keep him away until the next day. It had been a regular occurrence for so long that it became a joke between her mother and her. She smiled, recalling the time when Irène, having had a little too much to drink, had actually prompted her husband into action, asking whether he had forgotten about the urgent business matter that he had to attend to.

But Greenberg was speaking, and Nadine came back to the present.

'It's just that if you're not doing anything, I've taken a villa in Barbados for a couple of weeks. You're welcome to come along. No obligation to—' he began.

'Greenberg, you are a very special man,' Nadine replied, reaching across the table for his hand.

'I'm holding a few flights so you don't have to let me know straight away. Anyway, it's always quiet at this time until the schools go back.'

Greenberg sensed that she was seriously considering his offer. But then her expression changed again and he knew that she would decline.

'It's that other chap, isn't it?' he asked, no longer able to resist saying what was on his mind.

Nadine didn't respond straight away. She so wanted to be able to tell Greenberg how complicated her life was, but she knew it would destroy him if he learnt the truth.

Was her reticence also attributable to her own self-interest? she asked herself. The fact was that Greenberg had been the only one to find her regular work. Without his help, she would be completely lost.

'It's not what you think,' she replied awkwardly.

'You mean he's married?'

'How did you know that?' Nadine was incensed at the thought that he had been prying into her private life.

'I've known from the first time we met,' Greenberg admitted.

'And you still wanted me?'

'I fell in love with you. I just thought that in time you might learn to feel the same way.'

Nadine got up and went across to sit on Greenberg's lap, her small breasts showing through the opening of her bathrobe.

'You are the most adorable man,' she whispered, putting her arms around his neck. For one fleeting moment, she wondered whether she should have accepted his marriage proposal. Even though she wasn't in love with him, it was clear that he would do anything to make her happy. She then reminded herself that she had the responsibility of an eighteen-month-old son whose well-being had to come first. It wasn't Dominic's fault that he had been born to dysfunctional parents.

Nadine felt a sudden wave of exhaustion sweep over her.

'Goodnight, Greenberg,' she said abruptly, getting off and moving away.

Greenberg was again caught by surprise. Just as he thought he had got through to her, there was something he would never be privy to, pulling her in the opposite direction. If only he knew what it was.

'Do you want me to wake you for breakfast?' was all he could think of saying as she entered the small bedroom and turned to close the door.

11

The next morning Greenberg woke early. Last night's events were still playing heavily on his mind. He packed his suitcase and, not wishing to wake Nadine, passed quietly through the suite to go downstairs.

Just as he was about to leave the room, he caught sight of what appeared to be a handwritten note on the supper table. The spare key to his room was resting by its side. He picked up the piece of paper and quickly scanned its contents. All it said was that Nadine had decided to catch an earlier train back to London. She thanked him for the tour and wished him 'Happy Christmas'.

The position couldn't have been clearer. As far as he was concerned, he had tried everything to win her over. But this time he had reached the end of his endurance. He'd go away at the weekend, have a bloody good time in Barbados and come back at the start of the New Year feeling refreshed.

Of course, he wouldn't turn his back on her. If a suitable part came up, it would be churlish not to offer it to her. He wasn't the vindictive type. Due to the fact that it would take the best part of a year to get *All at Sea* ready for the West End, he had resigned himself to not seeing Nadine again – at least until the beginning of rehearsals in nine months' time.

*

It was already dark when Nadine dragged her suitcase through the front door of the Chelsea flat. She was surprised to see that there was no one at home. The Langleys knew when she would be back – so where was Dominic? However, the flat was warm, so someone had come in to put on the heating.

She took the carrier bag of Christmas presents that she had bought for Dominic on her way back from Euston station and placed them in the nursery. Uncertainty filled her mind. She was almost certain that she had informed Charles when she was returning. Perhaps the nanny had taken Dominic to see the Christmas lights in Regent Street. The little boy would have loved that. But it was getting late. Time for her son's dinner, bath and bed. Nothing here was ready for him.

Nadine passed along the narrow hallway to the kitchen and sat down at the table. A neat pile of post had been left there. Apart from the utility bills, which Charles had never let her contribute towards, the only unusual thing was an airmail letter from France dated 14 November.

She opened the flimsy envelope and started to read the diatribe from her father.

Dear Nadine,

You cannot imagine the degree of my disappointment I feel because I have had to resort to communicating with you by letter. Why did you not keep in touch by telephone? Did you forget about us so completely? Selfish girl. Your dear mother passed away peacefully in her sleep, two weeks ago.

Relentless efforts were made to contact you, but to no avail. It has always been obvious to me that your career comes before anything else – and perhaps my own example is to blame for that – but not to be at your mother's side during her final moments, when you appeared to be so close, is beyond my comprehension.

The funeral was a dignified affair attended by just a few of our closest friends. Her ashes, should you wish to know, are on the windowsill of my study overlooking the Bois de Boulogne, forever your mother's favourite park.

I don't know whether this note will ever reach you, but even if it does, please do not try to contact me, since I shall shortly be taking a holiday to try and get over my loss. I have already put the apartment up for sale. There are far too many cherished memories of our twenty-five years of marriage together to enable me to continue living there.

I hope in time that I can come to understand you better and that we can at least resume a courteous relationship.

Affectionately,
Your father

Nadine covered her face and wept uncontrollably. How was it possible that no one had told her? She had given a list of the telephone numbers to her nanny. Charles had all the information with regard to her itinerary, and he said he even knew some of the hotels where she would be staying. She felt numb.

Nadine rushed out of the kitchen to the telephone in the hall and dialled the Paris number. She could hear her mother's voice in her head. But there was no one at the other end of the line.

Staggering into the bedroom, fully clothed, Nadine got into bed and pulled the covers over her head to escape the nightmare of her tragic homecoming.

She must have dozed off because she dreamt that she was

in a church at a funeral service. A line of people were filing silently past the open coffin, which had been placed on a dais. When it was her turn to pay her respects, a corpulent man with a kind face took her by the hand up to the ebony coffin. But when she looked inside, it wasn't the corpse of her beloved mother she saw lying there. Instead she was staring at herself...

Nadine was stirred by the babble of a young child. She opened her eyes to see Dominic standing unsteadily against the side of her bed. She reached out for him and without resisting he came over to her. For a few seconds the warmth of her child's body offered her some respite. But when she looked into his pale blue eyes, his blank expression indicated that it had only been his curiosity that had brought them together.

Then there was the thud of officious footsteps as Miss Pinkham stalked into the room.

'I see you're back, Miss Bertrand,' she said, showing her disapproval. She then reached over and lifted Dominic from his mother's arms.

'Let him stay for a little while longer,' Nadine pleaded. 'I've just got home.'

'There will be plenty of time for that while I'm away,' the woman replied curtly.

It took a moment for Nadine to grasp what had been said to her.

'You do remember, I hope, that it's Christmas and that I shan't be working?' the nanny stressed, looking at her as if she was simple-minded.

'Yes, of course,' Nadine replied exhaustedly, gazing at the bag of presents in the corner of the room. For some reason, Greenberg's invitation to Barbados passed through her mind. The expression on his face seemed familiar but she didn't know why. Then it struck her. He was the man who had looked after her in her dream.

'Come along, young man, it's time for your bath,' announced the woman in her navy-blue uniform. 'Your daddy will be back from work soon to read you your bedtime story and we shan't want to keep him waiting.'

'I can give him his dinner,' Nadine said, trying to assert herself.

'Good gracious! Dominic has his supper at half past five. Mrs Langley has already dealt with that at the other house,' the nanny snapped. 'But he'll be needing quite a few things for the morning. You'd better get to the shops before they close. I've prepared a list,' she added, producing a piece of paper from her apron and passing it across to Nadine. She then left the room, with Dominic still in her arms, his arms clasped about her neck.

Nadine knew that she was being marginalised. Now she was back home she wanted to take over the care of her son but she was in no condition to argue. The sense of well-being that had accompanied her on tour had vanished. It was as if the last eight weeks hadn't existed. Instead, her old feelings of inadequacy resurfaced with even greater intensity. She lay her head back down on the pillow and shut her eyes. Once again, sleep overtook her.

The next thing she heard was voices speaking in the hallway. A few moments later, Charles strode into her bedroom.

'When did *you* get back?' he asked chirpily.

Nadine sat up. She should have felt pleased to see him but her father's letter had completely overwhelmed her.

'An hour or so ago,' she answered in a subdued voice.

'Looks like you've been overdoing it, old thing. Still, you're home. That's the main thing. Now, you can get some rest. Have you seen how much Dominic's grown? He is walking and climbing the little slide in the park.'

'My mother died,' she said, trying to hold back her tears.

'That's a bit of bad luck,' Charles responded, but showing scant concern. 'I expect you'll be going over for the funeral, won't you?'

'Charles, it was six weeks ago and I've only just found out,' she wailed. 'My father is really upset. He said he tried to contact me to let me know that her death was imminent.'

'Surely you're not suggesting that *I* knew anything about it. We weren't even here,' Charles blustered.

'Yes, I'm sorry. I just thought—' Nadine then remembered that her father would also have had her old flat number. She jumped out of bed.

'Where are you going?' Charles asked.

'I have to phone Sophie. I'm sure she'll be able to tell me something.'

'No, wait,' Charles called after her.

Nadine stopped and turned around.

'Look, I'm afraid that I haven't been completely truthful,' he muttered.

'What do you mean?' Nadine noticed that he had a strange expression on his face.

'It was only that if you had known, I mean, taking into account your fragile mental state—'

'It's my mother,' she cried. 'You had no right to keep it from me.'

'Sophie and I thought it was for the best. We knew how important the tour was to you.'

'More important than my own mother? So you persuaded Sophie not to contact me?' Nadine accused him, astonished that her best friend would have agreed to such deceit.

'Actually, it was the other way around. It was her suggestion. Please believe me. We only had your best interests at heart.'

The thought went through Nadine's mind that there was something going on between them. Charles had always said how attractive he thought Sophie was. But surely the other girl wouldn't have taken advantage of their friendship. It then occurred to Nadine that she had taken her pregnancy tests with her when she moved back to the flat in Belsize Park.

A shudder went up her spine. It was Sophie who had given them to Charles. Collusion. Betrayal. From those she had trusted. Nadine felt her world falling apart. Her first impulse was to snatch up her son and just go, as far away as possible.

She rushed past Charles to the nursery. Dominic looked up at her from his cot, saw her fierce expression and started crying.

'You've frightened the poor thing,' Miss Pinkham said tightly, taking the child into her arms and cooing, 'There, there,' until he quietened. 'Your coming home has obviously unsettled him.'

Nadine felt like a stranger in her own home. The trouble was, it *wasn't* hers and neither, it appeared, was the child with tear-stained cheeks staring warily up at her.

I've lost everyone I've ever loved, she thought blindly.

First my mother, then my father, who wants nothing more to do with me, and Charles. I can no longer trust a word he says. Even Sophie, who is supposed to be my closest friend, has turned out to be false.

Ignoring their stares, no longer seeing any of them, Nadine went to get her coat and bag and walked slowly and mechanically out of the flat. There was only one person left who she could rely on.

Meanwhile, Charles shrugged at the nanny, chucked his son under the chin and then strode out of the nursery. As he poured himself a whisky in the sitting room, there was an unconcealed expression of triumph on his face.

12

It was snowing. Huge flakes fell quickly upon the smart street in Marylebone as Nadine stood shivering outside the Edwardian mansion block. She pressed Greenberg's buzzer. There was no answer. She tried again, desperate now for the comforting presence of the man who loved her unconditionally.

Receiving no response, she tried again, then turned away, her head bowed. Ignoring the bitter cold and with no destination in mind, she eventually found herself trudging around Soho.

The sounds of live soul bands and David Bowie records blasted out from clubs that were already open for business. Moving in a kind of trance, Nadine descended a steep metal staircase at the end of a row of pornographic bookshops and entered Hedgehog, the discotheque where she had first met Desiree six months previously. Girls dressed in hot pants or long skirts and platform shoes, and guys in T-shirts and skintight trousers were grooving to the DJ's music on the dance floor in smoky air filled with the sweet, druggy smell of Moroccan hashish.

Pushing through to the bar, Nadine ordered a large vodka, which she drank down in just a few gulps. She immediately ordered another, determined to anaesthetise herself from the events of the last few hours.

A tall unshaven fellow in a long leather coat came up

and started talking to her. Her mind was a blur and his words just muffled sounds. He lit up a joint, took a long drag and passed it to her. The combination of alcohol and marijuana had an immediate effect. Her heart began pumping so hard she felt that it would break through her chest.

Feeling an irresistible urge to get up and dance, Nadine dumped her fur jacket and shoulder bag on the young man. Pulling off her calf-length boots, she climbed on the stage and began moving in perfect rhythm to the music. Soon she had become the focal point of the club, producing gasps of disbelief from the audience she had created for herself.

After an hour of an unrelenting routine, oblivious to the wound in her foot, which had struck a metal strut on the uneven surface, she had to be helped down from the stage. Wincing from the pain that had by now become intense, she hobbled back to the bar and accepted the offer of several more vodkas before passing out cold on the pavement outside the club a few hours later.

The young fellow who had befriended her earlier called for an ambulance from a phone box across the street. Then, covering her over with her jacket, he placed her bag around her neck, propped her head against the railings and promptly disappeared, worried that if the police were called they would find the stash of drugs on him that he had been peddling all evening.

It was 2 a.m. by the time Nadine reached casualty in University College Hospital. She was swiftly admitted to a ward and put on a drip since she was suffering from severe dehydration. In addition, she had broken two metatarsal bones in her right foot.

At around the same time, the last of Greenberg's guests left his flat. Arranging the impromptu dinner for two of his closest friends had worked wonders on helping to take his mind off Nadine. He was determined to get her out of his system once and for all. Philip had even offered to take back the diamond that he had supplied him with from his father's shop in Hatton Garden, since he had another customer for the gem. That's what good friends were for.

Georges, his other chum, had supplied the wine and the food from his Lebanese restaurant on Edgware Road. It was high-class, which was more than Greenberg could say for the three beauties, done up to the nines, who he'd picked up on the way. With his athletic build and Mediterranean good looks, Georges was a ladies' man through and through, but Greenberg thought that he must have had to scrape the barrel to come up with a female cast far better suited to play the three witches in a production of *Macbeth*.

Tomorrow he would finalise the travel arrangements for his pals and him to go to Barbados. Even though it would start off as a stag trip, it wouldn't remain that way for long.

Greenberg chuckled again as the picture passed through his mind of the boys stuck outside on the step with only the three glittering young women and metal foil containers of lamb shawarma for company. They had been ringing the bell and getting no answer. First thing in the morning, he'd thank the night porter for being sufficiently alert to spot his friends and let them in, and he'd get the managing agents to arrange someone to fix the faulty intercom.

Nadine woke on the third day to find herself in a ward occupied by fidgety old women, constantly complaining, and young girls barely out of their teens, lying perfectly still, with vacant expressions on their ghost-white faces. At first, she thought that she must be dreaming again. What was she doing in a hospital? Although her head was thumping and her mouth felt parched, she didn't remember being taken ill.

Slowly the events of her last conscious hours began unfolding in her mind. The letter from her father that had left her distraught, and then Dominic being whisked away by his cold-hearted nanny when she needed the warmth of his little body to comfort her for the loss of her mother.

The sound of merriment distracted her. Struggling to lift her head from the pillow, Nadine glimpsed a doctor, accompanied by two nurses in Father Christmas hats, dispensing gifts and goodwill to each of the patients in the ward opposite.

Nadine began to panic. Christmas… With a jolt she recalled that Dominic and Charles were due to spend the day with her. Now she wouldn't be there to give her son his gifts.

The prospect of once more letting him down, being unable to make up for the times she hadn't been a proper mother… She needed to speak to Charles urgently, to apologise for her rash behaviour last night and to ask him to wait for her.

Nadine tried to get up, but her right leg felt like lead and there was a dull ache in her foot. Drawing back the bedclothes, she saw that she was in plaster up to her knee. She vaguely remembered dancing alone on a stage, music playing, people laughing and the distinctive aroma of marijuana.

There must have been an accident but she couldn't remember anything about it. Feverishly, she began to search her bag, since it contained her medication, but it wasn't there. The hospital had probably assumed that she had taken an overdose.

'Please, someone help me,' she cried out, trying to draw attention to herself.

'No good shouting, dearie,' said a toothless old woman with wild hair from the next bed. 'The nurses will be at their Christmas lunch. Anyway, what's a pretty young thing like you doing in here with a bunch of old vagrants and loonies? You should be out enjoying yourself. I'm Maureen, but on the streets everyone calls me Mo.'

Nadine did not reply but instead began weeping bitterly. Stuck in this dreadful place, unable to move, she had never felt so low. Turning away, she pulled the sheet over her head.

'Please yourself. I'm only trying to be friendly. There'll be plenty of time for us to get acquainted,' her neighbour sniffed, then went into a coughing fit that shook her sparrow-like frame.

After a short time, she heard footsteps and peered out to see an unsmiling doctor in a white coat standing at the side of her bed, carrying a chart.

'Miss Bertrand? I'm Dr Franks. How are you feeling?' Not waiting for a reply, he inserted a thermometer into her mouth and at the same time, placed two bony fingers on the underside of her tiny wrist to take her pulse.

He then withdrew the thermometer, glanced briefly at its reading and muttered, 'Temperature's ninety-eight.

Just going to take your blood pressure… Good. Well, all seems normal. You've been lucky this time.'

'There's been a mistake. I shouldn't be here,' Nadine tried to explain.

'Sorry to sound cynical, but I hear the same thing all the time, especially around this ward,' the doctor said.

'You must believe me. It was just an accident,' Nadine beseeched him, trying to sit herself up. 'Please, I have to go home.'

'With the sheer number of drugs and the amount of alcohol you had ingested, that "accident", as you call it, could well have been fatal.'

'I don't take drugs,' Nadine protested.

'So you're telling me that the reason we found a large quantity of benzodiazepine in your blood was because someone spiked your drink?' The doctor gave her a disbelieving look, before continuing on his rounds.

Nadine fell silent, shocked at what she had heard. She knew that she had consumed a lot of vodka, and remembered smoking a couple of joints, but the accusation that she had taken anything more serious was just absurd.

'Wait, please,' she called out after the doctor. 'I can explain. I take medication for depression. That's all, I promise.'

The doctor stopped and turned around. His expression was anything but sympathetic.

'And you expect me to believe that any medical practitioner worth their salt would prescribe a drug as dangerous as this, let alone fail to warn you of the serious consequences when mixed with alcohol? I'm sorry, Miss Bertrand, but I'm a bit too long in the tooth to fall for that one. I shall ask a colleague to examine you, and if she is of the same opinion as I am, I'm afraid you can expect to be with us for a good time yet.'

'You mean that I'll not be allowed home?' Nadine whimpered, her worst fears confirmed.

'You can be assured that it's in your best interests to be under medical supervision until you get better. I suggest that we enroll you in our therapy group for substance abuse. Dick Chambers is a very experienced psychotherapist and produces extremely encouraging results. Hopefully, you'll be weaned off in a month or two and can go back to doing whatever it is that you do. In the meantime, Mr Roger Hope, our orthopaedic surgeon who operated on your foot, will be around later in the day to have a look at you. Happy Christmas,' he said more cheerfully, before going on his way.

So it's true, Nadine thought. *They believe I am a drug addict. I should never have admitted to suffering from depression, because now they think that I'm a danger to myself. If only Greenberg had been at home, none of this would have happened*, she said to herself fretfully, remembering the snow falling and the lack of response when she rang the bell three times. Of course, he must have left for the Caribbean.

Now Charles, who she no longer trusted, was the only one who could help her. She needed to get to a telephone. But with Christmas upon them, and staff shortages, no one seemed available to wheel the portable phone to her bedside.

Better news came later that day, from the orthopaedic surgeon – an older man with a warm smile, who was an altogether different proposition from the insensitive doctor who had prejudged her. Mr Hope said he had guessed that she was a dancer, having treated many similar cases.

Being enthusiastic about ballet himself, he understood how important her career was to her and was able to assure Nadine that, after a period of extensive physiotherapy, she could expect to make a complete recovery.

13

February 1977

Nadine found it hard to believe she'd been in hospital since just before Christmas. Apart from the recurring dreams about her mother and the convent, which left her disturbed, the despair that she originally felt about being unable to contact Charles at the Chelsea flat had, strangely, been replaced by an inner calm. That this had been brought about by the change to a more benign medication, she was in no doubt.

Although her foot was slow to heal, she was a regular attendee at the group therapy sessions and found them beneficial. She had also made friends with two other young women in her ward: Tessa, a homeless eighteen-year-old from Birmingham who had been sexually abused by her father, and Kelly, a waiflike girl from a well-to-do family who had got mixed up with the wrong sort of people and had drifted into prostitution to feed her habit.

They were the only ones, apart from her family, who knew about Nadine's son. Many a time, sitting around chatting in her hospital gown and thick woollen socks, she'd talk about Dominic and how her life in touring musicals had kept her away from him for long periods at a time. The truth was, however, that by now she had convinced herself she was unstable and that her child was better off without her. And perhaps Charles also knew that. And that was why he had made no attempt to find out where she had disappeared to.

On a cold morning at the beginning of March, Nadine was discharged from hospital. It could have been three weeks earlier, but she had resisted, having become institutionalised in this place where all decisions were made for her. The fact was that she had become a little too comfortable.

When the taxi drew up outside the block of flats in Chelsea, she paid the driver and, still having to get used to wearing her own clothes again, she made her way slowly up the steps of the building she had fled from three months earlier.

Her heart was beating fast at the thought of seeing Dominic. There wasn't a day that she hadn't thought of him. Only her medication had prevented her from falling completely to pieces during the prolonged separation.

She wanted her arrival to be a surprise. Thankfully, it was still too early in the morning for the toddlers' playgroup that Dominic had been enrolled in before Christmas.

Nadine took out her key but it didn't fit in the door. Maybe she had made a mistake and gone to the wrong floor. She tried again, without success. It then dawned on her that the locks had been changed. A shiver went down her spine and she hobbled back down the stairs to the porter's desk.

'Excuse me,' she said, addressing a man she had never seen before. 'I'm having trouble getting into apartment 25. For some reason my key won't work.'

'That flat was sold shortly after I started here,' the surly-faced individual informed her.

'I'm sorry, I don't understand,' Nadine babbled, desperate to know what had happened.

'If I'm not mistaken, there are a couple of suitcases in storage, with some other stuff that was cleared out from number 25. No one's been to claim them, so we was thinking of throwing them out.' The new porter gave a put-upon sigh.

'If you want to hold on, maybe it's going to be your lucky day.' He then went off to the storage room in the basement.

Nadine stood shaking, only now fully understanding the consequences of her rash action in walking out on the night of her return from tour. Accusations that she had abandoned her own child would be justified. She pictured Miss Pinkham gloating because she had been right all along when questioning Nadine's suitability as a mother, and Charles standing by, giving tacit approval to the nanny's vilification.

She needed to try and think clearly but now, with nowhere to live, how could she reclaim her son? He was no doubt well settled in with Charles and his wife Clare in Onslow Square.

Then the thought came to her of Kelly, the girl from hospital, who had been allowed home after Christmas. Kelly had mentioned that she had her own flat, which her parents had bought for her in Earl's Court. Perhaps she would remember inviting Nadine to stay.

Nadine rummaged inside her bag until she found the piece of paper with the phone number she was looking for.

Just then, the porter appeared across the hall, lugging

two heavy suitcases.

'These belong to you, miss?' he said, trying to catch his breath.

Nadine stood outside the run-down Victorian house in the area of Earl's Court known as bedsit land and pushed the bell to the top floor. An unshaven man stuck his head out through the dormer window.

'Yeah? What do you want?' he shouted down suspiciously.

'Is Kelly here?' Nadine called back. This was not the kind of response she had anticipated.

'If you're some type of social worker or something, you can piss off.' He swore at her before disappearing.

'No, wait, please. My name's Nadine. I'm a friend.'

A few seconds later, the front door opened automatically. Nadine, using all the strength she could muster, began lugging her suitcases up the six flights of stairs to the top floor.

'Kelly's asleep, so keep the noise down,' a brusque voice hissed from inside the flat.

Exhausted, her sore foot throbbing, Nadine entered the tiny one-bedroom apartment, already regretting that she had come. Obviously, the invitation had just been made out of politeness, without any practical consideration of how to accommodate an extra person.

'You can doss down on the sofa, if you want,' said the barefooted man, dressed only in a round-necked undershirt and badly frayed jeans. 'By the way, I'm Anton.'

'Nadine,' she repeated wearily, just wanting a place to sit down.

'Kell mentioned something about a dancer from France

she met while she was drying out. Reckon that must be you.'

Nadine nodded.

'I look after her like the rest of my girls, but sometimes they spend their money on gear and end up in hospital or the clink. Still, business is business,' he shrugged, lighting up a cigarette. 'Want one?' he said, passing across a crumpled packet of Rothmans.

'Thank you.' Nadine took one out for herself.

'There's some coffee left on the stove. Looks like you could do with it. Going to be staying long?' the thin-faced man called out from the kitchenette.

'Just until I can find work,' Nadine replied, flopping down on a grubby divan, the cigarette in her hand.

The place was basic but she really had no option but to try and make the best of it until she could afford a place of her own. Then, despite being ostracised by Dominic's nanny, she'd go to Charles and reclaim her child, which as his mother, she felt she was fully entitled to do. Nadine offered up a silent prayer that Dominic was still young enough not to have been permanently affected by the upheavals of his first years.

Remembering the words of advice that the two girls had given her while she was recovering in hospital – *Never allow yourself to be separated from your little boy again* – Nadine suddenly felt more confident that she would soon be able to get her life back together.

Greenberg, his whole body dripping with oil, slid off the massage table in the basement gym of the exclusive Mayfair hotel. Wrapped in two large towels, he sat down by the side of the swimming pool and waited for his order of tea and toast to arrive. It had been a hell of a day, what with another of his mother's theatrical outbursts when she had barged into the middle of a meeting with a group of investors wanting to buy into his business.

'That ghastly man has ruined my life. I am going to die. My life has no meaning,' she announced, making her grand entrance. Not that she was saying anything new, Greenberg reflected. The relationship between his parents had been rocky for as long as he could remember. How two such unsuited people had stayed together for such a long time was completely beyond him.

Fortunately, the businessmen saw the funny side of it and were in such good spirits and so inebriated after their long and mostly liquid lunch that they thought they were being treated to a private viewing of his new show.

Then he had Melissa on the phone in hysterics because he had forgotten her mother Maria's birthday. Greenberg and Melissa had got back together again after he returned from Barbados. Partying until two o'clock in the morning and having to make conversation with an endless string of young women who didn't know the difference between a theatre producer and a Hollywood producer really wasn't his thing. Even though he was only twenty-six, maybe Georges was right. He was just born old. They both had to laugh about Phil, who had fallen madly in love with a gorgeous Bajan girl selling batiks on the beach. When he told his old man that he could forget the diamond business because he wasn't coming home, Sylvia, his mother, had threatened to put her head in the gas oven.

Still, having taken delivery of his new Rolls and with his company turning in record profits, Greenberg couldn't complain, could he? Life was good.

Tearing off a large wedge of toast, he smeared it with a thick layer of butter and marmalade and relaxed back on his lounger, thinking about the evening engagement with Roland White. Greenberg had secured the services of the West End's most illustrious director for a three-show deal starting with *All at Sea*, which was due to open at the Shaftesbury Theatre at the beginning of June. There were to be three months of rehearsals, which for once wouldn't be his concern. Peace of mind, that's what you got when you were paying for the best.

Greenberg showered and dressed, tipped the attendant and left. Then, as he passed the entrance of the gym, he saw the giant figure of John the instructor supervising a young woman in a bright yellow leotard and black leg warmers. Was it…? No, surely it couldn't be. But when he peered at her again, there was no mistake. It was Nadine. Greenberg's first inclination was to let it pass, not to get involved again in something that had only ever caused him heartache.

Halfway up the stairs, however, curiosity got the better of him and he turned back. The gym was empty. He must have just missed her. Looking at his watch, he saw there was still half an hour before his dinner engagement and so, assuming she was getting changed, he decided to go back and wait for her to come out.

Ten minutes later she reappeared, a large Biba carrier bag slung across her shoulder. She looked thinner than the last time he had seen her and there was a haunted look in her eyes.

'Didn't expect to see you here,' he called out as she walked past him.

Nadine stopped and looked around.

'Greenberg!' she exclaimed, her face suddenly coming to life. 'Finally decided to get into shape?' she said to tease him, as she went up to kiss him on both cheeks.

'How have you been?' he asked the young woman who had never entirely left his thoughts.

'Fine, thank you,' Nadine said, smiling and giving no indication of the traumas she had suffered.

'Auditions for *All at Sea* start shortly. It'll be great if you're available,' Greenberg said dispassionately.

'Yes. I'm sure that I can make it. Will it be the same cast as the tour?'

'That's up to Roland White. He'll be directing. It's going to be his call.'

'Allowing someone else to make the decisions? That doesn't sound like you,' Nadine laughed.

'It's just better for everyone concerned if I remain detached.' Greenberg didn't reveal that Roland had insisted as a condition of his employment that he would have sole authority for hiring and firing the actors.

'Right, I've got to be off. I can give you a lift if you want. Coincidentally, I've got a meeting around the corner from your flat,' Greenberg said.

'Actually, I don't live there any more,' Nadine confessed as they walked out of the club together. 'After my mother died, I moved in with a friend in Earl's Court, but it's only temporary until I can find a flat of my own.'

'Nadine, I'm so sorry. I really had no idea,' Greenberg said with genuine sympathy as they reached the entrance to the street. Then, drawing the woman towards him, he wrapped his powerful arms around her.

'She'd been ill for some time. It was a release,' Nadine explained, withdrawing only slowly from Greenberg's embrace. She missed the warmth of this very special man. How different his reaction was to Charles's callous response.

'Look, you've got my number. Call me, even if it's just for a chat,' Greenberg said, walking briskly over to the Rolls parked in the mews opposite.

As he drove past her, he couldn't help but notice that she was walking awkwardly. Assuming that she had merely overdone it in the gym, Greenberg continued to his meeting with Roland White.

Hungry from her workout, Nadine ate a hamburger then went back to Earl's Court, wondering what new drama she would find there. She was gravely concerned about her friend. Kelly had gone back on heroin immediately after leaving hospital and appeared totally under the influence of Anton, who provided her with just enough work soliciting punters to pay for her drug habit.

Seeing the life slowly draining out of the young girl, Nadine had tried her hardest to get Anton to intervene on her behalf, but to no avail. To him, Kelly was just an expendable commodity, like the rest of his girls. He would work her until she dropped.

Nadine, on the other hand, was feeling more optimistic about her prospects. Her foot was getting stronger by the day, and bumping into Greenberg was a bonus. With auditions starting in a few weeks, there was a definite target to aim for. Her savings were dwindling, and she needed to retain the position of Main Dancer that she'd had on tour.

Then she and Dominic would be reunited. Soon she would no longer have to make do with standing out of sight on the corner of Onslow Square, waiting for a glimpse of her son on his way out of the house. There were even a few occasions when she had actually followed him and his nanny to Hyde Park, just to see his face filled with joy in the children's playground. Wanting to reach out and cuddle him, knowing that she couldn't, left her perilously near to slipping back into the abyss.

Nadine got off the bus on the Old Brompton Road and walked the remaining few hundred yards to her home. As she turned into the street, she caught sight of an ambulance drawing away from the house and saw that a policeman was stationed outside. There was the sound of shouting as Anton struggled and was led away in handcuffs to the waiting police van.

'Sorry, love, you can't go in the house,' the officer said as Nadine approached the front door. 'It's been closed pending our investigation.'

'I don't understand. I live here,' Nadine said, fearing that something terrible had occurred.

'There's nothing I can do about that. I suggest you try and find somewhere else to stay. I'll need your name and an address, though, so we know where to contact you.'

'Yes, of course,' she said, giving the policeman the contact details of the only other person she knew, apart from Sophie. 'Can you tell me what happened?'

'A young girl died in there this afternoon. Top-floor flat. Third one this week from drugs.'

Nadine just managed to grab hold of the street railings before her legs gave way.

'Kelly's dead?' she whispered in shock.

'But at least we've now got the ringleader who's been

making those poor girls' lives a misery,' the policeman said, his voice full of satisfaction.

'You mean Anton?' Nadine said in a faint voice.

'Oh, that's just one of his many aliases, love. We know him as Frederik Claasen. Been after the blighter for three years. Hopefully, he'll now lead us to the rest of his gang – although word gets around quickly, and it wouldn't surprise me if the others lie low until the heat's off. Mind you look after yourself, miss. Don't discuss this with anyone, all right? And keep well clear of this area for a while.'

It had started to rain again. Still dazed, Nadine wandered across the road to a phone box. Putting a coin in the slot, she dialled Greenberg's number.

'Whoever was that on the phone at this hour?' the bare-breasted woman whined, rubbing the sleep from her eyes.

'Only a business problem that's suddenly cropped up,' Greenberg told her, swiftly stepping out of the room so he could take the call in private.

'Tell them that it can wait and then come back to bed,' she pleaded.

A few seconds later, Greenberg reappeared, sheepishly clutching the handset against his chest. He said to himself, *Why did it have to be Nadine, tonight of all nights, when I've finally got it together with Melissa again?* It had taken him weeks to persuade his former girlfriend that there was no one else in his life. Now he had to find an excuse to get rid of her, and he didn't have much time to do it in.

The image of the two women suddenly bumping into each other flashed through his mind, bringing him out in a cold sweat.

14

Greenberg stood waiting at the door in his silk dressing gown, reeking of a woman's perfume and unaware of the lipstick stain on his right cheek.

'Sorry, Nadine, I was just about to get in the bath when you rang,' he lied, concerned by the change that had come over her in just a few hours.

'I hope you don't mind my coming here,' she said shakily, 'but I have nowhere else to go.'

'You'd better come in and tell me all about it,' Greenberg said, assuming that she must have had some kind of a bust-up with the long-standing boyfriend. 'Go into the lounge and I'll get you a drink. Better still, if you haven't had supper, we could have something to eat around the corner.'

'Thinking of your stomach again?' Nadine said, forcing a weak smile.

'So I like my food. Nothing wrong with that. Anyway, look, I've lost a few pounds since I've joined that club,' he said proudly, parading his still ample girth. 'Although I have to say, I didn't expect to see *you* there.'

'I needed to build up the ligaments in my foot. A friend introduced me to the instructor,' Nadine explained, wary that if she revealed the true extent of her injury, it might hinder her chances of getting a part in the show. 'John said that it was all right to pay him privately.' She didn't mention to anyone that the trainer was a friend of the recently arrested Anton, nor that he had propositioned her, in case it cost him his job.

Nadine made herself comfortable on the sofa, thinking how differently things might have turned out if Greenberg had been at home three months earlier. Maybe she could have learnt to love him in the same way as he desired her. But the opportunity was lost, and now it was too late.

Perhaps she had just got what she deserved.

At that moment Greenberg appeared, carrying a generous measure of brandy.

'Right. Get this down you,' he said, handing her the crystal tumbler.

'When I got back to Earl's Court, where I've been staying in my friend Kelly's flat, the police were there,' Nadine told him, 'and they wouldn't let me into the house.'

'In that area, it was probably a drugs raid,' Greenberg surmised. And when Nadine nodded, he said, 'But you didn't have anything to do with it?'

'No, of course not. The girl who owned the flat – Kelly – she was only eighteen,' Nadine said, beginning to sob. 'And now she's dead.'

'You mean that she took an overdose?'

Nadine remained silent.

'They were probably only after the blokes who were pushing the stuff,' Greenberg said gently.

'Anton was being taken away when I got there,' Nadine mumbled.

'Who is this Anton? Was he her dealer?'

'I don't really know what he did,' Nadine said vaguely, not divulging what she suspected. The problem was that all her belongings were still over there. She would have to find a way of retrieving her two cases, since she had been living out of them.

'Would you mind if we leave dinner?' she asked, suddenly feeling on the verge of collapse. 'I've had a shock and I'm really exhausted. If I can just stay tonight?'

'Yes, of course, you're very welcome. The spare room is made up and the bathroom at the end of the hall is all yours.'

'You're very kind,' Nadine said, and meant it. And then she got up and limped off to bed.

Greenberg locked up and went to his own room, feeling a mixture of emotions. It was clear that Nadine was desperately in need of help, but her re-entry into his life had come at a bad time. Did he really want to risk losing Melissa again – and also upsetting and insulting her family?

He went to sleep with these thoughts going around and around his mind, knowing full well that resistance was futile. Whatever troubles he brought down upon himself, Greenberg would end up doing anything for the perplexing blonde Parisienne who had found a way back into his life.

Greenberg was already dressed and finishing his breakfast when Nadine came barefoot into the kitchen.

'Good morning, Nadine. I trust you slept well?' he beamed. There was a look of delight on his face at the sight of the scantily dressed woman.

'Yes, thank you,' she replied. It was true. The luxury of being able to stretch out in a large double bed after being subjected to the uncomfortable sleeping arrangements in Earl's Court had come as a great relief.

'Go and help yourself,' Greenberg said, returning to the theatre magazine he was immersed in.

Nadine went over to the stove, poured out a mug of coffee, toasted herself two slices of bread and came and sat down near Greenberg. She had made up her mind to go and see Charles to explain about her protracted absence and to ask for his help. There must have been a perfectly good reason for him moving out of the flat in Chelsea, she thought. It certainly wasn't his fault that she had run off without telling him where she was going. He had obviously just done the responsible thing and had got Dominic and the nanny to move in with him and Clare again. What she had to do now was to convince Charles that she was not the wayward woman he imagined – and that they could be a family again.

However, there was still the problem of where she was going to live in the meantime. Even if it were for just a few more days, it wouldn't be right to take advantage of Greenberg's hospitality and let him assume that they could be together. She had far too much respect for him. He could do a lot better than getting mixed up with such an unstable person as her.

'There's a small flat next to the Regent Street office that might suit you for a while,' Greenberg suggested, as if he was able to read her thoughts. 'I use it to put up business people from abroad. It's not bad and it wouldn't cost you anything. Have a think about it,' he said, getting up from the table.

'You would really do that for me?' Nadine asked, reaching up and stroking the side of his face, which now carried no traces of the rendezvous that had been apparent when she arrived the previous evening. If her assumption was correct, Greenberg had someone else in his life, and she was happy about that. It made her feel less as if she was taking advantage of him.

'At least if you were there I could keep an eye on you,' he said, smiling. 'There's a key for this place on the side. If you go out, drop it off with the porters. Right. I need to get moving.'

Secretly, Greenberg was hoping that she would still be there when he got home. What to do about Melissa was another matter.

15

It was a warm June evening. Nadine was waiting on the steps outside the imposing white stucco house, drumming up enough courage to ring the doorbell.

Her efforts to contact Charles by phone had proven fruitless. She had even gone, a week earlier, to his office in the City, but the message that came back from his secretary was that he was tied up in meetings, giving no indication when he might be free. Clearly, Charles was avoiding her.

Feeling dispirited, she had returned to Marylebone with only one thing on her mind: to reclaim Dominic for his second birthday in two days' time.

Fortunately, Greenberg had forgiven her for giving his address to the police. Two officers had turned up early that morning with her suitcases from the flat in Earl's Court, confirming that she was in the clear from their investigation. There also appeared to be no hurry for her to move out from Greenberg's apartment, since he had been having second thoughts about letting her move into the flat next to his offices.

Now, taking a deep breath, Nadine rang the bell.

'Hello, I was wondering if Mr Langley is at home?' she said to the willowy woman who answered the door.

'I'm sorry. He's out for the evening. I'm Clare, his wife. Charles didn't mention that he was expecting someone,' she said, looking bemused.

Suddenly, there was the sound of a child's laughter coming from upstairs.

Nadine's heart jumped. She was sure that it was Dominic. He wasn't in bed yet. An uncontrollable desire came over her just to pick him up in his pyjamas and take him away.

'Sorry, that's my son playing up in the nursery. He's always a handful before bedtime,' Clare Langley said, looking embarrassed.

Nadine felt a sharp pain as if she had been pierced through the heart.

'Are you all right?' the woman asked, concerned at the deathly pallor of the visitor's face.

'I'm Nadine,' she whispered in a voice so quiet that she could barely be heard.

There was a silence before the tall woman said impassively, 'You'd better come in. We'll go into the drawing room, where we shan't be disturbed.'

They entered a grand room with high-corniced ceilings and two sets of sash windows that let in an abundance of light.

'Please sit down and I'll arrange for some tea,' Clare said, walking off with great poise to the kitchen.

Left alone, still trying to recover from the bombshell that had been dropped on her, Nadine understood that she had a fight on her hands. For some unknown reason, she had visions of her mother again, using up her last reserves of strength as she cycled out of the transit camp, determined to save her unborn baby. With everything she had been through, Nadine was not about to give up her child even if her life depended upon it.

'I suppose it was inevitable that we were going to meet one day,' Clare said, reappearing a few minutes later with a small gold tray. After placing it down on the coffee table in front of her she began pouring tea into two china cups and passed one to her visitor, who perched nervously on the edge of her seat.

'You're so much prettier than I was given to believe. I can quite see how Charles was taken in,' she remarked, sitting down opposite.

'I don't know what you mean,' Nadine replied, hurt by the insinuation that she had purposely set out to ensnare her husband.

'I mean ... you did know, did you not, that he was married?'

'Yes, but—'

'And that we were trying, unsuccessfully, to have children of our own?'

Unprepared for the interrogation she was being subjected to, Nadine had no choice but to let Clare continue. She noticed, however, that Clare's was not the rant of a person wanting vengeance but instead of someone who felt she had been deeply betrayed.

'I'm sorry. You also are not what I expected,' Nadine said, feeling more confident. 'When we met, Charles gave me the impression that your marriage wasn't going well.'

'Did he now?' Clare said, taking a sip of her tea. 'I suppose he also told you that his family were extremely rich and that he didn't have to work for a living?'

Nadine nodded, curious to know what else she was going to find out about Charles for the first time.

'My dear, I'm afraid you have been badly deceived. Please don't look so shocked. There have been plenty of others over the years. Believe me, you're not on your own.' Clare put her cup down and, while running a slim hand over her perfectly groomed hair, she gave a deep sigh.

'Charles was just a clerk in an insurance office when I first met him,' she explained. 'He was always very good at mixing with the right sort of people, and with the handsome looks that he was blessed with, he never had any trouble talking his way into any society event that took his fancy. We met at a debutante ball when I was nineteen. That was twelve years ago now. Of course, he completely swept me off my feet. Naively, I thought it was me he loved, rather than Daddy's money.'

'I don't understand,' Nadine said. 'Are you saying that he married you—?'

'Yes, to get to my father,' Clare interrupted. 'Daddy owns a rather large estate in Suffolk and Charles had designs on one day being lord of the manor. You see, I'm an only child. And, there being no male heir, Charles, the rascal that he is, thought that the position was his for the taking.'

'But that doesn't explain why you stayed together,' Nadine said, only now finding out the true character of the man for whom she had been prepared to sacrifice everything.

Clare Langley crossed her legs in a relaxed manner.

'My dear, it has been a marriage of convenience from the start. Or, should I say that it has been, as far as Charles is concerned. I can't count how many times I've rushed back to my parents in tears, vowing never to return. But I always did.' She paused for a moment then looked Nadine in the eyes. 'You see,' she told her, 'in spite of everything, I love my husband.'

Nadine found herself feeling enormous sympathy for the woman whose gaze was fixed on her. Clare's experience of marriage had great similarity to and resonance with her own parents' relationship. Hadn't her mother Irène also been prepared to put up with a philandering husband for the whole of her married life? Maybe that's what had attracted Nadine to Charles in the first place, that unconscious desire to emulate her parents' example.

But Clare hadn't finished.

'It's been made perfectly clear to Charles that unless he can provide a male heir, he won't be permitted to have anything to do with my father's affairs,' she said next, her gaze steady.

'But you mentioned that you have been unable to have children of your own?' Nadine said, horror dawning as new thoughts came into her head.

'Yes, but you see when Charles owned up to me that he had a son with another woman – a woman who was ill-equipped to look after the little boy – I talked myself into believing that we could eventually be a family.'

There was a look of defiance on Clare Langley's face as she spoke.

'But that's not true,' Nadine remonstrated. 'I had a difficult time after giving birth, but I got better and then I started working again.'

'Charles claimed that you were suffering from manic depression and he then accumulated indisputable evidence that you were neglecting the child.'

The image of Dominic with the packet of her medication flashed through Nadine's mind. And even though they were strictly confidential, Charles might also have gained access to her psychiatrist's reports from his doctor friend. She could see now that Charles had taken advantage of her illness – even going so far as to have her prescribed the wrong drugs. This must have been why he had always encouraged her to go away from home. It was so that he could get his hands on Dominic. Not out of love for his child but for his own future prospects.

Nadine shuddered. Her mother was right. Charles *did* have a secret agenda. He had only come to Paris once he discovered she was carrying his child. This was the opportunity he'd been looking for: to secure his own future financial security with his father-in-law. Lord of the manor.

It all seemed so obvious now.

I meant nothing to him, Nadine thought, *but I was too blind to see it*.

There was a long pause, full of tension.

What if they were not prepared to give Dominic back to her?

Nadine knew she urgently needed to convince Charles's wife that she had been the victim of a gross injustice. She was Dominic's birth mother. It was only right that she should be the one to have custody of her child.

'You can see for yourself that the accusation that I'm unfit as a mother is absurd,' Nadine protested, getting to her feet. 'I'm going to be auditioning for the main dance part in a new West End show. You can ask the producer if you don't believe me. If what Charles said was true, how would I possibly be able to carry on working?' She had become flushed, and despite the cool temperature in the room, could feel herself perspiring.

'Funny, I assumed that you were the type of dancer in one of those men-only establishments. I had no idea that you were on the West End stage,' Clare remarked carelessly, leaning back in her wing armchair.

She then went on, her voice steely.

'Nadine – I hope you don't mind me calling you that – I can appreciate that you are in a difficult situation, but there's little I can do to help you. Our legal advisers have informed us unequivocally that in the best interests of the child, Dominic should remain with his father. Which, as I've just explained, means here with us.'

Nadine could see that the way she had been described had given Clare a completely false picture. Yet another of Charles's attempts to discredit her. Having been found guilty, she felt that she was standing in front of a judge, awaiting sentence.

'Please don't take my son away from me, I beg you.' And, bringing her hands up to her face, Nadine began sobbing.

But it was no use. The die had been cast, she saw. She was the victim of a wicked and cunning plot to deprive her of her child. A plot that had succeeded, and there was nothing she could do.

She had lost him.

'I really don't think that there's anything more to say,' Clare said, getting up. She then escorted the distraught young woman out of the house. 'I do hope that your treatment will be successful,' were her last words before the door was closed firmly and the lock pushed home.

Tears running down her cheeks, Nadine stood gazing up at the top-floor windows.

'Dominic, it's Mummy,' she cried out. 'Dominic, it's Mummy,' as she tried desperately to attract her son's attention. But it was to no avail. The little boy was nowhere to be seen.

Aware that she had lost the most precious part of her life, the one that made it worth living, Nadine strayed up the Fulham Road towards the Embankment with only one thing in mind. Spotting a wine bar, she went inside, in no particular hurry to undertake her final performance.

After ordering a bottle of her favourite French wine, she took her diary out of her bag and began recording in detail the events of her last, fateful day. She then fished out the small screw-top jar containing her medication, tipped the contents into her hand and washed mouthfuls of the pills down with one glass of wine after another until the bottle was empty.

She allowed around twenty minutes for the pills to start taking effect. Then she got up from the table and coolly settled her bill, leaving her shoulder bag and diary behind on the seat – she had no use for them now – and walked out into the moonlit evening.

In the distance, she could hear the strumming of an acoustic guitar and the gentle sound of singing. As she drew nearer, she saw the large crowd was focused on a long-haired musician playing Bob Dylan songs.

The whole area was lit up, and Nadine gazed in a kind of wonderment at Wandsworth Bridge, the vast metal structure that spanned both banks of the Thames.

Unnoticed, she removed her outer clothing and her boots and climbed gracefully over the low parapet wall and up on to the ledge of the bridge. The sheer drop below did not perturb her. With a soft breeze blowing in her face, her red silk scarf billowing out behind her like unearthly wings, she felt herself transported by some magic. She was back onstage in front of her audience. And suddenly that was the only thing that mattered.

She would give them the performance of a lifetime.

Standing completely still, her head held high, she raised one arm gracefully, and pointed one arched foot in front of her.

The guitar player halted. There was a hush of alarm in the crowd.

'Come down. You'll fall,' a bright-eyed teenage girl called out from the front.

'No. Stay still. Don't move.' A well-built man extended a muscular arm in an attempt to reach her.

'Someone go and call the police,' a panicky voice shouted.

Oblivious to the crowd's concern for her safety, Nadine then stood *en pointe*, lifting one leg high above her head. For a few seconds she remained absolutely still, a smile fixed on her superb face, until the foot she was balancing on, the foot she had damaged, suddenly gave way and she was carried off in a gust of wind to the murky waters below.

The next day, the news reported that the body of a young woman had been discovered, washed up along the river at Battersea. Nothing was known about her, apart from the existence of a diary left on a corner table of the Lone Wolf wine bar in Fulham. It had been handed to the police by the manager who, overhearing some late-night drinkers gossiping about the tragedy, had recognised their description of the victim. It was the same young blonde woman he had served earlier in the evening with a bottle of wine that she had drunk on her own. No one would forget that woman, he said, because she was so beautiful.

Even though the diary had been kept meticulously updated, the erratic mood it conveyed gave police to believe that the entries were written by someone of a disturbed mind.

Not having a lot else to go on, details were released to the press in the hope that her next of kin might come forward to identify the body. In the meantime, as a matter of routine, a post-mortem would follow and then an inquest, although the cause of death was obvious to all.

Suicide.

16

Greenberg arose early the next morning, expecting Nadine to walk through the door at any minute. He prepared breakfast, setting out butter and rolls, and making sure to fill a large pot with the strong French coffee that Nadine liked to drink. She said it brought her to life.

Glancing through *The Times*, he paid no particular attention to some amateur photographs of what appeared to be a woman balancing perilously on Wandsworth Bridge. That changed a few frames later, when he saw the same figure pirouetting through the air, to the visible horror of those who had witnessed the bizarre episode from the riverside.

Shocked, but praying that it wasn't Nadine, Greenberg drove straight to the named police station.

Greenberg was accompanied to the mortuary at the Royal Brompton Hospital, where he went to view and identify the dead woman. His face contorted. There could be no mistake. Despite some discolouration, Nadine's face – at least to Greenberg – had lost none of its beauty. The cropped blonde hair, he saw through the mist in his eyes, was still damp from the Thames.

The enduring image he had always carried with him of Nadine dancing onstage in her blue dress – so graceful, so joyous – was erased forever. The sight of her on that cold slab would haunt Peter Greenberg until his dying day.

17

On a muggy late summer afternoon, a small crowd comprised of several members of the chorus of *All at Sea* who had been on tour with her, gathered outside the Jewish cemetery in south-west London, waiting for the arrival of the body of Nadine Bertrand.

Before long, a black hearse drove through the unobtrusive entrance, followed closely by a single car of mourners, driven by Raymond Greenberg.

The four male members of the Greenberg family immediately sprang into action and hefted the plain oak coffin from the rear of the hearse. Positioning Nadine on their broad shoulders, the Greenberg males entered the prayer hall, an old barracks-type structure with a steep pitched roof, while her favourite tune, 'Dancing in the Street' by Martha and the Vandellas, played quietly in the background.

The whole clan had rallied around Greenberg when they heard of the tragic news. He couldn't have asked for more.

'It's a tragedy, Peter. She was so young,' his father had cried with genuine grief. Even though they had only met the once, Ray had really taken to Nadine, and she to him.

'Right, we'll take care of the arrangements,' his two brothers had said, putting aside any petty animosity they might have harboured towards him. And they were as good as their word.

They had been unable to make contact with any members of Nadine's family. So, once the authorities had released her to Greenberg's care, his eldest brother Clive had arranged for the funeral directors to pick up her body, and Barry had found the cemetery that would be Nadine's final resting place.

Everyone did their bit apart from his mother, who was miffed that the younger woman had stolen the limelight from her in such a dramatic way.

'*Bravo.* That's how *I* should want to take my final curtain call,' Valerie Greenberg said resentfully.

A low-key service followed, led by a nervous young rabbi dressed in a suit at least three sizes too big for him, who kept referring to the deceased as Noreen, thereby offering some light relief in what was otherwise a desperately sad occasion… That, and the enormous spread provided afterwards by the two sisters-in-law, Michelle and Janine, who had gone into business together to cater for such events.

Nadine was then taken by the same pall-bearers into the cemetery and interred in a simple grave, witnessed in silence by those who had come to pay their last respects to a young woman who had touched their lives for too short a time.

Over the next few weeks, Greenberg stayed late at the office, buried in work to take his mind off Nadine. His innate optimism had been replaced by a deep malaise that he didn't even want to try to shake off. He found himself sneaking into the spare bedroom where her clothes were still hanging in the wardrobe, just so that he could smell her scent. Subconsciously it had become his sanctuary.

He allowed himself a period to grieve, which amounted to no more than an unlimited period to dwell on his misfortunes.

Then one day it was brought to an abrupt end when a large parcel was left for him at the porter's desk while he was at work. Inside were items of Nadine's clothing and her big handbag. Greenberg realised this sense of finality provided him with the jolt that he needed.

She was gone. It was over.

18

It was the opening night of the West End production of Greenberg's musical *All at Sea*. A huge sense of expectation could be felt in the packed 650-seat Apollo Theatre as the orchestra began playing the opening score. The curtain went up and applause rang out around the auditorium as the audience caught their first glimpse of the stage, which resembled an ocean liner. The lights homed in on the chorus of thirty young men and women in full naval costume, who began marching up and down the three parallel gangways in perfect time with the music.

Greenberg, sitting well away from the seats allocated to the press, had mixed emotions. With the electric pace of the show and the strength of the original score, no one needed to tell him that he had a major success on his hands. That was what you got, he acknowledged, when you employed a top musical director like Roland White.

The trouble was, the lanky Irish-American girl who had taken over Nadine's part gave everything she had to it but lacked the lightness of movement that had made her predecessor unique. Greenberg sighed. Nadine was no more and he had to get on with his life.

But then his attention was drawn to a very pretty dark-haired woman at the end of his row. She had spent the whole of the first half weeping softly, as if the performance had evoked a distressing memory. She didn't reappear after the interval and Greenberg, left reeling from the ecstatic reaction of the audience, didn't think any more about it. After the show, he went backstage to congratulate the cast, and then made a quick getaway. He was due to meet his friend Georges for dinner in Knightsbridge.

Waiting at the taxi rank, he noticed the woman who had left after the first half sitting in the window of a late-night coffee bar across from the theatre.

Curiosity, added to the fact that she was extremely good-looking, led him to go in and boldly introduce himself. Considering that it was a Saturday night, the place was surprisingly empty, apart from a solitary waitress and two young couples on a corner banquette, dragging out their cappuccinos.

'Excuse me,' he said, going up to her table, 'but I noticed you during the performance of *All at Sea* over the road at the Apollo. We were sitting in the same row and you seemed very upset. I am the producer of the show, and I was just wondering if everything's all right.'

'It's most kind of you. I wasn't aware of making such a spectacle of myself,' she replied in a thick French accent, trying to hide her embarrassment.

Greenberg sat down next to her.

'By the way,' he said, holding out his hand, 'I'm Peter Greenberg.'

'And I am Sophie. Yes, I know who you are,' she said, shaking his hand and looking directly at him. 'I saw you glancing at me in the theatre. Nadine described you perfectly.'

'W-what? How did you know—' Greenberg stammered, totally taken aback.

'Nadine and I shared a flat together when she first came

to London. We were very close friends until—' Tears filled her eyes again and for a moment she was unable to continue.

'Here, take this.' Greenberg took the clean handkerchief from the top pocket of his jacket and passed it across to the young woman. He found it odd that Nadine had never previously mentioned Sophie, but then Nadine had always had secrets.

'I feel partly to blame for what happened,' the young woman said as she wept.

'I don't understand,' Greenberg replied.

'It's complicated, but if I don't talk to someone about it soon, I think I shall go mad.'

Greenberg checked his watch. He was already late for his dinner engagement but he couldn't drag himself away. Unconsciously, he'd been looking for any thread to keep Nadine's memory alive – and with the appearance of her distraught French friend, he might just have found it.

'Wait. I'll be back in a minute.' Greenberg got up and asked the waitress if he could use the cafe phone, pressing a pound note into her hand as he did. He had the restaurant number on him, and left a message, hoping that Georges would not be too annoyed. His friend knew that on opening night, anything could – and did – happen after the show ended.

When he went back and sat down again at the table, the young woman had wiped her eyes and was smoking a cigarette.

'I'm not sure how much Nadine told you, but her life was very traumatic,' Sophie said, inhaling deeply.

Greenberg smiled sadly. He had often thought that that was partly what had attracted him to her in the first place.

A troubled soul that he imagined he could straighten out.

'I tried to get her to confide in me but there was something holding her back,' he said, feeling that he could open up to this young woman.

'She couldn't,' Sophie answered, defending her friend.

'Why, you mean because of that other fellow she was involved with?' Greenberg recalled the hurt he had felt, knowing that there was always someone else in the background.

'So you knew about Charles?'

'I assumed that the flat she was living in was his, but Nadine never mentioned it,' Greenberg said, learning the other man's name for the first time. 'Anyway, what was he like, this Don Juan?' he added with false heartiness.

Sophie remained pensive for a few moments. Then, changing tack she asked, 'Were you aware that Nadine kept a diary?'

'I received a parcel two months ago containing a few things that the police recovered from the wine bar where she had left them.' A lump came into his throat. 'But I don't think I remember seeing a diary.'

'Nadine battled with depression. She wrote *everything* down. It was her way of dealing with her problems, a sort of self-therapy.'

'The police never mentioned anything to me about it,' Greenberg said and shrugged.

'*O, mon pauvre!*' Sophie exclaimed affectionately, touching Greenberg's hand. 'I know about the things she wrote down. It was all true, but no one else would have believed it.'

'And that chap Charles, where does he fit into the picture?' Greenberg asked.

'He is the father of her child.'

Greenberg's face revealed his shock.

'I can see that it has come as a big surprise to you,' Sophie said kindly.

There was a moment of silence while Greenberg tried to come to terms with this new revelation.

'How do you know all this?' he asked gruffly, sounding completely subdued.

'When Nadine telephoned me unexpectedly and asked whether she could move back in with me, I knew that something must be wrong. She sounded very distressed. You see, she had just learnt that she was pregnant.'

'By Charles?'

'Yes, absolutely, but she didn't tell him.'

'Why not?'

'Because he had finished with her. Said he was going back to his wife.'

'Yes, I knew that he was married,' Greenberg said, not needing any reminding of how he'd waited in the wings in case that relationship fell apart.

'Nadine stayed for a short while and then returned to Paris.'

'She wanted the baby?' Greenberg enquired.

'Yes – and that is something I could never understand.'

'She must have had her reasons,' Greenberg muttered, clearly distracted. Now he understood the sickness and why she had disappeared after they met for the first time.

'The birth affected her terribly,' Sophie went on. 'She was mentally not strong enough to cope on her own.'

'Couldn't she have remained in Paris?'

'Her mother wasn't well and Nadine wanted to get fit and to resume her career,' Sophie replied.

'But none of this explains why you think you were responsible,' Greenberg said, getting to the point.

'I was having an affair with Charles,' the young woman said, biting her lip. 'I'm not proud of myself but it just happened.'

'Did Nadine know?' Greenberg asked, thinking the tragedy would make a good French film.

'No, of course not. She had already returned to France. The thing is, I had given her my word that if Charles came looking for her, I wouldn't tell him that she was pregnant.'

'So what happened?' Greenberg asked.

'He and I started seeing each other, innocently at first, but I found myself falling for him. I can see now that he was just using me to get back with Nadine.'

Greenberg sat silently, pondering about the type of man whose allure managed to attract so many beautiful women and trying to stop himself from feeling slightly envious.

'You see, he discovered her pregnancy tests in my flat. It was after she had Dominic, her little boy.'

'And that's when he found out?'

Sophie nodded.

'Charles pursued Nadine to Paris. He told me he felt responsible and wanted to let her know that he would support her. He even provided her with a nanny once she moved back to Chelsea because he wanted to be near his son. But mentally she was in a bad way. You see, she had a history of depression and the birth was traumatic. Charles paid for her doctor's bills.' Sophie smoked for a moment before saying sombrely, 'The only time she was really herself was when she was onstage – and then her anxiety seemed to disappear.'

Greenberg knew from first-hand experience that what the pretty Frenchwoman was saying was true. Hadn't he also witnessed the drastic change in Nadine when she wasn't working?

'Then, when Nadine went on tour, I did something very stupid.' Sophie stubbed out her cigarette. She looked Greenberg in the face. 'I betrayed her. I agreed not to tell her that her father had been in touch to say that her mother, Irène, had died. Charles tricked me. He said he wanted the news to come from him, that it would be better if he told her himself. And Peter, I believed him.'

Sophie, who had begun weeping again, took Greenberg's handkerchief and blew her nose.

'It cost me our friendship. Charles said that Nadine had worked it all out, once she received a letter from her father. I'll never forgive myself.'

'I tried to get in touch with him,' Greenberg butted in, 'to let him know what had happened, but I don't know where he lives, nor do I have any contact number for him. As far as I know, he probably still thinks his daughter is alive.'

'I assumed that's what you might have thought when he wasn't at the funeral,' Sophie said.

'You were there?' Greenberg asked, wondering why he hadn't noticed her.

'When I saw a report in the paper and it mentioned a diary, I knew then that the suicide victim was Nadine. It didn't take long to ring around to find the cemetery. There are not too many Jewish ones in London. I came in at the last minute and took a seat at the back.' She wiped her eyes. 'I just lacked the courage to come up and introduce myself.'

'And her father?' Greenberg queried.

'I went to Paris to see Monsieur Bertrand as soon as I found out that my dear friend had died. I only just managed to get to see him, for the apartment is up for sale. It was a very difficult meeting.' Sophie gave a shuddering breath. 'When he discovered that I was the one who had kept the news of her mother's death from Nadine, he was completely distraught. He told me that he had written a cruel letter to her, blaming her and severing contact. So he too then felt responsible for her death. In the circumstances, it came as no surprise that he couldn't bring himself to be there. His guilt was overwhelming.'

For a while, the pair sat in silence, each absorbing what had been said. Then, gathering herself together, Sophie got up and went to pay for her coffee, refusing Greenberg's offer to do so.

Turning to him before she left the cafe, her parting words were, 'Nadine often said how much you did for her and how sad she felt, not being able to return the affection you deserved. *Elle avait raison.* You are a good man.' She came around the table, kissed Greenberg on both cheeks – just as Nadine had used to do – and then walked swiftly out of the restaurant.

Slowly, Greenberg followed her and went home with only one thing on his mind.

Heading straight for the spare room, he located the shoulder bag that had been returned by the police. And, inside, he found what he was looking for. The proof he needed to substantiate Sophie's story.

Nadine's last diary.

PART TWO

Betrayal

19

London, 2012

Greenberg got out of his car in Seymour Place in Marylebone, put a few coins in the meter and entered the newly refurbished offices of his accountants, Nicolaou, Franklyn Stevens.

He was feeling on edge. Reminiscing about the past had left him unsettled and ill-prepared for what was bound to be a difficult meeting. His assistant, Issy, had put her head down following their frank discussion earlier and had produced her best results since she had started working for him. Nevertheless, it wouldn't surprise him if she was up to something.

'Good afternoon, Rebecca. Michael back from lunch yet?' he asked the woman behind the reception desk, just as a burly motorcycle courier in black leathers brushed past him, nearly sending him flying.

'It's been a bit of a madhouse, I'm afraid, Peter, with people traipsing in and out all day. Must be the heat,' the receptionist said, cooling herself by the fan humming soothingly by the side of her. 'Take a seat in the boardroom. I'll let him know you're here.'

Greenberg followed her to the stifling boardroom and sat down, wishing there was a fan in there too. Shortly afterwards, a tall man in a blue linen suit breezed in carrying a pile of papers.

'I'll be with you in a minute,' Michael Nicolaou said, not bothering to look his client in the eye.

Greenberg nodded. He was used to the offhand way in which Mikey always treated him. His school friend had always envied him. It went back to when they were kids because, unlike Mikey, who came from a working-class family and lived with his three sisters above their dad's greengrocer shop, Peter had money in his pocket, and also because Ray Greenberg drove a smart car. In Mikey's words, 'You have always had it easy.' But the two men went back a long way and, to Greenberg, loyalty was important.

'So, the accounts are done,' Mikey said, passing a copy to his client.

Noting the ill-disguised smirk on the other man's face, Greenberg suspected he was in trouble.

'As you can see, they don't make particularly happy reading,' the other man went on.

Greenberg looked at the figures and gasped. The situation was worse than he could ever have imagined.

'You'll see there is a shortfall of six hundred thousand,' the accountant went on spitefully. 'I suppose even for a man of your substantial means it isn't going to be that easy to make up.'

'What are my options?' Greenberg asked. Suddenly feeling constricted in the airless room, he undid the top button of his shirt.

'Liquidate and let your creditors stew?' came the glib reply.

Greenberg frowned, surprised by the other man's flippant attitude.

'You know that's not an option.'

Mikey shrugged.

'The company's ring-fenced. So long as your National Insurance payments are up to date and you haven't been fraudulent, I can't see a problem. It's been done before.'

'Not by me, it hasn't. I've still got my reputation to consider.'

The accountant's expression said it all. If it was a question of keeping a valuable client or seeing him ruined, when it came to his old enemy Peter Greenberg, as far as Mikey Nicolaou was concerned, it was a tough call.

'I suppose you could sell the house, move somewhere smaller. I assume the place is in both your names. You'd probably achieve a reasonable price, even in this market.' Mikey had always been envious of the mock Georgian six-bedroom mansion in Totteridge in North London where Greenberg lived with his wife Suzanne.

'I might get two million on a good day,' Greenberg estimated. 'After paying off the bank, it still wouldn't put enough money back in the business to keep it afloat. Believe me, I've done the sums.'

'It's up to you,' Mikey replied, getting up from his chair. 'Right, I've got a meeting out of the office at three, so if you wouldn't mind…' He pointed to the documents that required his client's signature.

Greenberg got out his pen, signed the accounts and handed them over.

'Rebecca will see you out. Keep me updated,' Mikey said casually as he disappeared along the corridor.

Mopping his face, Greenberg slowly made his way out of the building, wondering how the hell he was ever going to get out of this mess.

Less than an hour later, Michael Nicolaou parked his new silver Jaguar in the short-term car park at Heathrow Airport. Before getting out, he gazed into the driving mirror and smiled at himself. He had good reason to be happy. Everything was shaping up nicely.

Issy Williams had followed his instructions to a T. Getting her placed with Greenberg after her three weeks' work experience with his firm was a masterstroke. He knew how short of money she was. All it had taken to win the girl over was a paltry couple of grand – and the promise of a rise in salary – for her to agree to stash the landlord's rent cheque, unsent, in her drawer. He would now arrange for the short statement, showing her employer's financial position, to mysteriously find itself on the desk of the West End's most prominent producer, Ken Brookman.

Greenberg had often bragged to him that Brookman was itching to get his hands on the Duke's Theatre. Now, with his dire cash situation, it was only a matter of time before Greenberg would be forced to hand over the keys of his establishment to his major competitor.

Mikey grunted contemptuously. That would only partly pay him back, the greedy fat bastard, for screwing around with and then ditching Mikey's beautiful younger sister Melissa all those years ago, not just once but *twice* – probably just because, like her brother, she wasn't born with a silver spoon stuck up her arse.

Mikey got out of the car and proceeded to the British Airways counter in the departures terminal.

Standing waiting for him, clutching two airline tickets, was a slim, heavily made-up woman with red bouffant hair, dressed in a satin bomber jacket and tight black jeans. Just as Suzanne Greenberg took out her mobile phone and tapped in a number, her lover came around the corner, pulling a small suitcase.

'Took your time, didn't you?' the woman said in her distinct Welsh twang. 'They've already made the final call. I swear we're going to miss the bloody plane.'

'Suzanne, I'm sorry. The traffic was at a snail's pace out of London,' the accountant said, lifting his case on to the scales.

'So how did it go?' she asked expectantly.

'Your husband could well be facing bankruptcy proceedings unless someone bails him out.'

'And what are the chances of that happening?'

'I reckon the odds are about 80–20 against him. Shows you what a little bit of creative accounting can do.'

'But what if he goes and gets a second opinion?'

'Suzanne, sweetheart, I've been doing your husband's accounts for the last twenty-five years. He hasn't queried them so far.'

'So you could say that you helped ruin him?'

'Only so I could get hold of his beautiful wife.'

'Michael Nicolaou, you can be a right bastard sometimes. Do you know that?' Suzanne went up and pressed her body against him.

'Nothing that a long weekend in Estepona can't put right,' the accountant said, grinning, as they hurried to the gate holding hands.

He hadn't told her about the planned diversion to Gibraltar to make a substantial withdrawal from his offshore account.

20

Over the next few days, alone in a large empty house, knowing that his wife was gallivanting around southern Spain again with her two girlfriends, and with too much time on his hands, Greenberg began to reflect on their life together. His friend Georges had gone out with Suzanne before he got married to a Greek girl from a good family. Then, once he had a wife and three young children, Georges had tried on several occasions to fix Peter up with someone, saying – probably more out of envy for his single status than anything else, Greenberg thought – that ten years on his own was enough for any man and that it was about time he settled down.

He knew Georges was right. After Nadine, and to obliterate the pain he was feeling, hadn't he thrown himself into going to parties, clubs, and on holidays, in order to meet as many women as possible? Unfortunately, none of the relationships lasted more than a few weeks at the most.

Then one day, for a reason he couldn't fathom, Greenberg decided to get in contact again with Melissa. Thinking he could just pick up where he had left off, third time lucky, he made some enquiries. His discovery that she had been happily married for five years, with a little son and a new baby on the way, hit him hard.

Georges's offer of an introduction to Suzanne came out

of the blue. Having no one else at the time, Greenberg decided there was nothing to lose.

Although her claim about being a fashion model had seemed slightly wide of the mark, Greenberg soon found himself falling for the high-spirited young woman from Cardiff. He recalled the time when he took Suzanne around to meet his parents after he had proposed to her, and the looks of disapproval – so different from their reaction to Nadine, ten years earlier.

'She's just a floozie,' his mother hissed, when her prospective daughter-in-law's back was turned. And even Raymond, who normally saw only the good in people, struggled to hide his disappointment in his son's choice of partner.

Nevertheless, despite their twelve-year age difference, Greenberg had made up his mind.

The wedding was a raucous affair at the Hendon Hall Hotel, the same venue where the victorious England football team stayed during the 1966 World Cup. The event was attended by coachloads of well-wishers shipped in from the valleys of South Wales. Apart from Georges, his best man, Greenberg had serious doubts that anyone from his side would turn up. He couldn't have been more wrong. The whole clan, including his mother, better for the several drinks she had knocked back beforehand, turned out in force. His sisters-in-law, Michelle and Janine, had catered the whole affair (at cost) as their wedding present. As at the funeral of Nadine, his family had come up trumps.

He remembered Nadine's wistful comments about his family, and his father Ray's favourite saying came to mind:

'A happy occasion needs to be celebrated.'

That was all such a long time ago. How he missed the insanity of the family dynamics, now that his father had passed away and his mother's mental health had deteriorated. His regular Sunday visits to the private care home in Southgate had become less frequent. Now she no longer recognised him he would come away feeling too upset. And with his brothers having grown-up children of their own and no linchpin to keep them all together, they only saw each other at family functions.

Without the prospect of a new show, perhaps he should have gone to the villa in Spain, Greenberg mused. Suzanne had grown tired of asking him. When they were first married, they travelled all over Europe and to America together, but she was always more interested in adding to her already extensive wardrobe or lying for hours in the sun by the pool than soaking up new culture.

It might have been different had they been able to have children, but after three miscarriages, Suzanne's fertility was irreparably impaired and she was unable to become pregnant again. Adoption was mooted half-heartedly but, as he was approaching forty, they both considered that he was too old to be a first-time father.

The truth was, he and his wife had drifted apart, and it actually suited them both to have the occasional break.

It had finally stopped raining. Seeing that there was nothing in the fridge, Greenberg went out to clear his head and get something to eat at the new Thai restaurant that had just opened in the high street, half a mile away.

On the way back, he looked in a couple of estate agents' windows. Finding nothing to compare with his own property, he felt more optimistic about his chances of receiving a price that would clear his debt.

Perhaps now she had arrived in Spain and was relaxing in the sun, it would be a good time to try to get Suzanne to understand that the house in London had to go.

When he got home, he dialled the villa in Spain.

'Suzanne, it's me. Just wanted to find out if you're enjoying yourself.'

'Hello there,' she said, sounding vague on the other end of the line.

'There are a few things we need to talk about. But if it's not a good time, we can leave it till you come home.' By the sound of the music playing, Greenberg assumed that she was having a party.

'Sorry. I can't hear what you're saying,' his wife shouted into the phone. 'I'll turn the music down.'

Then Greenberg distinctly heard a man's voice asking Suzanne who it was.

'It's him,' Greenberg heard her whisper.

'Tell him you're busy,' the man in the background muttered carelessly.

'What if he suspects something?'

'He's got to find out sooner or later,' came the reply.

Greenberg cut off the call and just stood holding the receiver. That distinctive intonation belonged to one man alone: Mikey Nicolaou.

Everything started to fall into place, including the reason for Suzanne's diminished libido. She had told him it was due to her change of life, even though she was only just fifty. Then there were the afternoons when she was never at home when he rang. Finally, he understood why his accountant had sounded almost happy about the state of his financial affairs. He knew Mikey still blamed him for breaking up with Melissa, his younger sister, a second time, and had accused him of keeping her dangling until something better came along.

Greenberg wondered how long the affair had been going on.

Lying awake in bed, he didn't feel any of the normal sentiments of a man whose wife had been cheating on him. On the contrary, he felt a sense of relief that a divorce or separation, which was obviously next in coming, would make a splitting of assets that much easier. At least he still had the Duke's.

On reflection, he wasn't in the least bit upset. His love for Suzanne, he now admitted to himself, had died a long time ago.

The next day Greenberg rose early, with renewed energy. He was due for a change in fortune and was keen to get started on a new project. When he got to the theatre, however, he had the third major shock in twenty-four hours. The place was boarded up and there was a padlock on the door. There must be some mistake.

Just then, two men in dark suits appeared at the front of the building. Assuming they were from the property company that owned the freehold, Greenberg went up to them to see if they could tell him what was going on.

'Morning, gentlemen,' he said, trying his utmost to remain cool. 'Would you care to tell me why I can't seem to get into my premises?'

'You are—?'

'Peter Greenberg, and this is my theatre.'

'Sorry, sir. As you can see, the place has been closed

down. We are surveyors. These are our instructions from head office,' the older one said.

'But you can't do that. I have got a lease on the place,' Greenberg protested.

'That may be so, but you'll find that if the rent remains unpaid longer than ninety days, the landlord is within his rights to take back his property,' the other one stated.

Greenberg was certain that he had given the next quarter's rent to Issy to pay before the weekend. Even if she'd forgotten, surely the landlords couldn't have acted that quickly.

'Now if you will excuse me, we have to get on,' the first one said in a businesslike fashion.

Greenberg suddenly felt overcome with dizziness and had to grab on to the side of the building to stop himself from toppling over. He had lost everything. First his home, then his wife, and now his theatre.

He looked up at the grey sky. Perhaps he was being punished. But for what reason, he couldn't fathom. Even though he didn't believe in God, hadn't he always done his best to treat people fairly? There must be a reason why everything was collapsing around him.

Having no idea where he was going, he moved slowly away.

'Mr Greenberg, we'll need an address to serve the schedule of dilapidations,' the assistant surveyor called out after him.

Greenberg stopped for a few seconds, then, ignoring the question, he carried on walking.

This time with his head held high.

21

As Greenberg cleared away the breakfast things on a cold January morning, he reflected on how greatly his life had changed.

The house in Totteridge had sold quickly to an anonymous buyer, the divorce settlement with Suzanne had been agreed, and his company, PG Productions, had gone into voluntary liquidation.

As soon as she returned from Spain, Suzanne admitted to the affair with his accountant.

'I'm sorry,' she told him, her South Wales accent always prominent whenever she was stressed, 'but I've been unhappy for a long time, Peter. We've just got nothing in common any more.' To her own surprise, she felt quite emotional saying the words. 'Surely it would be better, for both our sakes, to go our separate ways.'

The poor woman was shaking with nerves as she repeated word for word the speech he was sure Mikey had written for her. Greenberg drew her into his arms and gave her time to recover. The fact was that he had been through so much himself that his only reaction was to offer comfort to his partner of the last twenty-five years, even though he was the injured party.

What to do about Mikey was a different proposition. Greenberg could definitely see the ironic side of carrying on as if nothing had happened. And if the betrayal had simply been confined solely to his wife he might seriously have considered it. But he had a strong feeling that it extended much further. Being vengeful wasn't normally in Peter Greenberg's nature, but his livelihood had been ruined and whoever was responsible would sooner or later pay dearly.

Looking around now at the sparsely furnished flat that had been his home for the last four months, he wondered whether he would ever adjust to his new circumstances. Not through choice was he living above a florist in Camden Town near the famous market that tourists flocked to in their thousands. Even at £250 a week for the tiny one-bed property, it was all he could afford. But, no longer answerable to anyone else, things could definitely be a lot worse. Fortunately, he had managed to avoid going bankrupt and had even ended up with twenty thousand pounds in the bank, courtesy of a life insurance policy that he had cashed in.

As usual, Greenberg dressed smartly, preparing to spend the day trawling literary agents in the West End, hoping to find the script that would enable him to rebuild his reputation. All he needed was a break and he would be on the up again.

Three hours later, after achieving precisely nothing, he found himself walking past the Duke's just as a well-presented young woman in a smart button-down coat and black patent kitten heels came out of the theatre.

'Mr Greenberg, is that you?' she called.

Jolted out of his stride, he looked up at his former PA. Issy was barely recognisable as the timid, clumsy girl who had worked for him up to a few months ago. Her hair been straightened into a ponytail and she was wearing make-up.

'Hello. I wondered when I might bump into you,' he said, glancing up at the theatre that had been wrenched from him.

'It's ... not what you think,' she stuttered, her face suddenly flushed with her old embarrassment.

'Issy, I'm sure you had nothing to do with what happened,' Greenberg said, forcing a smile.

'I didn't really have a choice. You do believe me, don't you? Look, it's nice seeing you and that, but Mr Brookman only gives us an hour for lunch,' she said, and began walking away.

So now he knew it for certain. Ken Brookman had taken over the place. It just all seemed far too convenient. He had been stitched up and there was nothing he could do about it.

A few yards up the street, Greenberg called out after her, 'Look, if you're not doing anything, I'll buy you lunch. There's a decent place I used to go to that's just up here.'

Issy Williams stopped and turned around. Not knowing how to refuse, she said, 'If you're sure, thank you very much,' and tagged along.

'Go and grab a table and I'll get the food,' Greenberg said, joining the queue at Sammy's counter as he had done so often over the years. 'Croque-monsieur all right?'

Issy nodded politely, undoing her coat to reveal a pretty V-neck wrap dress.

'So, what have you been up to?' Greenberg asked, returning a few minutes later with their lunch. He was hoping to tap her for any information that would reveal how that villain Ken Brookman had managed to get his hands on the Duke's so quickly.

'Things are going really well. Now I'm in charge of scheduling, we've taken on a junior to do all the donkey work,' Issy said proudly.

'And you get on all right with Mr Brookman?' Greenberg asked, taking a large bite out of his toasted sandwich.

'He seems very nice, though we don't see him that often.'

'It just seems strange that with so many larger theatres, he'd be so eager to add the Duke's to his empire,' Greenberg said conversationally.

'I don't really know why, although I do recall overhearing a conversation with a man in his office, shortly after I started, who said something about how Mr Brookman could stay as long as he liked, provided he kept the place warm.'

'I see,' Greenberg replied thoughtfully. 'I don't suppose you got his name – the other man, I mean?'

'No, I'm sorry, I didn't,' Issy said. Then, wiping her mouth, she added, 'I do hope I haven't said anything I shouldn't have.'

'Knowing Ken, he was probably just out to do the best deal he could for himself,' Greenberg replied calmly. His suspicions had been raised, however. Why on earth should the owners be so desperate to get the producer in at any cost?

'And how about you, Mr Greenberg? Are you keeping yourself busy?' the young woman enquired, her previous fears seemingly allayed.

'It's kind of you to ask, Issy. I've got a few irons in the fire. After you've been in the business as long as I have, you learn to cope with the occasional setback.' Greenberg was trying to sound sanguine.

'That's good,' she replied, sipping from her can of Coke.

There was a short pause while the pair carried on with their meal.

'Anyway, looks like you've landed on your feet,' Greenberg said, laying down his knife and fork.

'The work's interesting,' Issy said cheerfully.

'And I take it that you've been able to negotiate an increase in your salary?' Greenberg continued probing.

'Nothing was actually discussed with me,' Issy replied. 'All I was told was that I would be pleased with what had been decided. And, I have to say, Mr Brookman has been most generous.'

A few moments of uncomfortable silence followed.

'There's still all your things for you to collect,' Issy said, changing the subject. 'If you don't mind waiting, I'll go up and get them when we go back.'

Ten years of his life compressed into a cardboard box, Greenberg reflected. The unpalatable fact was that he was history. Forgotten, as if he had never existed.

'There's no hurry. I can pick them up the next time I'm passing,' Greenberg said resignedly. 'Would you like a coffee? We've still got fifteen minutes.' He was trying to extend their lunch a little longer, since he had absolutely no idea what he was going to do with himself for the rest of the afternoon.

'No, thanks, Mr Greenberg. I should really be getting back,' the young woman said, already on her feet.

The two had left and were making their way back up St Martin's Lane, when Issy suddenly exclaimed, 'I am sorry. I almost forgot. A man with a French accent called up this morning, asking for you – a Monsieur Bertrand, I think he said his name was.' She blushed. 'I hope it's all right that I gave him your mobile number. He mentioned that it was very important.'

The name at first meant nothing to Greenberg.

They parted outside of the Duke's, saying that they would stay in touch, neither of them believing that for a second.

Greenberg had just got back to Camden Town when his phone rang.

'Monsieur Greenberg, you don't know me. My name is Jacques Bertrand,' said a frail voice at the other end of the line. 'I'm in London for a few days and should very much like to make your acquaintance.'

It took just a few seconds for Greenberg to realise that he was talking to Nadine's father.

22

The winter sun had already started to go down on the tranquil South London cemetery, when in the distance Greenberg caught sight of a dapper man with a cane getting out of a black taxi and walking slowly towards him.

Jacques Bertrand had described himself perfectly. Medium height, with a full head of white hair and a tanned complexion. He resembled Alan Ladd, the 1940s Hollywood actor, Greenberg thought to himself. They had arranged to meet at Nadine's graveside. It was probably his last chance, Jacques said, to see where his daughter had been laid to rest and to beg for her forgiveness.

'Monsieur Greenberg?' he enquired a little breathlessly.

Greenberg nodded and shook Jacques Bertrand's gloved hand. The old man reached inside his coat and produced a handful of photographs.

'She was so beautiful,' he said, focusing on the images of his daughter. 'We were too similar – that's why we didn't always see eye to eye – but I adored her.'

'She never spoke about you,' Greenberg said honestly.

'I was away a lot,' the Frenchman continued. 'You see, as a young man, I felt that I had something to prove. As a consequence, I put my work before my family and I missed seeing my only child growing up.'

Greenberg was aware that this very elegant man must

be looking for some sort of absolution before he died, although why after all these years he, Greenberg, had been selected as the one to provide it, he wasn't sure. They set off for Nadine's grave, walking slowly, mindful of tree roots and the uneven path.

'I assumed that since Nadine appeared in your shows, you knew her well,' the old man said.

'I often thought so,' Greenberg told him, 'but she was a complex young woman.'

'And despite the fact that she was a troubled soul, you still had sufficient faith in her to find her parts?'

'Monsieur Bertrand—'

'Please do me the honour of calling me Jacques,' the older man interjected.

'Jacques, Nadine was extraordinarily talented,' Greenberg explained.

'*Sans doute*, but with her moods and the traumas in her private life, it didn't make things difficult for you?'

'I was very fond of her,' Greenberg said quietly, finding the other man's line of questioning rather strange. It was as if in some way his loyalty to Nadine was being tested.

At the graveside, both men placed a stone in remembrance of the young woman they both had loved in their different ways.

It was getting chilly and the cemetery was about to close.

Jacques was the first to break the silence.

'If you are agreeable, perhaps you would be my guest for dinner tonight at the Savoy and we could continue our discussion,' he said, looking intently at the man he'd travelled specially to see.

'I would like that,' Greenberg answered, grateful for

the opportunity of keeping Nadine's memory alive for a while longer.

Taking a last look at his daughter's grave, the old man walked slowly away, leaning on his cane, Greenberg at his side, and headed back to the taxi that had been waiting for him to return.

Greenberg entered the famous mirrored bar to the muted sounds of good-humoured conversation and the clinking of fine crystal glasses. Three barmen in crisp white jackets were busy mixing a variety of exotic cocktails for their sophisticated clientele. He found Jacques Bertrand sitting at a corner table, making notes on a small pad.

'*Très bien*. You are on time,' Jacques said, beckoning his guest to come over and join him. 'I've made a reservation in the Grill Room. I hope it's to your taste.'

Greenberg sat down, feeling self-conscious. He couldn't keep track of the times he had entertained in the renowned establishment and yet, all of a sudden, he felt like an impostor. That was how far he had fallen from the success he had always taken for granted.

'You would care for an aperitif before dinner, perhaps?' the host enquired. 'I'm afraid that these days I have to confine myself to sparkling water – doctor's orders.'

'No, thank you,' Greenberg replied. It was clear to him that he was in the presence of a wily individual and sensed the need to remain alert.

'I ran a theatre during the war, you know,' the Frenchman unexpectedly divulged. 'In Valence, just south of Lyon. I was eighteen years old.'

'I thought you were in business,' Greenberg said, recalling what Nadine had once told him about her father.

'That part of France was under the Vichy government then,' M. Bertrand went on. He paused, and became visibly distressed. 'It is not a period of which I am particularly proud. Innocent men, women and children were being rounded up daily by the Nazis and sent off to concentration camps, while I, and many like me, just stood by and continued with our everyday lives.'

'Why did you stay?' Greenberg asked, wondering why Jacques had chosen to talk about his past.

'For the same reason most people simply turned a blind eye – money. I was working for my uncle in commodities – oil and petroleum – and, with sources of supply that no one knew about, we did very well out of the Germans. Then, after the war, with the contacts and the capital I had accumulated, I started my own company.' He sighed. 'I sold up and got out ten years ago. They wanted me to stay on, but these days it's a young man's game.'

'You mentioned a theatre?' Greenberg reminded him, curious.

'*Oui.* The only venue for live entertainment in the town, it was packed every night. There was a young woman called Solange, who I was involved with. Her family were the original owners but they were Jews, and when the war started the place was going to be closed down. I agreed to take over the running of the theatre with Solange. She was their eldest daughter.'

'But surely she must have been risking her life.'

'She gambled on the fact that, while we were together, the Nazis would leave her alone.'

'And did they?'

'Yes, until her father fell ill and their family's hiding place in the basement got discovered. The entire family,

167

including my Solange, were arrested by Pétain's thugs and handed over to the Germans.' The elderly man rubbed a hand across his eyes, before continuing bitterly, 'If that wasn't bad enough, I was forced to carry on being there every night as if nothing had happened.'

Clearly still affected by the memory of over seventy years ago, it took a few moments for the old man to regain his composure. Then, taking a large gulp from his glass of water, the colour slowly returned to his face.

'And so how did you meet Nadine's mother?' Greenberg asked, finding himself totally absorbed in the old man's tale.

'Irène and Solange were first cousins. Solange made me promise that if anything were to happen to her, I would see that Irène was taken care of.'

'And that included marrying her?' Greenberg said, more flippantly than he had intended.

'After the war ended, I found myself in Paris on business and, more out of curiosity than anything else, I went to the address that Solange had given to me. Immediately seeing the strong physical resemblance between the cousins, I deluded myself into believing that I could recreate in Irène what I had lost in Solange.' Jacques looked Greenberg in the eyes. 'Too late, I came to see that it was a big mistake.'

'And Nadine?'

'She suffered unfairly because I was caught up in an unhappy marriage.'

Greenberg thought about the similarity with his own life. How after Nadine died, he would subconsciously look for her in the other women that he met.

'Of course,' the elderly man rambled on, 'I had no idea at the time how greatly Irène had suffered in the war. For most of our married life, she was convinced that she was going to be dragged away in the middle of the night again because she was Jewish.'

'But, as you saw yourself at the cemetery, Nadine knew she was Jewish too,' Greenberg interjected.

'Yes, quite so,' Jacques replied. 'But being married to me, a churchgoing Catholic, enabled Irène to hide her religion as long as she could, to protect her daughter from suffering the same fate. The thing is, I never did fulfil my promise to Solange, and now I need to make amends.'

'I don't understand how I can help you.' Greenberg was sympathetic to the man's predicament but had no idea what he had in mind.

'That's why I went to so much effort to meet you,' Jacques was saying. 'Now if you wouldn't mind helping me up, over dinner I will explain everything.'

Jacques Bertrand ate little. The journey from Paris and the emotional upheaval involved in revisiting the past was taking its toll on his frail, ninety-one-year-old body.

Greenberg couldn't believe what the other man was proposing. The chance to put together a major musical production based on his daughter's life seemed completely surreal. It was, in the old man's words, his 'last opportunity to try to make up for the despicable way he had discarded Nadine when she had needed him most'.

'*Alors*, Monsieur Greenberg, do we have an agreement?' the old man said, suddenly coming to life.

'Jacques, it's very kind of you, but I'll need to give it some thought. What you are asking is a huge commitment.'

'Forgive me for being, as they say in French, *présomptueux*, but I was of the opinion that your business

169

affairs have recently taken a turn for the worse.'

'I see that you are very well informed,' Greenberg said, embarrassed.

'Let us just say there are times when a great deal of probing is required to get what one wants,' Jacques stated, a crafty look on his still magnificent face.

'What I don't understand, though,' Greenberg said frankly, 'is why you want me when there are several West End producers I could name who are better suited for the job.'

'But none who loved Nadine the way you did,' came the swift response from across the table.

Greenberg felt tears come unexpectedly into his eyes, and blew his nose. How could Jacques possibly know how he had felt about his daughter? Then it came to him. Although he struggled to recall her name, he remembered the meeting with Nadine's friend after the opening of his show, *All at Sea*. She had been the one to break the news to Jacques. What he hadn't realised was that they would have discussed the part he himself had played in the dancer's tragically short life.

'You are aware that my daughter had a child by another man? Clearly, it was a tempestuous relationship,' Jacques said.

Greenberg nodded, remembering the shock when he had discovered that Nadine's friend was telling the truth.

'I don't suppose you know my grandson's whereabouts, do you? I am aware that I have left it rather late in the day to make my peace with my Maker, but I can assure you that I wish to do so.'

'I believe that as a child, he went to live with his father,' Greenberg answered cagily. Jacques obviously didn't know about the conspiracy to remove the boy from his mother. After all, Greenberg was the only one privy to Nadine's diary.

'I've been trying to trace my grandson for a long time. Even with Sophie's help – she was Nadine's friend, who told me that my daughter had died – we didn't manage to obtain any leads. It is as if Dominic has disappeared from the face of the earth.'

Of course. Sophie. That was the name of the young woman he had met that night. But something didn't make sense. If she were still in contact with Nadine's father, surely it wouldn't have been difficult for her to find out about Nadine's son, unless there was something preventing her from doing so…

Then he remembered her confession about having an affair with Charles, the father of the child, and how ashamed she was of deceiving her closest friend. That must have been the reason why she didn't actively pursue Dominic's whereabouts, in case her contribution to Nadine's anguish regarding the relationship with Charles became known to M. Bertrand.

'But I'm grateful to her nevertheless, for her assistance in contacting you,' the old man said, smiling weakly. 'Now forgive me, but I'm getting tired. If you agree to help me, I will transfer one million pounds to you from my account here in London so that you can start on the project immediately. It will be up to you to use the funds as you see fit.

'There's only one request I have of you,' he went on, 'which is that my daughter's show must open before the end of the year. The doctors are not prepared to commit themselves further than that. Peter, my plane to Paris is not until midday tomorrow. I should appreciate receiving your decision before I leave.' The old man signed the bill for dinner and got up from the table.

'*A demain, alors,*' he mumbled, patting his guest's arm before leaving him.

Greenberg remained seated, slowly drinking a brandy and reflecting upon the life-changing events of the last ten hours.

23

Michael Nicolaou stuffed the last bundle of notes into his attaché case and closed the lid. He looked over at the naked woman snoring quietly in the king-sized bed behind him and smiled. Then, stealthily, he proceeded down the stairs, put on his coat and scarf and left the house.

Mikey had a lot to be happy about. It had only taken a small incentive for the manager of the local estate agent's in Totteridge to advertise the property for sale, and then to withdraw it the very same day in order to secure the place. Mikey's closest friend was Paul Wakeman, a sole practitioner solicitor and therefore perfectly placed to formulate the paperwork. Peter Greenberg's name was summarily removed from the Land Registry and replaced with his own as joint proprietor of the manor house in Totteridge Lane.

Since the luxury home had been advertised as *Price on application*, no one knew that he had paid a fraction of what it was worth, nor that the money came from an offshore account in Gibraltar. As far as the outside world was concerned, it was all kosher and above board. He had handled it beautifully, if he said so himself. Thanks to Paul, he had sidestepped having to deal personally with his client when he returned from Spain.

That was five months ago. Greenberg was now history.

And, as for Suzanne, they would get married as soon as Mikey's other business commitments afforded him the time.

Later that morning, Mikey was waiting on the quayside at Dover as three heavily built men wearing caps and with their collars turned up approached him.

The Jaworski brothers were the scum of the earth as far as he was concerned, but he'd learnt from experience that you couldn't always choose who you did business with. Whether he liked them or not, they were his partners in Eastern Europe, mostly supplying cheap labour from Latvia, Lithuania and the rest of the Baltic States for the British market. For three thousand pounds key money, young people in search of a better life were provided with a roof over their heads and casual jobs rarely paying more than the minimum wage of six pounds an hour.

Supplying accommodation was Mikey's idea. He had discovered that there was a healthy demand for scores of these slum buildings scattered around London and the Home Counties. Each house consisted only of a number of single rooms with shared kitchen and bathroom facilities, which would otherwise cost too much to convert to self-contained units. With no capital outlay, even he struggled to keep up with the vast amounts of cash the operation had generated from day one.

The tenants were not so lucky. Often finding themselves broke and unable to afford the exorbitant rents that they were being charged, many of the men resorted to petty crime, while their women were forced into prostitution to try and make ends meet. But that wasn't his problem. Mikey's view was that he was merely providing a service.

'Good morning,' said Tomasz, the eldest brother, grinning as he shook hands with his most important customer. Tomasz had a huge scar running down one side of his face and part of his left ear was missing, thanks to a fight over a business deal that had gone sour.

'The fifty grand is all here,' Mikey responded, lifting up the bulging attaché case. Even though to him it was only petty cash, this was the part of the business he liked the least. But he had to make the payoffs, otherwise the transport arrangements and the working papers for the next shiploads of people would come to a halt.

'The normal place?' he asked, glancing at the Premier Inn by the Eastern Ferry Terminal.

'I could do with a full English breakfast,' Marek, the tallest of the three, remarked.

'And some of that coffee of yours that tastes like cat's piss,' Grzegorz, the last one, said, causing all the brothers to burst into laughter.

Mikey led the way into the hotel. While he accompanied Tomasz to the gentlemen's lavatory, the others headed for their first meal of the day. It was the routine he'd insisted upon. The transaction swiftly completed, Mikey and his Polish business associate took up their places in the dining room.

'The price has to go up,' the fair-haired Marek announced abruptly.

'But the delivery schedule hasn't been completed yet,' Mikey reminded the youngest brother.

'Conditions are improving in these countries. It's not going to be so easy to get hold of the stock,' Grzegorz said.

'What's that got to do with our agreement?' Mikey was beginning to get annoyed. He'd always been wary of doing

175

business with Poles, but this was the first time they'd tried to vary the terms halfway through a contract.

Something told him that they were getting greedy. He'd done his research, and there was no way that wages in those Eastern European countries were anywhere near those in the UK. He didn't like being held to ransom, but he was a businessman. And if it meant going along with them in the short term until he found alternative sources of supply, so be it.

Then he'd go over there himself and make new contacts. The prospect of a Baltic cruise sounded most appealing. It could be his honeymoon with Suzanne. Since they planned to get married in the spring, it would kill two birds with one stone.

'I'll give you 10 per cent on the next shipment,' he offered.

The three brothers started talking together in Polish. By the expressions on the faces of Marek and Grzegorz, Mikey detected that they were clearly unhappy. More of a concern was the fact that Tomasz remained impassive. This was a problem, since he was the one who made the decisions.

'It must be twenty per cent, or we take our business elsewhere,' Marek announced sternly.

'I can't go higher than fifteen per cent, once the present contract has been fulfilled,' Mikey retorted.

There was another lull in the negotiations while the brothers mulled it over. Then Tomasz said, smiling, 'We have a deal.'

After handshakes and a general feeling of camaraderie had been restored all around, they finished their meal and the party dispersed.

Mikey knew that once the brothers got paid, they'd go on the town in London and blow most of the money on girls and booze. It would be a surprise if they left England with little more than the fare home. That was their prerogative. As far as he was concerned, it wasn't a bad deal. Since each contract was negotiated separately, all he had done was settle the price upfront for the next one. That is, if he hadn't replaced the Jaworski brothers before then.

Once he was sure that the last member of staff had left for the evening, Mikey returned to his office to await the conference call scheduled for 6 p.m.

Suddenly his mobile phone rang.

'Hello, Raj, you just beat me to it,' Mikey said, happy to let his most important client think he was in control of their lucrative business relationship. 'Right, let me bring you up to date,' he went on.

'Please do,' the softly spoken man on the other end of the line replied.

'I've just agreed the schedule for the next shipments from Eastern Europe,' Mikey boasted. He avoided mentioning the adverse effect on profits of the extra prices he'd been forced to pay the Jaworski brothers to keep the operation moving.

'And how are the new people you found for the Duke's working out?' Raj Patel enquired, more concerned about presenting a respectable front for the huge quantity of slum housing scattered around the capital, which was the reason why he had purchased the trophy building in the first place.

'Everything's fine on that front,' Mikey assured Patel.

It had been far easier than he had anticipated. All it had taken was one phone call to Ken Brookman. The famed producer had been so keen to take over the place that it was as if his personal vendetta against Peter Greenberg was even greater than Mikey's own.

'That's good to hear. I'm sure you don't need reminding that I mustn't be seen to have any association with those particular properties,' the client stressed.

'Raj, with the network of nominee companies registered offshore that I've set up, I can guarantee there's no possibility of any comeback on you – which brings me to the question of formalising our agreement.'

'Ah, yes, of course. There's never any chance of a free lunch where accountants are involved, is there?' the other man said smoothly. 'However, we've already settled on your 25 per cent, have we not?'

Mikey was taken aback. This was far less than had been intimated. After all, he'd saved the man millions of pounds in tax.

'Sorry Raj, we did actually agree on 45 per cent.'

The smooth voice hardened.

'It will be 30 per cent. And that's final. And don't forget the hundred thousand retainer you managed to wheedle out of me on top. I'd think about it very carefully if I were you. It wouldn't go down too well if your other partners got to hear of the large amounts of money you were raking off on the side.'

Mikey was speechless. It was obvious that he had seriously underestimated the fellow.

'When you've drawn up the papers, you can bike them over,' Patel said, before the line went dead.

24

Greenberg still had difficulty digesting what had been offered. A show of his own, all the financing in place and a heart-wrenching tale that, if he didn't know better, could only have been the product of an overactive imagination. He should have bitten the man's hand off. But there was something holding him back from agreeing there and then. Sitting in his overcoat in his cold flat, no closer to being able to solve his dilemma, he poured himself a large whisky and went to bed.

The next morning, feeling refreshed, he suddenly understood what was troubling him. It was that he was the only one who knew everything about Nadine. Hadn't he, for his own peace of mind, gone over and over every entry in her diary until he knew her as well as he knew himself? The problem facing him was how to portray an accurate image of her life, one that would do her justice, when there were several episodes that would show her in a less than favourable light.

It came to him that for the sake of her elderly father, he would have to tell him that he just couldn't do it.

Greenberg put down his phone. Overcome with emotion, he could still hear Jacques Bertrand's words in his head.

'Of course I expected you to decline,' he had said. 'Your humility, the self-doubt... That's precisely what makes you the only man worthy of recreating my daughter's life onstage. Trust me. You must do it for all those who knew her and loved her. Not only for me but for her mother, for Dominic, her son – and also, my dear, dear man, for your good self.'

Greenberg had his mind made up for him. He gave Jacques his bank details, even though he suspected it was a tall order to have the show ready by Christmas 2013. It was still only early February but he would give the project his best shot.

The first thing he needed to do was to get hold of his personal items at the Duke's, the ones that Issy had put aside. He had always trusted her with a key to his office. With luck, there wouldn't be anything missing. Nevertheless, he needed to contact her to say that he would be dropping by to collect them.

Trying to dispel the fear that Nadine's diary might have disappeared, he dressed quickly and took the number 29 bus to Trafalgar Square. By the time he reached the theatre, Issy was standing outside with an old suitcase.

Everything was there: the diary, the awards he had received, even the cash deposit box containing the diamond engagement ring. He felt a huge sense of relief.

When he got home, there was a message on his landline answerphone from Barclays Bank saying that a large amount of money had been transferred into his account and they needed him to confirm that it was in order. They wanted him to arrange a time to come in and discuss how to invest it.

Jacques had done what he'd said. Now it was up to Greenberg to keep to his side of the bargain.

Trying to prioritise what needed to be done was harder than he had anticipated. He hadn't worked in nearly a year, and what had always been second nature in the past – starting on a new show – now seemed a daunting prospect. Switching on his computer, and working from memory, Greenberg started on a résumé of the unique woman he had been charged to bring back to life. He had a weird sensation that Nadine was with him again in spirit, as if to guide him through the enormous challenge he had committed himself to.

Next, he had to engage a writer who was able to truly empathise with the main character.

Armed with the synopsis, Greenberg marched into the office of Dawson McClintock, the most respected literary agent in the West End, a couple of hard-working days later. This was his first setback. Naively he had assumed that, now he had an important project in progress, he could rely on his reputation of old, and that doors which in the past had automatically opened for him would continue to so. He could not have been more wrong.

He was informed that Pauline, whose father had started the business, was in back-to-back meetings for the rest of the day and would be unable to spare him even a few minutes. Her personal assistant suggested that he email them with a proposal instead and mark it for her attention.

Refusing to feel despondent, he kept on, with his next destination firmly in mind. The firm of J. Levy had been around ever since he could remember and occupied a small space on the top floor of a shabby building on the Charing Cross Road.

Greenberg pressed the buzzer. A crackling sound signalled the release of the front door.

'Jules, how are you?' Greenberg called out as he struggled up the last flight of stairs.

'Thought I was getting old till I saw you,' quipped the slight man with a strong European accent, who was waiting outside his office.

'It has been a long time, hasn't it?' Greenberg agreed, shaking hands with the agent he had dealt with for more than thirty years. Jules beckoned him in.

'So come in and tell me where you disappeared to.'

The two entered the small reception area, a cramped space overlooking the busy main road manned by Annie Stein, a jolly grey-haired lesbian whose job, Greenberg remembered, was to spend the entire day on the phone pacifying anxious writers who were desperate to make a name for themselves.

Greenberg acknowledged her with a pleasant smile as he walked past and entered a sparsely decorated office.

Typical Jules, he thought. Never spent a penny that couldn't be justified. That's why he was still in business when many others like him had folded.

'So, my dear, what can I do for you?' the agent asked, positioning himself behind a cluttered desk.

'I'd like your view on this,' Greenberg said, handing him the synopsis that he'd been working on. 'It will require a good writer.'

Levy put on his specs, sat back on his chair and began reading. When he'd finished, he put the paper down, looked up and said, 'Is it true? Not that it really matters.'

'Every word of it. Why do you ask?' Greenberg said, hoping for a positive response.

'It's an interesting story. You might have something if it's handled properly,' the canny agent concluded, keeping hold of the piece.

Greenberg smiled. For Jules not to discard something straight away meant that he probably loved it.

'I've got just the boy for this,' the agent said, standing up abruptly. 'Annie, get Jake Simmonds on the phone,' he screamed across the office. 'Tell him to come in at four this afternoon, will you? And if you need a place to work,' he said, turning to his long-established client, 'there's always space here. Nothing to be ashamed of because you've been through a tough time. Remember, it only takes one success.'

'Thanks, Jules. I really appreciate the offer. I'll have a think about it.' Greenberg got up to leave. 'I'll say goodbye to Annie.'

And he clumped back downstairs, feeling far more confident than when he had arrived.

A month passed. At the end of it, Greenberg was presented with the first three scenes of his new musical. Once he'd read it he saw that Jules's assessment of the young writer had been entirely accurate. Jake had got to grips with Nadine's character immediately.

Knowing from experience how important it was to convey the right image in the theatrical world, Greenberg took a serviced unit in Covent Garden that offered full secretarial facilities and the use of a pleasant meeting room. He formed a new company, Peter Greenberg Productions, printed a full set of business stationery and employed a website designer to establish his presence on the Internet. His brass nameplate gleamed prominently on the door of his new office, whose walls were lined with the memorabilia of thirty years in the theatre business.

Greenberg had returned to the only world he felt truly alive in.

At first he considered it only right to keep Jacques updated with how things were progressing. Unfortunately, four weeks later he received the news that Nadine's father had suffered a serious stroke, leaving him semi-paralysed and confined to a wheelchair. Greenberg was genuinely upset. Even though they had only met once, he had grown very attached to the old man. It was nothing to do with the amount of money Jacques had placed at his disposal for his daughter's show.

Greenberg knew then that, unless he got a move on, the old man wouldn't live long enough to see the opening.

25

The detective inspector, a shifty-looking individual a few years off retirement, glanced at the police report on his desk.

'Too many bloody threads and nothing to join 'em up, that's the trouble,' he muttered to himself, scratching his head.

But Brian Morley had cracked harder cases than this and wasn't about to give up. He knew all about the Dover operation and the scores of entrants from the Baltic. His boys had picked up many of them on the streets around the capital, and they all claimed they had been thrown out of their lodgings and had nowhere else to go. Even though their papers were faultlessly in order, they were too frightened to supply the names of those who had organised their passage. The most he was able to glean was that they had used up all their savings getting to the UK and wanted to return home.

Yes, there was no question that he was dealing with a bunch of professionals, but DI Morley knew it was only the tip of the iceberg. An operation on this scale required money, and a lot of it. He needed to find out who the ringleaders were – who were lining their pockets at the expense of these naive, unsuspecting people.

"Ere, Connolly, got anything to report on the fire at the house in Newham?' he called over to the trainee investigator sitting at the other side of the open-plan office. Newham was a deprived area of inner-city London.

'Yes, sir,' the spotty young man replied. 'Three fatalities so far, five still in the house, and the remainder seem to have made a run for it. Appears it was caused by a gas leak. Fire Officer Eddie Lawrence, area manager from Tower Hamlets, told the local press that it's a miracle the whole place hadn't gone up in flames.'

'Any clue about the landlord's whereabouts?' the detective asked.

'None, except it's one of those overcrowded dwellings, six-to-a-room jobbies. Occupied mainly by Eastern Europeans, from what I hear.'

'Right, lad, get on to the Land Registry and find out who owns the place. I want full names and addresses.'

Brian Morley opened his expensive leather diary and took out the two tickets he had been given to the Duke's Theatre for Saturday night. It was ages since he'd taken his wife for a posh night out, and Saturday was her birthday. Michael Nicolaou was a decent enough bloke. He could get tickets to anything – which was handy because, like Brian, the bloke was sports mad.

The detective cleared his paperwork away, got up and put on his coat.

'Oh, and make sure to put the airports, including the private ones, on alert. I don't want anybody doing a runner before we get to them. Right, I'm off,' he announced. 'See you lot in the morning.'

The other members of the team knew that was Brian Morley's way of saying that he was going down the pub for a few gin and tonics before heading for home.

*

At the same time an emergency meeting of the executive board of Patel Enterprises had just begun in the group's plush Queen Anne offices overlooking St James's Park.

Michael Nicolaou looked at the ten anxious faces around the table and could see that each man was wondering why, in the absence of their chairman who had been delayed by adverse weather conditions in Mumbai, they had been summoned to a board meeting at such short notice. He had no intention of telling them the real reason why he himself had been asked to attend. The fact was that news of a potentially damaging investigation into the suspicious circumstances surrounding a fire at one of their properties had somehow reached Raj, and he urgently wanted steps put in place that would distance him from any wrongdoing.

He stood up and cleared his throat to gain their attention.

'Gentlemen, it appears that we've got a problem on our hands,' he said glibly from his position at the head of the table, and proceeded to bring them up to date about the fire. Mikey himself remained unperturbed. He was sufficiently knowledgeable on matters of company law to be aware that, not being a director, there was no action that could be brought against him.

The other members looked at each other with shocked expressions. An eerie silence filled the boardroom.

'Ahem,' exclaimed a distinguished man in a grey pin-striped suit, standing up. Matthew Foux was the in-house company lawyer, and ostensibly Raj's second-in-command.

'Yes, Matthew? I'm sure the rest of us would be interested to hear what you have to say.'

'I can assure everyone,' Matthew began, puffed up with

his own self-importance, 'that although it's extremely regrettable that this fire occurred, we are fully insured. I'm not really sure, therefore, what there is to worry about.'

'How about the fact that the property was not fitted with adequate fire escapes?' commented another board member at the table.

'And when was the last time the gas installation was serviced?' added the young fresh-faced surveyor.

'Listen to this,' said the nervous-looking finance director, who began reading the headline of the *Evening Standard* newspaper that he was holding up.

Gas Explosion at House in East London. Eight Dead, Ten Others Missing.

Police Launch Criminal Investigation Against Owners.

He looked around the table and said in a panic, 'We're all going to end up being sent to prison.'

Tension gripped the room. Forced to contemplate that they were jointly culpable, through their negligence, for the deaths of so many innocent people, the entire board of directors froze.

Mikey Nicolaou didn't give a toss about the victims. He found it all highly amusing and was already working on a plan of how to turn the situation to his advantage. He knew that if he could make the investigation go away, his value to Raj would increase enormously and net him a substantial sum of money in the process.

All might not be lost, he thought. It was odds-on that his good friend Detective Inspector Morley of Scotland Yard would be handling the investigation. A chance for him to get his name in the papers would prove too hard for that publicity-seeking prat to resist. If Mikey was correct, there was more than one way of ensuring that a prosecution against Raj Enterprises never saw the light of day. All of a sudden, the dinner that had been arranged weeks ago to celebrate Catherine Morley's fiftieth birthday had taken on an extra-special significance.

The meeting broke up as the participants, a sense of foreboding hanging over them, filed despondently out of the boardroom and returned to their duties.

'Mr Nicolau, may I have a quick word?' the in-house lawyer requested.

'OK, Matthew, but do make it quick. I've got another meeting to get to,' Mikey replied.

'Since I'm just a few months away from retirement, I trust you'll put a good word in for me with Mr Patel,' Foux said humbly. 'I can assure you that I had no involvement whatsoever in this dreadful incident.'

'Very well,' Mikey said condescendingly, giving a sneer as the lift doors closed on the lawyer.

26

Greenberg put the script down and let out a huge sigh of relief.

'Not bad, not bad at all,' he muttered to himself. Working into the early hours night after night had paid off. A decent first draft had come of it, which even Jules admitted had all the bones of a sensational story. The boy had done well. Of course they'd had their disagreements. Which writers weren't overprotective of their work? The difference with Jake was that he wanted to make Nadine's character his own and didn't always appreciate that her unpredictable nature (which he, Peter Greenberg, knew better than anyone) would capture the public's imagination.

Greenberg glanced at the coloured wallchart that gave him a detailed breakdown of every component part of the show. Few outside the business were aware of the military-style precision required in bringing all the elements together for a West End production.

It was still only the beginning of May, and eight months might have seemed sufficient time – apart from the fact that he hadn't started looking for a theatre yet, let alone applied his mind to the cast – and then there was still the score to be arranged.

The reality of having to commit to a long run at a West End theatre suddenly came home to him. Consumed with self-doubt, the confidence that as a young man had enabled Greenberg to splash out tens of thousands of pounds of his own money without thinking twice now appeared to elude him.

It had been a piece of cake when he owned the Duke's, for it meant he had his own place to try out a new show or could transfer it there when he had had the opportunity to tour it first. But this was a different proposition altogether. The prospect of going in completely cold was unnerving, to say the least.

For a brief moment he wondered whether he had been foolish, allowing himself to be talked into this venture. Then, remembering how he had never shied away from a difficult situation, his courage slowly returned. He'd made a commitment and he wasn't a man to go back on his word.

With renewed enthusiasm Greenberg spent the week on the phone, trying to secure a four-month slot for his show. He called all the premier theatres in the West End first, and then some of the smaller, less well-known venues.

He was left bitterly disappointed. With those like the Shaftesbury and the Wyndham's, which weren't already booked, he found he no longer held any sway. The reaction was always the same:

'Tell us who the director is and which *names* you've got for the cast and we'll give it our due consideration.'

He'd come up against a brick wall.

Eventually, Greenberg reluctantly concluded that he would have to return Jacques Bertrand's money and tell him that he wasn't able to put the show together.

A feeling of huge disappointment enveloped his whole being as he picked up the phone and began to tap in the Paris number. Just then, he recalled what the shrewd old man had said to him over dinner about the lengths he had gone to so he could find him in London. Surely, if Greenberg was prepared to throw in the towel that easily, Jacques Bertrand would have good reason to regret that he had selected him for the job.

There was no time for despondency. He needed to find a solution. Impulsively, he began flipping through the 200-page script.

All of a sudden, Greenberg stopped. Inadvertently, he had found what he was looking for. It had been staring him in the face the whole time, but he'd been too blind to see it. Dominic, Nadine's son. Dominic Langley was the key to making the show a reality.

What he had to do now was find a way of getting to him, the hottest director on Broadway, and persuade him to read his script. The other problem was that he needed to be able to verify to Dominic that the script was about his birth mother. The only two people who knew Dominic as a baby, apart from Charles and his wife, were Nadine's friend Sophie, and more importantly, Jacques Bertrand, Dominic's grandfather. He needed to pay the old man a visit.

Greenberg booked himself on the 6 a.m. flight to Paris the next day. When he telephoned to find out whether it would be possible to see Jacques, he was told that the old man was making a remarkable recovery after spending many weeks in a nursing home.

On arriving at the apartment in the exclusive Avenue Foch, Greenberg was shown into a splendid drawing room. At first he wondered why a man on his own, even one as wealthy as Jacques Bertrand, would need such a substantial place to live. Looking around the apartment, the answer immediately became clear. The shelves were full of photographs of Nadine and her mother Irène. This was the family home that Nadine had described so vividly in her diary, where she had returned to have her baby after they had first met. Contrary to what her father had said in that unfortunate letter, informing his daughter of her mother's death, he had obviously had second thoughts about selling the place.

Before long, Jacques appeared in his wheelchair accompanied by a pleasant-looking young woman in a green and white nurse's uniform. Greenberg was shocked by the extent of the other man's deterioration. The stroke had left his face horribly distorted, and a withered left arm rested helplessly on a cushion on his lap.

'Hello, Jacques,' Greenberg said gently, trying to sound cheerful.

The patient looked up, forcing a lopsided smile.

'Excuse me,' the nurse said politely in English, 'but if you could make the visit brief… Monsieur Bertrand only returned home yesterday.'

'Yes, yes, of course,' Greenberg responded sympathetically.

'Monsieur Bertrand has to write everything down with his good hand because his speech is still impaired,' she explained, pointing to the pen and pad resting on the wheelchair tray. 'Just talk to him normally. He will respond. His mind is still alert.'

Then, leaving the two men alone, the kindly nurse left the room.

'Jacques, it's good to see that you're getting better,'

Greenberg began, but he felt at a loss. There was so much he had planned to say. But, because of the old man's condition, he now felt it would be impossible to achieve his mission.

Jacques was busily writing on his pad. Sensing his visitor's predicament, he had quickly realised that he was the one who would have to take the initiative.

Greenberg went over and gazed down at the questions the old man had been unable to communicate verbally. Getting straight to the point, he wanted to know whether the venue had been arranged and who had been selected to play the part of Nadine in the show.

Greenberg was on the spot. If he skated around the subject and painted a better picture than really existed, he would be deceiving Jacques. But if he told him about the dilemma he was facing, the old man would surely feel that he had been badly let down.

Jacques wrote something else.

Is money the problem?

Greenberg sighed.

'The only issue outstanding,' he said obliquely, 'is to find a director who can really relate to the show.'

Jacques adopted a puzzled expression as if to say, 'That was the last thing I thought you'd have a problem with.'

Greenberg carried on.

'I know who I want for the job, but I need to find a way of getting him to agree. It's Dominic Langley – Nadine's son. Your grandson.'

Jacques looked at Greenberg and his face lit up. Tears poured down his cheeks. His mouth opened and closed several times. Greenberg rushed forward to wipe the face of the man who might, if Nadine had reciprocated his love, have been his own father-in-law.

Then, a little recovered, Jacques began scribbling hectically. He wrote what a fantastic idea it would be to have Dominic work on a show about his own mother. He came to a halt as a new thought entered his head. Writing more slowly this time, he added the comment that Dominic would surely need proof that Nadine *was* his mother. Afterwards he sat back, exhausted, and closed his eyes.

Assuming that he had drifted off to sleep, Greenberg gently wiped more tears from the sick man's wrinkled cheeks. There was a tear or two in his own eyes. He was about to tiptoe out of the room and find the nurse when Jacques roused himself. Picking up his pen, he wrote the words *Certificat de naissance* on his pad and handed it to his visitor. His face flushed with excitement and, gesturing as best he could, he directed Greenberg to wheel him somewhere else in the apartment.

Pushing the wheelchair along the hallway, they reached the old man's private study. With the blinds down and the musty aroma that pervaded the place, the room gave the impression that time had stood still.

Greenberg switched on the light and waited with great anticipation for Jacques to make the next move, but he just sat staring at the line of bookcases that ran around the room. It was as if he couldn't recall why he wanted to be there. Greenberg waited patiently and it wasn't long before his host perked up and scribbled a series of numbers down on the pad. The combination to a safe.

Mustering just enough energy to raise his good hand, Jacques pointed to a unit in the corner. Greenberg went over to the cabinet which, from a few feet away, looked just like the others. As he got closer, however, he observed that it had a false front. Intuitively, he slid it to one side and there, set in the wall, was the safe.

Glancing at the piece of paper, he spun the dial once to the left, then twice to the right, and the metal door sprang open. Turning around, he looked for the old man's approval before sifting through a small pile of documents on the bottom shelf. And there it was. An official copy of Dominic's birth certificate was soon in his hand.

Just then, there was a knock on the door. Greenberg closed the safe, then the cabinet door, then called out, 'Please come in.' The nurse reappeared with a glass of water and a vial containing her patient's medication.

Conscious that he had taken enough of the sick man's time, Greenberg bent down and kissed Jacques warmly on both cheeks, promising to let him know as soon as he'd been in contact with his grandson. Then he left the apartment and went back out into the wide avenues of Paris.

In no hurry to leave the beautiful city, Greenberg bought a savoury baguette and a juice from a food stall and wandered into the Bois de Boulogne. As he stood gazing at the still water on the lake, with the laughter of young children playing in the background, he thought about Nadine and what might have been. The opportunity to immerse himself in her again was, he acknowledged, merely an escape for a man who had lost everything except his memories.

One day, he didn't know exactly when, he would have to wake up and start rebuilding a life for himself.

27

It was after midnight when Greenberg arrived home. The flights back to London were overbooked and it was a miracle that he had managed to get a seat on the last plane out of Charles de Gaulle Airport.

Passing into the small kitchen of the Camden flat, he rustled up some scrambled eggs and poured himself a large measure from the litre bottle of Johnnie Walker whisky that he had purchased at the airport. The experience with Jacques and feeling Nadine's presence in the background had left him emotionally drained.

The next morning, however, he was back in the office and raring to get to work on the production.

A few years ago, when he was still a somebody, Greenberg would have jumped on a plane to New York, marched straight into somewhere like the William Morris Agency and told them to get him the best musical director on their books. Nowadays, he had to settle for networking with the few contacts who were still prepared to do business with him. Thankfully, he could rely on Jules Levy. He had called Jules from Paris to ask for his help in contacting Dominic Langley.

Jules's response was that his US associates would be far better suited for the task. As an initial step, he suggested mailing a hard copy of the script to his old friend Arlene Davidson at Goodkind Davidson in New York, saying that if she liked it and could see a way of involving her firm in the project, could she ask Dominic to at least read the piece.

'Do nothing for a couple of weeks,' Jules advised, 'and wait to hear.'

The trouble was, Greenberg had forgotten about the pantomime season. Those lucrative productions took over London theatres and seemed to start earlier and finish later each year. It was cutting things very close.

Greenberg poured himself another cup of coffee from the percolator that was refilled every morning as part of the service agreement. Sifting through the post, he found correspondence from a firm of solicitors he'd never heard of. Opening the long brown envelope, he saw that it was his copy of the decree absolute, formally ending his marriage to Suzanne. A tinge of sadness came over him, but he wasn't sure if it was about the wasted years of his life or the ignominy of losing his wife to someone who, until recently, he had always considered his oldest friend.

Greenberg sighed. As far as he was concerned, if it hadn't been Mikey, Suzanne would have found someone else. No, the only thing that still grated on him was that if his accountant was capable of such deception in his private life, it was more than possible that he had had a hand in pushing Greenberg's business off the end of a precipice. Some instinct told Greenberg that although he was no longer a client of the West End firm of Nicolaou, Franklyn Stevens, he hadn't heard the last of Mikey Nicolaou.

Nor, he thought, had Mikey Nicolaou heard the last of him.

*

The next two weeks went by slowly. Trying to focus on other aspects of the show proved difficult, when the fact that he still hadn't got hold of a director was preying on his mind. Greenberg frequently found himself short of breath and feeling a tightness in his chest.

Worried that he was about to suffer a fatal heart attack, he made an emergency appointment to see the doctor. Apart from being told what he already knew, that he was grossly overweight and needed to take more exercise, he was diagnosed with nothing more serious than stress. This time, however, he knew it was a warning sign to start looking after himself.

Then, at the beginning of the third week, he received the news he had been waiting for: an email from the PA to Arlene Davidson inviting him to attend their offices in New York at 9 a.m. on Wednesday, 12 June to discuss his script.

At the exclusive seafood restaurant in Leicester Square, the accountant got out his Platinum American Express Card and paid the bill for dinner. The party of four then got up from the table and, after collecting their coats, walked in opposite directions back to their cars.

Mikey thought the evening had been a great success. Getting Suzanne to wear her most revealing low-cut dress had worked wonders. Brian Morley couldn't keep his eyes off the breasts leaning provocatively across the table. The inspector's plain wife Catherine, on the other hand, whose fiftieth birthday they had supposedly come to celebrate, had sat with a blank expression, barely uttering two words all night while concentrating on clearing her plate of all three courses. Her husband's gift of a pearl choker, most probably paid for by another of his 'benefactors', was lost around her pudgy neck and left her looking like a trussed chicken.

Heading back towards North London, Mikey was surprised that it had only taken a hundred grand in cash and free use of the villa in Estepona to gain Morley's agreement. The bloated scoundrel had even tried to justify taking the bribe, saying that the evidence Scotland Yard had received so far, which implicated the owners of the property, was insubstantial and probably wouldn't stand up in court. As far as he was concerned, DI Morley said, the case was now closed.

As the silver Jaguar entered the drive of their three-acre detached residence, Mikey said instinctively, 'Something's not right.'

'What's the matter?' Suzanne asked, bleary-eyed and suffering the after-effects of the six rum and Cokes that they had got through over dinner.

'I thought I told you to leave the lights on before we went out,' Mikey said.

'I did. I'm certain of it,' Suzanne replied defensively.

'Right, stay here. I'm heading inside to see what's going on.' Mikey got out of the car and proceeded determinedly towards the house once owned by Greenberg.

'Be careful, precious,' Suzanne called out after him.

It only took Michael Nicolaou a few seconds to confirm that they had been broken into. The front door had been forced open, but other than a few footprints visible on the cream carpet that ran the entire length of the ground floor, the place had been left in good order, which made him think that there was more to it than just an attempted burglary. What was strange, though, was that the alarm hadn't gone off. Perhaps it had been tampered with.

The upstairs floor was a similar story. The only proof that someone had been in there was a thick piece of cardboard nailed crudely on the wall in the master bedroom suite above their bed. On it was written a threat: unless he paid two million pounds by the end of the month, he and Suzanne would die. Further instructions would follow in a few days.

Mikey immediately suspected that it was from the Jaworski brothers. Either they had stumbled on how much money Raj was making out of them, or else someone inside his company had fed them the information. In any event, they obviously thought they were being exploited and this was their way of trying to get even.

Mikey tore down the notice and put it in his pocket. Ignoring the marks on the carpet, he turned off the lights and went back downstairs. Fortunately, Suzanne had failed to lock the deadbolt on the front door, so he was able to secure the premises.

'You took your time,' Suzanne remarked casually when he returned to the car, while adjusting her make-up in the passenger mirror.

'Nothing to worry about, love. Probably just a bunch of kids looking for drugs. I'll get a locksmith down first thing in the morning,' Mikey said, not wanting to cause her to panic. He had never seen the need to divulge any of his business dealings to Suzanne, and he certainly wasn't going to start now. As far as he was concerned, the less she knew the better.

Mikey put the key in the car's ignition and the Jag responded immediately with a roar of its engine as it pulled smoothly away from the house.

'Michael, where are we going?' she asked curiously.

'How about that small hotel off the M1, where we used to go when that idiot of a husband of yours thought you were at the gym?'

'You are so romantic,' Suzanne replied, leaning across and pecking her lover on the cheek.

When it came to hiding his feelings, Michael Nicolaou was an expert. The truth was, the experience at the house had left him seriously rattled. He could hardly go to the police and say he was being threatened by a bunch of thugs when he was involved with them up to his neck. What he needed to do was to extricate himself from the Eastern European operation completely, and as quickly as possible.

Raj would be back in London in a few days. Mikey would tell him that, for a price, he had persuaded the police to drop the potentially damaging case against the company, and that the directors were now off the hook. Then he would explain that at sixty-two he was retiring from his accountancy firm and therefore wouldn't be able to continue as his financial adviser.

Mikey knew he had more than enough money in banks spread all over Europe and would never have to work again. He would sell up and move to Spain.

In the meantime, Detective Inspector Morley would be waiting a long time for his free holiday in the sun.

PART THREE

Day and Night

28

The American Airlines 747 landed exactly on time at New York's JFK Airport. Greenberg recalled his first ever visit, when he was invited by Ray Lester, then the most prominent musical producer on Broadway, to discuss bringing over his show *All at Sea*, which had premiered in London a few months after Nadine had drowned.

Here I am, back again after all these years, and this time trying to get Nadine's son to do a show about his mother. Ironic, isn't it? he thought to himself as he reached down his small suitcase from the overhead locker. After clearing customs, he found himself amidst the early morning hubbub of one of the world's busiest airports.

Getting into the back of a yellow cab that had barely come to a halt, his solitary piece of luggage slung carelessly on to the backseat, Greenberg tried to get comfortable as the car moved swiftly away in one fluid movement, heading towards the Manhattan skyline. Because he had been restricted in the plane to a small seat that prevented him from getting any sleep during the eight-hour flight, Greenberg felt grubby and exhausted. He could have done with a shower and with changing his crumpled suit, but there was no time.

The sun had broken through the clouds when the taxi pulled up outside an elegant stone building. With its arched windows and grey slanting roof it was more like a nineteenth-century French chateau than commercial premises on the fashionable Madison Avenue.

Greenberg paid the driver and entered the offices of Goodkind Davidson. He gave his name to an alert young man who, after checking his list of the day's appointments, sent an electronic message to the executive suite on the floor above. Within moments, a tall black woman with striking features appeared on the staircase from across the hall.

'Good morning, Mr Greenberg, and welcome to New York. I'm Tamara, Arlene Davidson's PA,' she said in a mild Southern accent, extending a slender hand to her visitor. 'Arlene sends her apologies. She has been delayed in a breakfast meeting. You can leave your bag. It'll be safe with Christopher.'

Greenberg smiled and passed his case to the receptionist, who was already on hand to take it from him.

'This way, please. I trust you have no objection to taking the stairs.'

'No, not at all,' Greenberg lied, trying to keep up with the much younger woman.

'We have the whole building, but Arlene is on the first floor.'

They stopped outside a spacious air-conditioned room with tall French doors that opened out on to a small patio.

'This is her office. You go on right ahead and make yourself comfortable. Would you care for some refreshment while you're waiting?' the PA asked.

'Thank you. That'd be great.' Greenberg went over and sank down on a stylish leather sofa. Having eaten little on the flight, he was feeling ravenous.

He wasn't disappointed, for almost immediately the aroma of coffee and freshly baked pastries wafted in from outside and a young female employee appeared with a trolley stacked with food.

After helping himself to a large selection of what was on offer, Greenberg sat back to enjoy his breakfast. Munching on a buttered croissant, he wondered about the woman he was waiting to see. Judging by the art on the walls and bronzes placed strategically around the tastefully decorated room, it was apparent that even if its occupant didn't actually own the company, she was certainly its prime mover.

Over the years he had normally only dealt with men, but he knew from the few female producers he had come into contact with that in business they rarely responded to charm. On the contrary, they could be as hard as nails. Something told him that he would have to be at his most alert with Arlene Davidson.

Greenberg suddenly became aware of the waft of expensive perfume as a woman in a white linen dress breezed in carrying a Burberry document holder under her arm.

Arlene Davidson was in her mid fifties, but with her slicked-back hair and intelligent face she could easily have passed for ten years younger. There was an intensity about her, which indicated that she didn't suffer fools gladly.

'I'm so sorry,' she said, giving Greenberg only the briefest of glances on the way over to her roll-top desk. 'I'll be with you in just a minute.' Opening up her paper-thin laptop, she peered down to read her emails, pausing for a moment when one attracted her attention.

'So, Peter, how do you know Jules?' Arlene asked

eventually, still preoccupied with other matters.

'We've dealt with each other for over thirty years. He has the knack of coming up with good new writers,' Greenberg replied from the other end of the room, draining the last of his coffee.

'Yes, of course, you are a producer. He did tell me.'

Greenberg got the impression that this was going to be one of those meetings that had been set up purely to maintain the goodwill between two parties who went back a long way together. He suddenly felt weary of the whole process, or maybe he'd been out of the cut and thrust of business for too long. If the only way back was to rely on favours, he seriously doubted that he had the will to persevere.

'Right, I'm with you,' Arlene said, now giving her full attention to the man who had flown more than three thousand miles to see her.

'So,' she went on, 'I have shown your script to a few people here and the feedback has been mainly positive. Let me say straight away, Peter, that you can forget all about Dominic Langley.' A frown crossed her face. 'From what I hear, he's contracted for the next three years, and even if we could get to him, I can't see him being interested in a piece like this. However,' she went on, 'what I thought would be useful, while you're in New York, is to meet with Brad de Winter. He's one of the directors represented by Goodkind Davidson, and talk in the theatre world is that he's going places.'

Greenberg sat back, feeling deflated. Palmed off with someone other than Dominic Langley, even if that someone was extremely talented, was not at all what he had in mind. His first reaction was to get up and leave. The three-day trip could easily be cut short.

'With all due respect, I think you've completely missed the point,' he said, trying not to let his disappointment show.

'Oh, really?' Arlene replied, rising to the challenge.

'This is a show that has been commissioned by Dominic's maternal grandfather. It's a tragedy based on his daughter's life, a woman that her son knew practically nothing about. Surely you can appreciate that Dominic is the only person who could do justice to the production,' Greenberg emphasised.

'Yes, if you say so,' the agent conceded crisply. 'And if you're insistent that Dominic is the guy you want, naturally I'll do what I can to ensure that he at least gets to see it.'

'Please, if you would. I'm only in New York until Saturday,' Greenberg told her, aware now that he had been foolish to expect that this would already have been done. It was also obvious that he had been too optimistic in thinking that a director like Dominic Langley would just fall into his lap.

There was an uneasy silence while the two attempted to gain the measure of each other.

But then Greenberg had a change of mind. What if trying to lure Dominic proved impossible? Wouldn't he be better to at least see this chap de Winter? He might be a budding genius and if he was, it might save a hell of a lot of time.

'How's tomorrow looking?' Arlene called over, consulting her calendar.

But before her visitor had a chance to answer, she'd got up and gone across to where he was sitting and casually positioned herself next to him.

'Say you'll meet him here at three tomorrow afternoon. Give you a chance to catch up on some sleep,' she said, helping herself to a piece of croissant that Greenberg had left on his plate.

'Sorry. I'm starving,' she confided. 'Trying to keep to a diet is miserable if you're me and you like your food.' On seeing that the hard-nosed businesswoman had suddenly become far more affable, Greenberg began to feel at ease.

'I don't know, you look pretty good on it,' he replied, trying to divert his gaze from the shapely legs that were being exposed through the opening in her dress.

'A flatterer, no less. Jules didn't say anything about being wary of a smooth-talking Englishman.'

'He was quite a ladies' man in his time,' Greenberg remarked.

'Yes, he was,' Arlene agreed, giving him a sideways glance.

Greenberg thought he detected a momentary flash of sadness in her eyes. Was it perhaps the memory of a broken love affair? he wondered. Normally his discretion would have prevented him from enquiring further, but there was something about this woman that intrigued him. Unconsciously, he found himself looking for a ring to indicate whether or not she was single.

'It was a long time ago. Jules wanted to marry me and I have to say I was tempted, despite the age difference.' Arlene laughed, as if she had been able to read his thoughts.

'What happened?' Greenberg asked.

'I was very naive in those days and got seduced by all the wrong things. My husband Harold was a banker, fabulously wealthy…had a penthouse apartment overlooking Central Park, a house in The Hamptons, the 'whole deal.'

'And it didn't work out?'

'Twenty years and three children later, I discovered I wanted something else.'

Arlene noticed her visitor looking over at the wooden-framed photograph on the sideboard.

'We lost a son in a car crash,' she said, pre-empting his question of why the family picture of her included only a boy and a girl.

'I'm sorry, that must have been awful,' Greenberg sympathised.

'It was fifteen years ago this week.' The expression on her face showed that time had not diluted her pain. 'Anyway, I'd always been independent and that didn't go down well with Harold's family. It remained a bone of contention between us.' Arlene turned to look at her visitor. 'And you. What's your story?' she asked.

'Me? Oh, I fell in love with an elusive French dancer who, I'm afraid, spoilt me for anyone else,' Greenberg divulged. It was clear by her blank expression that Arlene hadn't recognised that he was referring to the main character in the script. Now he knew for sure that she hadn't read it.

'You must tell me about her some time. She sounds most alluring.' Then, reverting to her former businesslike manner, the woman suddenly stood up. 'Great, so you will get together with Brad tomorrow. The meeting room will be booked out for you,' she said, indicating that their own meeting was at an end. 'Where did you say you were staying again?'

'A hotel not far from here. I think it's called the Library,' Greenberg replied, aggrieved that he was being dismissed.

'Great restaurant. I use it a lot,' Arlene remarked. 'Well, Peter, it was good of you to come all this way. I'm sure Brad will let me know how it goes.' She showed her visitor out. 'Tamara will call you a cab,' she added, smiling at her PA, who had arrived exactly on cue.

Greenberg collected his case and, not expecting the scorching temperature outside, chose to walk to the hotel, unsure what, if anything, he had accomplished. Thirty minutes later, his clothes sticking to his body and convinced he was suffering from sunstroke, he checked into the four-star hotel next to Grand Central Station and was directed to his room on the tenth floor. After dousing himself all over with cold water and raiding the minibar, he collapsed semi-clothed on the bed.

At the same time, a fit-looking man strode confidently out of an exclusive $15,000 a year Fifth Avenue gym, threw his Hermès sports bag on the back seat of his white open-top Mercedes and sped away in the midday traffic, heading west across Central Park. He pulled up outside a run-down residential building in 96th Street and checked his watch. He was in good time for his therapy appointment.

Despite appearances, Dominic Langley was deeply troubled. The break-up from Alejandro, his Puerto Rican lover, had affected him profoundly. He had thought the gorgeous twenty-three-year-old fashion model was different from all the others: young guys who had looked on him purely as a meal ticket. He certainly hadn't expected things to turn nasty when the passion eventually fizzled out of their three-year relationship. Alejandro knew from the start that, for Dominic, being monogamous was out of the question, and it hadn't been a problem when Dominic started dating Werner, a young German dancer from his hit musical *Jumping Through Hoops*.

Now, however, Dominic was facing a claim of thousands of dollars for lost support, a problem he could well do without. In addition the recent letter from his mother, begging him to return to London, had added to Dominic's gloom. After the bombshell of her diagnosis of Alzheimer's, she wrote that there were things she needed to tell him before she became too disorientated or died. But how could he just get up and leave halfway through auditions for the new play, even if he did have serious doubts about the quality of the production?

Looking at himself in the driver's mirror, for once he didn't like what he saw. Despite only being thirty-seven years of age, albeit only for another three days, he saw that his face had become lined and the first strands of grey were clearly visible around the edges of his short brown hair. He was the most sought-after director on Broadway, had more money than he knew what to do with, and yet he felt like shit.

Dominic got out of the car and proceeded up to the seventh floor, as he had done every week without fail for the last six months. At least in Sandra Cohen he had found a shrink who at last understood his issues.

'Good afternoon, Mr Langley. How are you today?' the receptionist said cheerfully. 'Go right ahead. Sandra's waiting for you.'

He entered the drab room, which had an academic feel from the medical books and journals that filled every inch of spare wall space, and sat down on a frayed armchair, waiting for the elf-like woman in round black spectacles to finish writing up her notes. Dominic had often wondered why anyone would choose to spend the whole of their working day in such uninviting surroundings. Perhaps the deliberately depressing aura of the place was a well-thought-out accompaniment to its clients' moods.

Putting down her pen, Sandra Cohen moved agilely over to a simple wooden chair in the middle of the room from where, for the last thirty years, she had engaged with her patients' concerns.

'So, Dominic, tell me how things have been,' she said, glancing at the clock on the wall that indicated the start of the fifty-minute session.

'Not brilliant,' he replied, sounding despondent.

'Last time you said you were happy with how everything was going with Werner. What's changed?'

'That's all fine, but my mother's unwell. She wants me to go back to London. There's some revelation or other that she apparently needs to share with me before it's too late.'

'And you find that upsetting?'

'I prefer New York to London and avoid going back there if I can possibly help it, so I can't say that I'm overjoyed by the prospect.' Dominic knew from experience that it only took the slightest jolt to his highly structured life to throw him off balance.

'Too many bad memories?'

Dominic shrugged but didn't reply.

'Maybe we should spend today talking again about your childhood,' suggested the therapist.

'Which part in particular?' Dominic said guardedly, unaware that he was clenching his fists.

'I remember you telling me that you had a strained

relationship with your father. That could be a good place to start.'

Dominic grunted.

'As I told you, he just wanted to get shot of me, so at ten years old I was sent away to boarding school.'

'And before that?'

'He was rarely at home. And, when he was, he was always arguing with my mother.'

'What about?'

'Money, mainly.'

'You mean about the amount she was spending?'

'No, far from it. My mother's family were very wealthy and he felt that he was entitled to a share of it.'

'Didn't he have a job?'

'From what I remember, he was more interested in having a good time than earning a living, and then probably at someone else's expense.'

'It can't have been much of a life for your mother.'

'I often wondered why she put up with it for so long when he had that other woman on the go for so many years. Sophie. She was French.' Dominic grimaced. 'My mother knew all about her but she chose to turn a blind eye.'

'It happens quite often when one partner loves the other.'

'But it was never reciprocated,' Dominic said.

'That doesn't seem to matter. In fact, when it's one-sided, it can often become even more intense,' Sandra Cohen explained.

'You mean like an obsession,' Dominic said, thinking about his own relationship with Alejandro.

'Exactly. And you were caught in the middle.'

'I was always close to my mother, which turned my father even more against me.'

'You're implying he was jealous of you?'

'Hardly. When he realised I wasn't the type of son he had envisaged, he lost interest in me.'

'You mean when you told him you were gay?'

'No, long before that. It was when I was diagnosed as bipolar.'

'How so?'

'The doctors said that the condition often travelled in families.'

'I see. In other words, it was hereditary. And your father took it as a personal affront?'

'He said they were talking rubbish. It was just before I went to Eton.'

'That was your boarding school, wasn't it?'

Dominic nodded, his expression clearly reflecting the unhappy episode in his life.

'It was his way of dealing with things. Get me out of his sight so I couldn't remind him of my problems. Then when I was asked to leave because the school couldn't deal with my mood swings, he became even more hostile.'

The therapist remained pensive, and after a moment she said, 'Dominic, didn't you ever wonder why you were an only child?'

'Apparently, there were complications during the birth, or so Mother told me.' Dominic wondered what Sandra was getting at.

'It just seems as though your father was hiding something, and that you in some way reminded him of it. Of his guilt.'

'Something – or someone?' Dominic said.

All of a sudden, he recalled the image of the little boy at the window. It was years since he had been plagued by that recurring dream. Maybe it was the thought of returning to his parents' house in London that had brought it all back. Who was that child? And what had he seen that had caused him to feel so sad? And why, whenever he tried to talk to his parents about it, were they always so evasive?

'You seem distracted,' Sandra Cohen observed.

'Just something that came back to me, something that happened when I was a child.' He cleared his throat.

'Do you want to tell me about it?'

'It's really nothing,' Dominic muttered, shrugging off the possibility that the dream bore any relevance to his present state of mind.

'All right. We were talking about your father. Then what happened?' the woman asked gently.

'When they divorced, he used to come around to the house quite regularly.'

'Because he felt guilty for the way he had treated you?'

'Oh no, nothing to do with that. No, it was because he was still obsessed with the idea that he had been unfairly dealt with. Even though, according to my mother, he had been offered a very generous settlement.'

'So how old were you at that time?'

'Eighteen. I had just left sixth-form college and I wanted to be an actor.'

'That didn't go down too well with your father, did it?'

'Thinking how much he would have disapproved actually drove me on,' Dominic admitted. 'That, and the chance to escape the painful experience of my childhood by reinventing myself, did seem incredibly appealing.' He sighed and rubbed a hand across his face.

'Anyway, the last I heard, he had got remarried and was living in France, probably with that woman he had been with all those years. Fortunately, my mother had the means to support me. Grandfather had died and bequeathed the major part of his estate to her. So money wasn't a problem.'

'Then what happened?' prompted the therapist. Even though she'd heard the story several times before, there was always a chance of new discoveries, memories resurfacing.

'I managed to get into the Royal Academy of Dramatic Art to study drama. RADA is the English equivalent of Juilliard in New York. We've spoken of this before.'

'Of course. Tell me, Dominic, how was the relationship with your mother during that time?'

'I was all she had left in her life. When my father cleared off, she bestowed all her affection on me. There was no one else, only her dogs.'

'It must have been very lonely for her.'

'When I qualified and said I wanted to go to New York to further my theatrical studies, she almost fell to pieces and started drinking heavily. But you know all this already. Why are we bringing it up again?' Dominic asked irritably.

'We're getting there. Just stay with the process,' the therapist said. 'How did you cope with that?' she continued.

'Basically, I learnt to toughen up.'

'You were actually glad to get away?'

'Cornell was like a breath of fresh air. I wasn't answerable to anybody else. For the first time in my life, I could be myself.'

'And you made friends quickly?'

'One boy of the same age. Josh. Our birthdays were actually on the same day.'

'You've not mentioned him before.' Sandra Cohen

looked closely at her patient. 'I wonder why.'

'I didn't think it was that significant,' Dominic lied.

'And … were you close?'

'Yes, more than I had been to anyone else up to that time.'

'But it ended?'

'After university we just went our separate ways,' Dominic replied, the finality in his tone of voice indicating an unwillingness to expand further.

'We've still got a few minutes. Is there anything else on your mind?' the therapist asked.

'Just that when I had my first Broadway success, I hoped that my father might have read the reviews.'

'You were still seeking his approval?'

Dominic sighed but didn't offer a reply.

'Well, I certainly found that useful,' Sandra Cohen said, getting up from her chair to show her patient out. 'Perhaps, if you are able to spare the time, you should really think about going to London, especially if it can throw some new light on your past.'

'I'll think about it,' Dominic replied without much conviction. He settled the $300 fee for the consultation in cash and made an appointment for the same time the following week.

As he took the lift down to the street he was in a better frame of mind. Not because his previous concerns had been alleviated, but because they had been replaced by thoughts of his father. And by the unrealistic, ever-enduring hope that Charles Langley might still get in contact.

29

Greenberg woke up in the Library Hotel feeling seriously jet-lagged. He'd been asleep for almost ten hours. Unable to recall his last decent meal, he picked up the phone and ordered something from the room service menu on his bedside table. He then got out of bed, flicked on the television and had a quick shower while he waited eagerly for his food to arrive.

Being alone in unfamiliar surroundings had never really bothered him, but he suddenly felt desperately lonely. Although Suzanne and he never shared a great deal in common, she was good company. He had in the main been a one-woman man, and at that moment in his life there was no obvious candidate to take her place.

Feeling better after his three-course dinner, he decided to go out for a few hours. Recalling from previous visits that Manhattan worked on a grid system where the avenues ran north to south and the cross streets ran east to west, Greenberg came out of the air-conditioned hotel into the clammy June evening to find the streets still bustling with tourists in summer clothes and carrying cameras, making the most of their time in the city that never sleeps.

The stench from the rubbish piled up on the pavement filled his nostrils as he headed past Park Avenue's exclusive apartment blocks and soaring glass office buildings. Then, after passing through Lexington's more eclectic mix of less formal establishments, he reached Third Avenue, with its fashionable bars and restaurants.

Finding all the places he peeked into either far too young or too noisy, he settled for the more sedate surroundings of the bar at the Waldorf Hotel, a few blocks uptown from where he was staying. It was late, approaching midnight, when Greenberg found a small table a few feet away from the pianist, who was playing Cole Porter's 'Night and Day'. As he ordered a Dewars on the rocks, Greenberg wished he had a Cole Porter on hand to write the numbers for his show about Nadine.

Later, back at the hotel, Greenberg lay in bed wide awake. The pretzel he had bought from a food cart an hour ago was lying on his chest and he couldn't get comfortable. He began to think about Arlene Davidson. That brief glimpse of vulnerability she had displayed, speaking freely about her personal life before clamming up, had left quite an impression on him.

None of this helped, however, to solve his dilemma regarding Dominic Langley. Naturally, he could see that Arlene wanted to have one of her own clients involved in his production. Why wouldn't she? It was business, and one he imagined she was highly proficient at. The problem was, they had vastly different priorities.

The sound of the ambulance siren intensified as it screeched to a halt outside the former shoe factory, now turned into the exclusive apartments where Dominic lived. He stared anxiously down through the full-length window that offered an uninterrupted view of the Hudson River, praying that help would come in time.

Just then, two paramedics jumped out of the back of the vehicle with a stretcher and raced into the building.

The dinner with Larry Druckman, New York's most influential producer, had gone as Dominic expected. Larry wanted him to option for a revival of Billy Wilder's *Some Like It Hot*, which he was planning to take on a States-wide tour in the spring. Dominic had made all the right noises, and while he would have jumped at the chance a few years ago of being at the forefront of such a high-profile production, these days the thought of being on the road for months and living out of a suitcase had totally lost its appeal. Perhaps because he could now afford to pick or choose, he had lost the hunger that had always driven him on.

After the dinner, he had gone on to a gay club to meet Werner and a few of the members of the cast of the musical that Werner was appearing in, before leaving alone at 2 a.m.

Dominic looked over at the naked body of his former lover sprawled out on his king-sized bed, a partially used vial of cocaine next to him. It was clearly the last desperate attempt of a man to make a stand. He berated himself for his stupidity in giving Alejandro a key to the apartment. Thank God he was still breathing. Dominic knew that the police would have to be notified. He just hoped that he wouldn't be embroiled in a criminal investigation.

Two minutes later, an oxygen mask over his face, Alejandro de la Rosa was on his way to the New York Presbyterian/Lower Manhattan Hospital.

Dominic went over to the fridge, took out a bottle of Diet Coke and swallowed a couple of pills to calm himself down. He then changed into a pair of jeans and began clearing up the place. Soon there was not a trace of the incident that had confronted him when he returned to his apartment. The trauma of it had, however, lodged itself firmly in his mind, causing him more than once to wake up panicking when he finally fell asleep, convinced that Alejandro was lying dead next to him.

The next day Dominic walked resolutely into the emergency department of the hospital Alejandro had been admitted to.

'I'm enquiring after Alejandro de la Rosa. He was admitted early this morning,' Dominic announced to the young woman at reception.

'Are you a relative?' she asked, fluttering her eyelashes at the attractive man.

'My name is Dominic Langley. I'm a very close friend.'

'One moment please, sir, while I check our records.' She began running her forefinger down her computer screen. 'My information indicates that he left ICU at 7 a.m. and is presently under sedation in a private room on the fourth floor.'

Thank heavens he was alive.

'Take the lift at the end of the corridor. There'll be someone up there who can help you out.'

'Thank you, thank you,' Dominic said, hurrying away, his trainers making a screeching noise as they crossed the vinyl floor.

It was mid afternoon by the time he had satisfied himself that his former lover was out of danger. Dominic gave his name as next of kin and instructed the patient accounting department to bill him for the full cost of Alejandro's treatment. It was the least he could do. When the doctor in charge had said that Alejandro's heart had stopped en route to the hospital and that he had needed to be resuscitated, Dominic was gripped with a terrible fear that his friend wasn't going to make it. Instead, the doctor told him, the patient had eventually woken and had immediately burst into tears and begged for forgiveness.

Fortunately, since the quantity of the Class A drug in his bloodstream was minimal and it had been his first offence, the police, who had immediately been informed, assured him that Alejandro would probably get off with community service rather than the possible year in prison. Dominic breathed a huge sigh of relief that they had believed his statement that he hadn't been party to the misdemeanour, and that he wouldn't be facing charges.

Hastening away from the hospital, Dominic glanced at his Panerai watch, which registered 1.50 p.m.

'Bugger it,' he swore to himself. Half the day was already gone. He dashed over to the car park opposite, collected his car and then drove uptown, weaving his way in and out of the lunchtime traffic to reach his next appointment.

The modern brick four-storey building on Seventh Avenue housed a small hundred-seat theatre, a dance studio and a number of rooms that were hired out for different artistic purposes.

Against his better judgement, Dominic had agreed to help out on a musical production of *David, the Warrior King*. Murray Lyon was a decent enough guy for a producer. At least, unlike many others he could name, Murray wasn't deluded into believing that he had any artistic flair. He was purely in it for the money and had already sunk a load of it into a show that was going nowhere. Dominic didn't have much faith in the piece, but he wasn't going to turn down thirty grand for eight weeks' work. As part of the deal he had also been given a free hand to come up with a cast, and since he had no intention of taking the gig himself, to recruit a competent director to take his place.

Armed with his copy of the script and his fastidious directorial notes, Dominic crept down from the back of the raked auditorium to his usual position in the middle of the third row. He needn't have bothered. The stage was empty and the cast, completely oblivious to his presence, were congregated in small groups, stuffing their mouths with sandwiches from the deli next door or else busy jabbering on their mobile phones.

As far as he was concerned, actors were a breed apart. Irrespective of how talented or famous they were, basically they were all just a bunch of children, needing someone to keep them in check and make them feel appreciated.

Dominic called down to the cast to get their attention.

'Right, everyone, I'm glad to see you've been keeping yourselves occupied. We've a lot of work to get through this afternoon so we'll make a start with David and Jonathan, Act One Scene Six.' He also spoke directly to a lean black youth and the lead, an angelic-faced young man with a neatly trimmed beard.

'And Leroy and Zac, if I'm not interrupting something more important—'

The two actors quickly consumed the rest of their lunch, picked up their scripts and moved to take their positions upstage.

'Remember, Jonathan is warning David that his father, King Saul, is intending to kill him. Start whenever you're ready,' the director called out.

Dominic gave them a free run, which to him felt like an eternity but, in reality, was no more than about thirty seconds. Then, unable to restrain himself any longer, he jumped to his feet.

'Stop!' he ranted at the two performers. 'Leroy, look, this is supposed to be one of the most poignant parts in the play. Jonathan is distraught that something is going to happen to the person he loves deeply, and you're playing him with as much feeling as if he's making a fucking restaurant reservation. If you're not up to it, I suggest you pack up your things and get out. I want real passion and if you can't give it to me, you can all leave now and I'll recast the whole sodding show. Now do it again *properly*.'

Dominic sat down again, feeling much better for his outburst. It was good to be back at work.

30

Greenberg left the offices of Goodkind Davidson and returned to his hotel. As he had anticipated, the meeting had been a complete waste of his time. The young director was a nice enough fellow. But he obviously hadn't grasped what the tale was about, nor was he able to relate to such complex characters and their mixture of emotions. It made Greenberg appreciate how perceptive Jules had been to recommend Jake Simmonds to write the script in the first place. It proved what Greenberg already knew: that age wasn't relevant if you had the ability and, in his estimation, Brad de Winter was seriously deficient in that department.

Perhaps he was so personally involved with the story that he'd overestimated the commercial value of the piece, Greenberg wondered as he fretted. What was certain, however, was that Ms Davidson hadn't taken him or his project seriously.

Greenberg went up to his room and packed. After summoning a bellboy to fetch his case, he then went down to the front desk to find out about changing his ticket back to London. The long flight home would, he hoped, provide the opportunity to try and pick up the pieces.

All the flights to the UK, he was informed, were full, but the concierge suggested that he should go to the airport anyway, just in case he could get on via standby. There was nothing else keeping him in New York, Greenberg thought, so what did he have to lose? If the worst came to the worst, he could always spend the night in a motel near the airport.

Using the lightweight cotton jacket over her head as scant protection against the torrential rain that had gridlocked the centre of Manhattan, Arlene quickened her step, trying to dodge the Fifth Avenue shoppers. Lunch at the Writers Guild had dragged on, and she couldn't wait to get away.

Her clothes sodden, she eventually reached the building that bore her name. Already knowing the outcome, she didn't bother looking in at the meeting room and proceeded on up to her office.

Getting Brad to agree to set himself up was the only thing she could think of. She wasn't proud of herself. The Englishman seemed a nice guy and he deserved better. She wished to make amends, but when she tried calling his hotel room there was no answer. He obviously hadn't picked up his messages.

The photograph of her children and the talk about family had brought everything back. Also, it would have been Josh's birthday on Saturday. Arlene had spent the evening alone in her Upper West Side apartment with a glass of chilled white wine, absorbed in Peter Greenberg's script. She lay awake, convinced that it was purely a work of fantasy. But what if it were true? What if, for all these years, she had been wrong about Dominic Langley?

'Tamara, what happened with Brad and Peter Greenberg?' she asked, bumping into her PA, who had been waiting around for her superior to return.

'I don't really know,' the assistant replied, sounding embarrassed. 'When I went in to see if they needed more coffee, the meeting had already broken up.'

'Get Brad on the phone for me right away,' Arlene instructed.

Tamara produced her mobile from inside her jacket pocket and brought up the number.

'It's going straight to voicemail. Do you want me to try Mr Greenberg at his hotel?'

'Yes. Do that, will you?' her boss replied, having already written off getting any work done for the rest of the day.

The PA put her head around the door of the adjoining office a minute or so later and said, 'It appears he checked out about an hour ago.'

'Shit!' Arlene exclaimed. She had to get to him before he left New York. Then she asked, 'Tamara, what's the quickest way to get to JFK?' In her head she was putting money on the fact that the man she was now so desperate to see was already on his way back to the UK.

'We're hitting rush hour right about now, so it's probably best if I drive you. I live in Queens, so it's really not out of my way,' the assistant suggested.

'Girl, I'm all yours,' Arlene said, eager to get started.

Arlene darted into Terminal 8 at JFK Airport, suddenly recalling how, when they first exchanged emails, the producer had mentioned that he was flying with American Airlines. Even so, locating him would be like trying to find a needle in a haystack, but she had to start somewhere.

Looking up at the electronic departures board, she saw that there was a flight to London at 10 p.m. She glanced at her watch. It was just after six thirty. Hopefully the gate wouldn't be open yet. As Arlene approached one of the American Airlines check-in counters, she knew that she would have to be at her most inventive to get what she wanted.

'Excuse me, I wonder if you could help me. I'm trying to find out whether a Peter Greenberg is travelling on your flight to London this evening.'

'I'm sorry, ma'am, we're not able to divulge that type of information,' replied the pretty young ground stewardess, who had just sat down to start her shift.

'Yes, I understand, but it's a matter of great importance,' Arlene stressed. 'You see, he asked me to marry him and because he thinks I've turned him down, he's cut his trip short. If I don't manage to stop him, I'm afraid I'll have lost him for good,' she said dejectedly, taking out a handkerchief to wipe away imaginary tears.

'Look, I'll see what I can do,' the young woman replied sympathetically, casting her eye down the list of passengers for the ten o'clock flight. 'I haven't told you this, but there's no one of that name here. It's too early for standby. Can I suggest that if you want to come back in an hour, maybe your man will show up?'

'Yes, yes. Thank you for trying,' Arlene said, moving away from the queue that had begun forming behind her.

She then went over to the information desk in the middle of the concourse. Perhaps, if they called his name over the public address system, it might produce results. But at the risk of creating a public spectacle she opted instead to wait around for a miracle.

At a quarter to nine and several cups of black coffee later, Arlene caught sight of the man she was waiting for, two positions away from where she had made her inquiries. Thankfully, he had saved her the embarrassment of being caught out about her earlier pretence.

Not having the faintest idea of what she was going to say, Arlene went over to where he was standing. She couldn't be certain, but it appeared that he had not been able to find a seat. She just hoped that he would give her the opportunity to explain.

'Hello, Peter. I'm so glad I caught you in time.'

Greenberg looked around, an expression of bemusement on his face. Arlene Davidson was the last person he expected to see.

'Arlene, there's really nothing to say,' he responded flatly. 'I can't get on a flight until the morning but it's no big deal. The airline has given me the name of a couple of hotels nearby. Don't be too concerned that it didn't work out. These things happen. It's just business,' he said, touching her hand. 'It was good to meet you. I'm sure we'll run into each other again.' He then walked away, pulling his suitcase behind him.

'It's about Dominic Langley,' Arlene called out after him.

Greenberg stopped, not sure whether he had heard correctly.

'If you will just allow me to explain, there may still be a way of getting what you want.'

Greenberg was intrigued. If the woman had taken the trouble to follow him to the airport it couldn't just have been because she felt she had let him down. There must be something else to it, he thought.

'All right, where do you want to go?' he said.

'Let's get a taxi back into the city. I'll pick up my car and we'll go out for dinner. Hope you like Italian.'

'Sounds good to me,' Greenberg said, his spirits lifted.

Just then, the young woman behind the first counter, recognising Arlene as she passed by, mouthed, 'I hope it works out for you both.'

The rain that had lasted all day had finally ceased and brought with it a refreshingly cool evening. Unlike the bedlam that had greeted him when he arrived two days before, the airport was quiet and Greenberg found himself with a clear run into Manhattan, sitting next to the woman who, until a few minutes ago, had been responsible for his abortive journey to America.

'I'm afraid I have not been exactly candid with you,' Arlene said meekly.

'Oh. And how's that?' Greenberg asked curiously.

'There was a reason why I kept you away from Dominic Langley.'

Greenberg frowned, wondering what was coming next.

'It's complicated. You see, it concerns Josh.'

'The son you lost?' guessed Greenberg.

'Yes. He and Dominic were very close. They met at university. Josh wanted to be an actor. He was really very talented.' Arlene's voice was filled with emotion.

'What happened?' Greenberg asked.

'When it ended – you see, they were more than just friends – Josh was inconsolable. It was his first serious relationship.'

'And you blamed Dominic?' Greenberg said, learning for the first time that Nadine's son had been gay.

Arlene took a moment to gather her thoughts.

'He could have helped Josh, but he never gave him a chance. Everything Dominic touches turns to gold. You

232

don't get where he is without being ruthless, I'm aware of that. But I didn't expect that when their relationship ended, Dominic would drop Josh like a stone.'

Arlene raised her voice.

'He could have found him parts in any number of his productions but he wouldn't even let Josh audition for him. As far as he was concerned, it was as if my son didn't exist.'

Greenberg was trying to empathise with Arlene's predicament, but maybe it hadn't occurred to her that her son just wasn't good enough. In which case there was no way that Dominic, the professional that he undoubtedly was, would have chanced taking him on to a production when it was *his* reputation that was at stake. Surely, being in the business herself, she could understand that.

'There are plenty of other directors in New York,' Greenberg said diplomatically. 'I'm sure there would have been work for a talented young actor.'

'Josh managed to get a few small parts in films when he moved to LA, but nothing could make up for the disappointment of not appearing on Broadway. Theatre was his first love. It would have been his birthday in two days' time. It still seems like yesterday,' she said, giving Greenberg a sorrowful look.

Greenberg wished he could offer her a modicum of comfort for what she was going through but he knew, deep down, there was none.

The taxi passed swiftly through the toll at the entrance of the Queens-Midtown tunnel that linked the borough of Queens with Manhattan. They surfaced at 42nd Street and headed towards the Goodkind Davidson offices on Madison Avenue.

'Just here, please,' Arlene said to the driver, sliding open the glass passenger divider. 'I've got it,' she smiled at Greenberg as she handed over the standard $55 fare from the airport. 'Tonight's on me, by the way,' she announced, walking over to the grey Fiat convertible parked in her private parking space.

'I don't suppose there's any point in me arguing,' Greenberg retorted, squeezing into the passenger seat of the pint-sized car.

'None whatsoever,' Arlene replied in a playful mood, giving Greenberg a flirty look.

31

It was almost 11 p.m. by the time Arlene had asked for the bill.

'I don't know about you, but that red wine must have been really heavy. It's left me feeling quite woozy,' she said, looking glassy-eyed at the empty bottle in the middle of the table.

'You still haven't told me what changed your mind,' Greenberg said, savouring the last remnants of wine in his glass. He, by contrast, was completely sober. His only concern was that they had spent the entire meal talking about restaurants and their favourite plays and foreign films, interrupted by the occasional gaze into each other's eyes, as their mutual attraction grew. There was no doubt that they had connected. But they had only skated around the subject of Dominic Langley.

'I kept thinking about the little boy in your story who never got to know his real mother,' Arlene responded. It was clear by the expression on her face that she was deeply moved by what she had read.

Greenberg didn't quite understand what had motivated her to mention the script, since he was certain that she had only just read it for the first time … unless she was somehow seeking closure on the tragic death of her eldest son, and the only way she could achieve it was to make her peace with the person she had blamed for his death.

Dominic Langley.

Arlene suddenly leant across the table so their faces were practically touching. Greenberg felt her breasts brush tantalisingly against him.

'I'm too shit-arsed to drive you back tonight, so I suggest you stay in my apartment and I'll run you back in the morning – if you're still intent on leaving New York,' she said with a mischievous look.

Greenberg could hear his heart beating hard through his shirt. Arlene was obviously used to getting her own way, but at the same time, he sensed that behind the brusque exterior was a gorgeous, warm-hearted woman wanting just to be loved. He had no problem putting himself forward as a suitable candidate. He just hoped he'd get the gig.

'I admit it does sound a bit more attractive than an airport hotel room,' he said, returning her smile. 'Would you like me to drive?'

The small Fiat stuttered to a halt outside the smart Upper West Side apartment block. As a uniformed doorman approached, recognising the car, Arlene said, 'I told you it was no big deal, Peter,' and planted a kiss on Greenberg's cheek.

'That was pure hell,' Greenberg blurted out, trying to stop himself shaking. 'Cars coming from all different directions ... I must have been completely out of my mind to have offered to drive.' He got out of the car, taking a moment to breathe in the evening air.

'Don't worry. I'll make it up to you,' Arlene called back as her guest followed her and the doorman into the exclusive residence.

After taking the lift to the fifteenth floor they went through a marble entrance hall that branched off into a series of interconnecting rooms.

'How much space have you got here?' Greenberg asked, looking around a vast drawing room that seemed to go on forever.

'Harold didn't want anyone living next to him so he bought the whole floor and made it our home,' Arlene said, busily flicking switches that brought the palatial apartment to life.

'And you live here alone?'

'Except on the rare occasions when the children come. Sheri stays with me whenever she's in New York. She's a TV producer in Beverly Hills,' Arlene said proudly. 'I hardly see Darren, even though he works with his father in Manhattan. That's how it is with kids.' There was a look of profound sadness in her eyes. 'Now, how about a nightcap?' she suggested, recovering her buoyancy.

'I think I've had more than enough for one night,' Greenberg replied.

'Wait … I've got some special cognac you must try. A client of mine gave it to me when he came back from Paris.' Arlene moved nimbly over to a bar area, which was partially visible through a pair of frosted glass sliding doors. 'Make yourself comfortable. I'll be back in a minute.'

Greenberg went and stood at the window that offered a panoramic view of Central Park and the silhouettes of the buildings dominating the sky like some impregnable fortress. He thought of the similarity with the apartment Jacques owned on the Avenue Foch and felt pangs of guilt. It was two months now since they had seen each other. He resolved to call his number in Paris before he left New York.

'Spectacular, isn't it?' Arlene remarked, appearing with two large balloon glasses. 'Here,' she said, holding out one of them to her guest. Placing her own on a coffee table made out of an Indian tea chest, she then kicked off her high heels and sank back into a deep-seated sofa that enveloped her completely.

'It reminds me a lot of Paris,' Greenberg mused.

'What was she like?' Arlene enquired cheekily, reaching for her glass.

'Actually, it was a he,' Greenberg said.

'*Chacun à son goût*, as they say.'

'It's a long story,' Greenberg told her, the inference going completely over his head. He joined Arlene on the settee. 'Here's to a productive relationship,' he went on, toasting the woman who was beginning to get under his skin.

'I'd prefer something a little less formal. How about "To us"?' Arlene countered with an inviting look.

Greenberg, requiring no further encouragement, put down his glass and, drawing Arlene to him, he kissed her gently on the lips. Then, when there was no resistance, he kissed her again, more passionately.

'That's better. Much, much better,' she gasped, wanting more.

And Greenberg took her to him and made love to her. For a while afterwards, they lay in each other's arms, not wanting the moment to end.

'You see, my instinct was right,' Arlene murmured finally.

'In what way?' Greenberg wanted to know.

'About wanting to keep you in New York.'

'I thought that was because you had second thoughts about Dominic Langley.'

'Is that man always going to be the main topic of conversation between us?'

'I didn't mean—' Greenberg started to explain.

'It was only a wisecrack. Don't be so sensitive.' Arlene dug him in the ribs, then yawned. 'Come on, let's go to bed. Don't forget, I've got work in the morning.'

Turning off the lights as they passed, the two new lovers went off together around to the other side of the apartment where the master bedroom and three other guest suites were situated.

'Sod it. I've left my case in the car,' Greenberg suddenly remembered.

'Well, you can't go down looking like that,' Arlene remarked, glancing at the stocky man dressed only in his birthday suit. 'Surely you can sleep without pyjamas this once.' And she led him by the hand into the darkened room.

'I'm bushed,' she said, immediately falling into the double bed, whose covers had already been turned down.

'Christ, it's two o'clock in the morning,' Greenberg muttered, noticing the clock on the flat-screen TV opposite him. He then settled wearily down next to Arlene, who was already fast asleep, with the bizarre goings-on of the previous day still playing on his mind.

When Greenberg awoke feeling disorientated at 10 a.m., rays of sun filled the room. He looked over at the other side of the bed. Arlene had gone, leaving him alone in her apartment. How had he allowed himself to get caught up in an adventure with a woman he had only just met? And who knew what her agenda was? He still couldn't fathom why she was so keen to keep him from returning to London. All he knew was that if he didn't get any answers in the next twenty-four hours, he would be on the flight home tomorrow.

Greenberg got up and showered. Passing into the dressing room, he was amazed to see that his suitcase had been brought up from the car and his clothes from the night before had been ironed and left in a neat pile. By the side was a note that simply read,

Meet me at the Metropolitan Museum at 12.30. Arlene. By the way, you talk in your sleep.

Dressed and ready to face the challenges of the day, Greenberg made his way along the hall. He could hear the sound of someone singing, and reaching the kitchen, he saw a round woman, her hair tied in a multicoloured scarf, on her hands and knees polishing the quarried tile floor.

'*Buenas dias, Señor,*' she called up at the man standing at the entrance. 'The clothes, I bring to your room, you are happy?' she said in her best English.

'Yes, thank you, but there was no need. I didn't want to trouble you,' Greenberg answered, embarrassed by the effort that had been taken on his behalf.

'I work for the señora seventeen years. It no trouble. She good lady. You want coffee, eat something, maybe? Manuela bring.' Not waiting for a reply, the cleaner got up and went over to prepare breakfast for the visitor.

As Greenberg slid along the banquette of the colonial-style kitchen, he couldn't help wondering how many other men like him the cleaner had had to look after in the morning when her mistress had left for work. What was worse was that Arlene was taking over his thoughts. True, it had been more fun than he had had in years, but the trip wasn't intended to be a holiday. He needed to pull himself together and refocus his efforts, within the short time he had left, on salvaging his show.

'You like the señora?' Manuela said, grinning as she placed the French toast down on the table.

'Ye-yes,' Greenberg stammered, taken aback by the cleaner's forthrightness.

'She needs good man. Not right for her to be alone.'

'You knew her husband?' Greenberg asked casually.

'Señor Goodkind is bad person. He only interested in money,' the cleaner spouted out, a look of disdain on her expressive face. 'Cuban men understand make family happy first, money come after.' She waved her hand contemptuously. 'He go, she look after children.'

'When was that?' Greenberg enquired, his interest aroused.

'After their boy, he—' she began sadly. 'I find his body.' Murmuring a few words in Spanish, the cleaner crossed herself.

Greenberg thought a moment. Hadn't Arlene said that Josh was killed in a car crash? And if what Manuela was saying was true, why would Arlene still choose to reside in a place filled with such terrible memories? He recalled wanting to run away from his flat in Marylebone after Nadine had died, and she had just stayed for a few weeks. Something didn't add up.

'The señora, she work too much. I tell her it no good but she says she has no choice.'

'But how is that possible? I mean, she has a magnificent home,' Greenberg said, gazing at the kitchen, which alone was the size of his Camden flat. It was clear, however, that

Manuela knew a great deal about the family's affairs.

'The apartment,' she said, opening her fleshy arms wide, 'it belongs to the señor.'

Greenberg was shocked at the revelation that Arlene had not benefited, as he had imagined, from a substantial divorce settlement, and had instead to work to support herself. He wondered what type of man would have been prepared to leave his wife in that position.

Greenberg put down his cup and, wiping the toast crumbs from his mouth, got up from the table.

'Thank you for breakfast, Manuela. Right, I have to go.' He actually had an hour to kill but as it was a beautiful morning, he relished the opportunity of a leisurely stroll to clear his head before meeting Arlene.

'You're welcome,' the cleaner replied with a broad smile, using the phrase she had picked up in her adopted country. 'You come to stay with the señora again and Manuela can keep job, no?' she said, returning to her chores.

Not knowing how to respond, Greenberg just nodded and went back to the room to finish packing, feeling great sympathy for the Cuban woman who for some reason assumed that he held some sway in maintaining her employment. Then it came to him. Arlene's husband was probably paying the cleaner's wages, and perhaps he had been threatening to put a stop to it. If her mistress were to find someone else, the new man would no doubt take Manuela on and relieve the ex-husband of the burden.

One thing was certain, the more Greenberg learnt about Harold Goodkind, the more he detested the man.

Following the map that he had picked up from the concierge at the hotel, Greenberg proceeded along 86th

242

Street into Central Park. Once he had crossed a pretty footbridge amidst a riot of colour and the fragrance of freshly cut grass, he felt as if he had stepped into a French Impressionist painting.

Then, after encountering an endless stream of joggers and street performers entertaining audiences of all ages, he passed by the side of the Jacqueline Kennedy Onassis Reservoir, a stretch of water the size of a large boating lake with a backdrop of Manhattan's distinguished prewar buildings.

So much was going on in that one vibrant segment that it wasn't hard to understand why, with its other more tranquil areas and green, wide open spaces frequented by sunbathers and picnickers, that New Yorkers valued their city retreat so highly.

How different, he thought, from the public parks in London, that seemed stark and uninviting in comparison.

Taking the Fifth Avenue exit, Greenberg looked up and saw the grey pillars of the Metropolitan, the world's most visited art museum.

As Arlene left her office and hailed a taxi to take her to her midday rendezvous, she was feeling particularly apprehensive. Brad de Winter had eventually returned her call from the day before. Even though he readily admitted that he wasn't the man for the job, he said he had been captivated by Nadine's story. Brad had also conceded that Dom Langley was the only person who could do it justice. Ironic, since she hadn't confided in Brad that it was based on Dominic's mother's life. Arlene hadn't known it herself until she met Greenberg in person. All Jules had said to her was that it was a script that she might be able to do something with. To her it had seemed just another good story.

Now, forty-eight hours later, everything had changed. She had now become smitten with the man she had only agreed to see as a favour to a dear old friend, even though she suspected that she was not his main priority. She hoped he would prove her wrong. Brad went on to say that Dom Langley had wanted him for a production that he was nursing back to health and had suggested that they could discuss it further at the Met, since Dominic wanted to take in the Picasso exhibition that had just opened. If she and Greenberg just happened to be there at around midday, Brad said, the two could meet 'accidentally'.

Arlene, already fifteen minutes late, hurried up the steps of the museum, no longer needing to psych herself up about seeing Dominic Langley, but instead merely hoping that Greenberg had read her note.

32

Greenberg wandered aimlessly through the first-floor rooms of the busy museum. Then, just as he had decided that he had waited long enough, he saw Arlene making haste towards the queue that had gathered outside the Picasso exhibition.

'You made it,' Greenberg said, going up to her.

'I'm sorry, Peter, there was a last-minute problem at the office,' she said to excuse herself, kissing him quickly on the cheek while at the same time keeping one eye open for Brad and Dominic Langley.

'Arlene, why did you want to meet here?' Greenberg asked, sure that she was up to something. The conversation with the cleaner had stayed with him and had, if anything, just increased his respect for a woman who, despite all the trappings of affluence, had to work hard for a living.

'I wasn't certain, after last night, whether you would come,' Arlene admitted.

'Why would you think that?'

'Well, for one, your trip to New York hasn't exactly produced the results that you were looking for.'

'So, a quick fling before I cleared off back to London was your way of making up for it?' Greenberg said indelicately.

Arlene winced. A hurt expression appeared on her face.

'That was unkind, I'm sorry,' Greenberg said quickly, to help retract his tactless remark.

'It's just there's a lot that you don't know about me, and I wanted the opportunity to—' Arlene began to try to explain. But, before she finished speaking, Brad de Winter and Dominic Langley breezed past them on their way out of the exhibition.

Arlene knew that she had to think quickly, otherwise the opportunity would be lost.

'Brad,' she tried calling, but it was too late. The men had disappeared amongst a crowd of art students and office workers on their lunch break. By this point she was in despair, but then she heard her phone buzz with a message, which read,

In the Met Store.

'Peter, do you mind if we skip the Picasso?' she said hurriedly. 'I seem to have developed a pig of a headache. I just need a little fresh air.'

'No, not at all. There must be somewhere we can sit down and have a drink,' Greenberg said, unsuspectingly.

'There's nothing here,' Arlene said. Taking Greenberg's arm, she led him swiftly back to the ground floor.

'Wait … I think that's Brad,' she exclaimed, making out the slight figure in the museum shop ahead of them. Next to him, facing their way and talking on his mobile, was a much taller man, dressed in a T-shirt and white jeans. At that moment Arlene thought she had never seen such a perfect face.

'I really should go in and say hello,' she said, turning to her companion, 'just to make sure that there's no bad feeling about yesterday.'

'I'll wait here,' Greenberg said, not thinking anything of it.

Arlene eased her way past a small group of shoppers

246

with their Metropolitan Museum of Art carrier bags to where the youthful-looking man was browsing at the shelves of lithographs.

'Hey, there. I thought it was you, Brad,' she said as she greeted him, kissing him on both cheeks.

'Hello, darling. Didn't expect to see you,' the young man blurted out, feigning surprise. 'The Picasso was great. Shame I can only afford limited editions,' he joked, holding up an image of a woman and child.

Just then, the man who had been on the phone came up to them and said, 'Sorry, Brad, I've got to split.'

'Dominic, you remember Arlene?' Brad said, realising that he had to delay his companion's departure a little longer.

'Yes, of course,' he said, extending his hand graciously to the woman who he knew had held a grudge against him for many years. 'It's been a long time.'

'Too long, Dominic,' Arlene responded quietly, indicating with her gentle look that she was ready to put the past behind her.

'It was good to see you, but I have to run. I'm having a party for my birthday tonight, and there's a hell of a lot to organise,' Dominic said hurriedly. 'If you're free, Arlene, do come along. Brad knows my address. Ciao.'

With that, Dominic, sockless in his Prada loafers, rushed back to his rehearsals, feeling happier now that he had arranged for Brad de Winter to replace him on the production of *David, the Warrior King*.

'Busy guy,' Brad remarked, stepping across to the checkout to pay for his Picasso print. 'Arlene, are you going to come tonight?'

'I'll call you,' she replied cagily. She then went out

to rejoin Greenberg, wondering how she was going to persuade him to stay a while longer in New York.

'What was that all about?' Greenberg asked, put out at being left alone.

'Don't be a grouch. It was just some business I needed to catch up on. Come on, there's a place that does great food near here. And anyway, it's your turn to pay.'

'I thought you had a headache,' Greenberg said, still wondering what was going on.

They entered a Mexican coffee shop cum diner heaving with lunchtime trade, and found the last two stools at the counter. Dispensing with the need for menus, Greenberg followed his companion's recommendations while waiting patiently for her to tell him what she was up to. Arlene, however, was content to bide her time, and identified and pointed out many members of the famous clientele who were known to frequent the establishment instead of enlightening him.

They didn't have to wait long for their food because, just as Greenberg felt he couldn't restrain himself any longer, two plates heaped with beef and chicken fajitas were placed in front of them.

'Feeling better?' Arlene asked, touching Greenberg's hand as he took another large bite out of his taco.

'I would if I knew what was going on,' he mumbled.

'Well, I've got some good news,' Arlene beamed, taking a swig from her bottle of Corona beer.

'Don't tell me. You're pregnant,' Greenberg said sardonically.

'Now that would be something,' she laughed, unwilling to let anything spoil her good mood. 'Actually, we've been invited to a party this evening.'

'And that's the reason you've been trying to humour me?'

'I thought that, given the opportunity to meet Dominic Langley in person, it might make a difference, yes.'

'And how did you manage to arrange that in the last three quarters of an hour?' Greenberg, recovering some of his warmth, wanted to know.

'Brad,' Arlene replied. 'He's just been asked by Dominic to work on a production he's involved with.'

Greenberg remained silent, his expression conveying a high degree of scepticism.

'Look, whatever you may have thought of Brad, he loved your script. In fact, he hasn't stopped talking about it.'

'And you're suggesting that he thinks Dominic might be interested in it?'

'That's what he told me.'

'Fine. As you say, it's worth a try,' Greenberg said, perking up.

'What are you doing for the rest of the afternoon?' Arlene enquired.

'I thought I'd see if there's a show I can get tickets for. Why, what did you have in mind?'

'I thought we might carry on where we left off last night,' she said, whispering softly in Greenberg's ear. Then, seeing his astonishment, she said to tease him, 'Don't look so surprised. I'm assuming that it wasn't purely by accident that you forgot your things in the apartment.'

Greenberg hadn't considered that leaving his luggage at the apartment to collect later would have given that impression. Nevertheless, he didn't need a lot of persuasion to alter his plans.

'In that case, I suppose Broadway will just have to wait,' he said, grinning.

Greenberg paid for their lunch. Then, holding hands, the couple walked through the park back to the apartment on 79th Street.

Once inside, they headed straight to the bedroom and quickly undressed, both impatient to make love.

'That was fantastic,' Arlene gasped. Rolling over, she rested her head on Greenberg's heaving chest.

'With all the noise we were making, aren't you worried about the maid?' Greenberg panted, running his hand down Arlene's spine.

'Manuela doesn't work in the afternoons. She's wonderful. I don't know what I'd do without her.' There was an anxious note in Arlene's voice that made Greenberg want to reassure her.

'She told me that she's been with you a long time. I'm sure there's no problem.'

'What else did you talk about?' Arlene said, lifting up her head, worried that the cleaner might have breached her confidence.

'Only that you work very long hours—'

'Did she say why?' Arlene interjected.

'No, not really,' Greenberg hedged, sensing that she was getting upset and that he had to tread carefully.

Arlene sat up abruptly and moved to the edge of the bed, facing away from the man she had just made love with.

'Everything you see is a facade,' she said fiercely. 'The apartment, the office, me… It's all one big fucking pretence.'

'I don't understand.' Greenberg was shocked by the unexpected outburst.

'Harold never forgave me for walking out on him after Josh died. He threatened to fight me all the way if I went through with the divorce.'

'And so you are beholden to him?' Greenberg muttered, already aware of the situation.

'He challenged me over custody of the children, saying that I was an unsuitable mother. He claimed because I doted on Josh that I neglected the other two. It was only because he couldn't deal with the fact that his son was gay that I felt I had to overcompensate. Josh had no one else,' she whimpered. 'And I still wasn't able to save him.'

'But surely your other son—' Greenberg interjected, trying to comfort her.

'Even though we have joint custody, Harold, the bastard that he is, tried to turn them against me. It's taken me years to have any type of relationship with Darren.'

'And your daughter?'

'Sheri had her own issues. But at least, with her father supporting her, she was able to move to LA. Now she's self-reliant, we get on OK, although I suspect deep down she'll never forgive me for not showing her enough love when she was growing up. And being stuck in this place, filled with dreadful memories, it's as if he wants to carry on punishing me.'

Greenberg recalled the cleaning woman describing how she had been the one to discover the youngest boy's body.

'Surely you could move somewhere else,' he said, wondering whether what Manuela had told him was true.

'Part of the settlement was that I would continue to

live here, only so that my husband could continue to boast to his wealthy friends how generous he had been in giving his wife such an expensive home.'

'But wasn't the apartment in joint names?' Greenberg asked curiously.

'It still is, but it can't be sold without the agreement of the other. So you see, I'm locked in,' Arlene said resentfully. 'Plus the fact that I'm expected to pay for half the outgoings, which comes to a fortune each month. Why else do you think I work every hour God gives?'

'And the office?' Greenberg asked.

'Owned by his company. I pay them rent.'

'I'm sorry. I had no idea.'

Greenberg was aghast at what he had heard. Moving closer to the distressed woman, he took her in his arms. Suddenly, he experienced a feeling of déjà vu. He was in his old apartment in Marylebone, and Nadine had just turned up, asking whether she could stay. She wore the same look of helplessness, had the same craving to be loved, and the hitherto brittle exterior was now only paper-thin.

Perhaps that was what he had found so attractive when Arlene opened up to him in her office the first time they met. The similarity, at least at that moment, was unmistakable. But was this relationship also destined to end in failure? he wondered. There was no doubt that he was fond of Arlene, but Greenberg reminded himself that in less than twenty-four hours he would be on the way back to London. And before then, he needed to convince Dominic Langley to direct the show.

'You know, I don't make a habit of doing this,' Arlene said, turning to Greenberg and recovering some of her previous edge.

'What do you mean by that?' Greenberg asked, jolted by this new change in her mood.

Without answering, Arlene got up and went to take a shower. A few minutes later, she returned with a large bath towel wrapped around her. The expression on her face was far from conciliatory.

'Is something wrong?' Greenberg asked, getting out of bed and going over to her.

'Only that I can't believe how guileless I've been, baring my soul to someone I hardly know. Not that it matters, since there's not much chance of us seeing each other again after tonight,' she said, dripping a small pool of water on to the carpet.

'What do you expect me to say?' Greenberg replied, keeping his distance.

'You've said enough. It's all right, really. Look, it was great while it lasted, but you have to get back to your main priority of getting your production put on and I have to start trying to make a life for myself.'

'What's brought all this about? I thought we were getting on so well,' Greenberg said, nettled.

'I think, maybe, it's better if you go to the party alone. I'll sort it out with Brad. He'll understand. I'll phone the address through to your hotel. Where will you be staying tonight?'

'I hadn't given it any thought,' Greenberg said, having taken it for granted that they would be staying together in her apartment.

'Probably best to try the Library again. They're sure to have a room and it's only a short taxi ride downtown. The party's in Soho,' Arlene proffered as she dried her hair.

'And that's it?' Greenberg said.

An awkward silence ensued. Arlene went out of the bedroom, leaving Greenberg alone to ask himself how everything could have gone so horribly wrong.

After getting dressed he collected his suitcase and left the apartment. He had wanted a final chance to speak to Arlene, a conversation that might have thrown some light on her strange behaviour, but she was nowhere to be seen.

33

Greenberg looked up at the red-brick building. The sound of a large gathering of people enjoying themselves, reverberating from the top floor, indicated to him that he was in the right place.

Armed with a presentation box of champagne that he had purchased from a wine merchant's opposite the hotel, he entered through a heavy glass front door. His encounter with Arlene had left him completely stunned. Why the sudden change towards him? Had she been left feeling exposed by his conversation with the cleaning lady concerning her private life? Talking about her unhappy past, along with the prospect of being thrown together with Dominic after such a long time, must have been the tipping point.

She'd left the note under the door of his hotel room containing the address of the party, which made him feel she clearly wanted nothing more to do with him.

Feeling more settled from the two drinks he had downed before leaving the hotel, Greenberg took the lift to the loft apartment. He passed through what looked like a pair of swing bar doors, whereupon a beautiful Native American girl with a feather headband was immediately on hand with shot glasses of tequila. Another followed behind with bowls of chilli con carne and nachos covered with melted cheese.

Greenberg looked around, amazed at the space that had been transformed to resemble a Wild West film set. Men wore wide jeans, checked shirts and cowboy boots, while their female partners, in low-cut velvet dresses, their hair half-pinned up, Wild West-style, in sausage curls, stood eating and drinking at a long wooden bar, above which hung a painted sign saying *DOM'S SALOON*.

A number of card tables had been scattered around the place. Shady-looking individuals in star-studded cowboy hats sat at them, playing poker, with their replica Smith & Wesson .45s at the ready. And in a corner of the room a man in a bowler hat and armbands was playing honky-tonk piano.

Greenberg helped himself to a plate of food, wondering which of the men in costume was Dominic Langley and whether there would finally be an opportunity to talk to him. He didn't feel at all optimistic, however. No doubt the whole thing was a mistake and he shouldn't have come.

Spotting his awkwardness through a cluster of guests, a long-legged girl in calf-length boots appeared, wearing only a skimpy animal-print top and shorts and carrying a box of extra outfits. Before Greenberg had a chance to finish his mouthful of nachos, his jacket was yanked off him and replaced with a suede waistcoat with tassels. Offering no resistance, he allowed a bandanna to be tied around his neck and a rodeo cowboy hat to be stuck on his head.

The cowgirl stepped back to inspect her work, and seemed satisfied that the bulky man who had previously been in the staid grey suit now looked the part.

When a small fellow with shoulder-length hair came up to him, Greenberg quickly recognised Brad de Winter behind the drooping moustache.

'Howdy, pardner. Glad you could come,' Brad said, extending his hand, showing that he bore no animosity regarding their brief meeting the previous day. 'Sorry that Arlene couldn't make it – although I can't say I'm surprised,' he added.

'Oh, really? And why's that?' Greenberg was eager to hear what the little chap had to say.

'Arlene is complicated.'

'And don't I know it,' Greenberg sighed.

'Come on, cowboy, let me buy you a drink,' Brad drawled, doing his best John Wayne impersonation.

Greenberg accompanied the unlikely-looking gun-slinger to the bar. However, before he could tell Brad what he wanted, the barman, a stout fellow in a striped waistcoat and long white apron, pushed a bottle of Wild Turkey and then two glasses down the bar in their direction. Grinning, Greenberg deftly caught them and poured out two measures of bourbon. He was starting to enjoy himself.

'Brad, you were saying?'

'My mother and Arlene were sisters. When Mum died, Arlene kinda adopted me. In some ways, she was closer to me than to her own children, except for Josh.'

'Yeah, she told me about him,' Greenberg replied. 'I know they were extremely close.'

'Cousin Josh was a no-good bum who took advantage of her any way he could,' said Brad, his voice harsh, as he divulged this to Greenberg.

'I didn't get that impression,' Greenberg said, taken aback.

'He got busted for being out of control on at least two

occasions. His mother didn't even know,' Brad went on. 'Dom Langley flew to LA especially, went to court and vouched for his good behaviour. Both times Josh got off with a heavy fine, and it wouldn't surprise me if Dom had settled them for him. They were very close at one time. Dom's like that. Always standing by a friend in trouble.'

'And Arlene?'

'Look, I love her dearly but she couldn't cope with the fact that Josh looked to Dom before her.'

'But that still doesn't explain—' Greenberg started to say.

'When Arlene feels that she is getting too involved with someone, she sort of goes cold,' Brad said perceptively. 'She's been hurt so often, she just puts up a barrier.'

'I think I understand,' Greenberg answered. Again, he thought of Nadine and wondered whether the same mechanism was in play when the young Frenchwoman thought she was getting in too deep with him.

'Look, Peter, I think your script's great. What I didn't realise till afterwards was that it was a true story. That's why, at the time, certain things didn't work for me. Now I can see why you want Dom. He's the obvious guy to do it.'

'Have you talked to him?' Greenberg asked, feeling more sanguine.

'Yeah. I gave him a copy when we saw you at the Picasso exhibition.'

'I didn't know he was there with you. Arlene never mentioned it.'

There was a moment of embarrassed silence as Greenberg now realised that the rendezvous at the museum had been set up to look like a coincidence. Arlene had done her best, but something hadn't gone to plan.

Thinking about it further, he did recall a good-looking man hurrying out of the museum store, but had no idea that it was Dominic Langley.

'Do you think he'll read it?' Greenberg asked.

'I wish it were that simple,' Brad answered guardedly. 'The thing is that Dom's in a higher stratosphere from the rest of us. You've no idea quite how successful he is. He collects theatre awards the way the rest of us accumulate air miles.'

'But if he knew that it was based on his mother, surely he would take it seriously,' Greenberg said, sounding desperate.

At that moment, the subject of their discussion moseyed over to the bar. Tonight, Dominic was dressed all in black and sported a large silver sheriff's badge on the breast pocket of his frock coat. Being dragged along by a rope in a mock arrest was a young man in handcuffs.

'Hi, Brad. Having a good time? You know Alejandro,' Dominic said, pretending to sneer at his captive.

'Sure,' Brad replied, acknowledging his host's partner for the evening. 'Dom, this is Peter Greenberg.'

'Hi,' Dominic replied, his vague expression indicating that he had never heard of him before.

'The script I mentioned?' Brad reminded him.

'Looks good,' the man in black said unconvincingly. 'You're from England, Brad tells me.'

'That's right,' Greenberg said. 'I'm a theatre producer.'

'West End?' Langley asked, gauging the other man's credentials.

'I've been involved in a number of musicals in the West End,' Greenberg concurred, not wishing to give a false impression of his current standing.

'It's all true. The story, I mean,' Brad interjected.

'Are you thinking of London or New York?' Dominic asked, oblivious to his protégé's comment.

'London to begin with, then hopefully have it adapted for Broadway,' Greenberg replied, holding his breath.

'OK, I'll take a look at it and get back to you. Brad, take Peter's contact details before he goes.' Dominic then moved away with Alejandro to rejoin the party.

'Well, at least you got to see the great man,' Brad said, trying to sound upbeat. 'When's your flight back to England?'

'Early tomorrow morning, so I'm afraid I have to go.' Fumbling around for a business card, Greenberg suddenly remembered that they were in his jacket. A few minutes later, he came back wearing the clothes he had arrived in two hours before.

'I'll do what I can,' Brad said, taking Greenberg's card, 'and have a safe trip back home.' He then left the bourbon and went off to get himself a beer.

'Thanks, and please say goodbye to Arlene,' Greenberg called after him, just as the man at the piano, joined by a banjo and a fiddle, started to play a foot-tapping tune, and the guests hastened to the dance floor.

The next morning Dominic looked over at his lover sleeping peacefully before leaving the apartment, which still showed the traces of the previous night's party. The last guests hadn't left until 2 a.m., and what with having to settle up with the theme company responsible for making the event such a success, he hadn't got to bed until four.

However, there was something he had to do before going to the gym. Thankfully, Alejandro would be there to supervise the clean-up. Acknowledging that they still had strong feelings for each other, he was glad that they were now living together and was looking forward to the trip he had arranged to Europe, especially as it was an opportunity for him to share the joys of Italy with his lover.

Dominic left his car on 72nd Street next to the Dakota Apartments, where John Lennon had lived. Jogging past Strawberry Fields, the memorial to the former Beatle, he quickly reached Bethesda Terrace, a classically designed promenade in the middle of Central Park, whose main focal point was a stunning fountain with a sculpture known as the *Angel of the Waters*. Shortly after arriving in New York he'd discovered this place, and he returned there again and again. Something about it comforted and consoled him.

As Dominic approached he saw Arlene, sitting gazing up at the eight-foot bronze angel. When he had unexpectedly bumped into her after so many years, Josh's mother had remained on his mind. Was this an opportunity, at long last, to make up for any bad feeling she had towards him? But when she hadn't appeared at the party, Dominic knew that he had to be the one to take the initiative. Brad gave him her mobile phone number and Dominic had texted her immediately, asking her to meet him at this special place.

'I'm glad that you agreed to come,' he said, breathing deeply.

'I've been incredibly stupid to let it drag on for so long,' Arlene responded, making no attempt to move from her spot.

'So we can be friends?' Dominic asked, full of emotion.

'Yes. I just hope I can make it up to you.' Arlene's eyes filled with tears.

Dominic sat down next to her and put his arm around her. He kissed her gently on the side of her head, bringing the distance between them to an end. They sat together just enjoying the warmth of the morning sun, wrapped up in their own thoughts of the past.

'He seemed nice, the guy who came to the party,' Dominic said, breaking the silence.

'Yes, he is,' Arlene agreed, glad for the opportunity to discuss the other reason for their meeting.

'Brad was very taken with his script. Thought I should have a look at it,' Dominic commented casually.

'It's something else, believe me.'

'Well, in that case, since I respect your judgement, I'd better make a point of reading it.'

'Is that Dom Langley the director fobbing me off, or will you really read it?' Arlene said with a knowing look.

'It's a promise,' Dominic laughed, knowing that he had met his match. 'Can I buy you breakfast?' he said, getting up.

'Thanks, but I'll have to take a rain check. I've got a meeting in the office at nine.'

'All right. Next time then,' Dominic said. 'I'll call you.' He then sprinted away, leaving Arlene to contemplate whether she had succeeded in making amends to the two different men that she had offended.

Dominic Langley. And Peter Greenberg.

34

November 2013

The rain splashed against the windowsill of the chilly flat in Camden Town, disturbing the man who was trying to get back to sleep. Greenberg rubbed his eyes and felt for his watch on the bedside table. Five thirty, the middle of the night. In London, winter had struck with a vengeance. Pulling a blanket around his shoulders, he got up and made himself a cup of coffee, wondering again how he was going to fill the day.

Another excursion into Regents Park, half a mile away … the same people taking their dogs for their morning walk, smiling politely and then giving him a wide berth so as not to have to engage this lone man in conversation. He found himself resenting them for their sense of purpose. Then there were others like him, a handful of forlorn individuals with nowhere else to go and for who time bore no relevance.

Greenberg passed a hand over a face blighted by several days' growth. A man in decline. Worse, for the first time in his life he had started to lose his self-respect.

Returning from New York in June with such a high level of expectation, believing that it was only a question of time before Dominic got back to him, he had gone straight to work. True, he would be unable to reach the deadline agreed with Jacques of the end of the year, but at least now there remained an outside chance that auditions could begin before that time. He had tried calling Paris to advise Jacques of the delay, but when there was no answer from his apartment Greenberg decided that he would be better going to see him in person, once Dominic had confirmed that he was on board.

Even the lunch with Jules Levy, a few days later, failed to dampen his spirits, although the agent was not as positive as Greenberg would have liked in treating the show as a foregone conclusion. In fact, he seemed more interested in hearing about Arlene. It was clear that he still had strong feelings for her, and the last thing Greenberg wanted was to cause Jules any discomfort by disclosing that he and Arlene had had a brief intimate relationship.

Then, impatient to move things forward, he had contacted the same West End theatres that had turned him down to put them on notice that he was hopeful of securing the services of an award-winning Broadway director – and would they please confirm their availability to him in writing?

That was four months ago. In the meantime, he had heard absolutely nothing. Stupidly, he had neglected to ask Brad for his number, and the only way to get it was from Arlene – which, after the way she had dismissed him, he was in no mind to do. In the end, after hanging around for another three weeks, he gave up. It was obvious that Dominic had only agreed to read the script out of politeness and had forgotten about it soon afterwards. Jules, never one to gloat, suggested two other London directors, but they both knew these were poor alternatives.

Greenberg looked at the stack of unpaid bills on the kitchen table. His savings had dwindled to almost nothing. It was clear that unless something changed very soon, he would find himself out on the street. Ironic really, when there was a little less than a million pounds sitting in his bank account. In any event, since it was unlikely that the production would ever see the light of day, he had already made up his mind to return the money to Jacques, minus a few legitimate expenses such as the cost of the office and the trip to America.

How he was going to make a living was another matter. Show business was all he knew. The prospect of trying to find something else at his age simply terrified him.

A few days earlier, Mikey Nicolaou had entered the disused East London warehouse and placed the black Adidas sports bag behind a stack of old wooden pallets. Again, he'd followed the instructions to a T. The five hundred thou was the final instalment of the two million pounds the gang had demanded. That, together with the hundred grand transferred to Inspector Brian Morley's account in the Isle of Man, had all but cleared him out. But what choice did he have? The chances that those East European thugs would now leave him alone were slim to none. He knew from experience that, when you are involved with people of this type, there is never an end to their extortion.

Fortunately, Suzanne was none the wiser. After the first night in the hotel off the motorway, they had spent the rest of the week in a five-star spa hotel in the New Forest. Mikey had travelled up to London during the day for business. Then they had moved into the three-bed flat on the top floor of his office. He had cleared it with his partners, saying it was only pro tem while some emergency repairs were carried out at their home.

By eleven this evening, Suzanne would be in Spain, out of harm's way. The ten thousand that he had had to scrape the barrel to find would tide her over until he joined her. Then he would access whatever was left in the offshore account in Gibraltar, buy a bar in Sotogrande and live out his retirement in peace.

Meanwhile, he put the sale of the fully mortgaged house in the capable hands of James Mahoney, the agent who had secured it from Peter Greenberg.

Driving back up to Central London, Mikey reflected nostalgically on the fact that the bribe he had offered the bloke to get the deal agreed by the close of business that day would be the last one he would ever make in England.

Around about the same time, an overweight man in a peaked cap and an Aquascutum raincoat presented his ticket to the steward and made his way into the private members enclosure for the lunchtime meeting at Kempton Racecourse.

To Brian Morley, a few G and Ts, some smoked salmon sandwiches and a flutter on the horses was a good day out. Of course, there was a much more important purpose to his visit, which would hopefully provide him with enough security so he would never have to do a day's work again for the rest of his life.

There, waiting for him alone in his private box, was an immaculately dressed man, who was studying the racecard.

'Ah, Inspector, glad you could join me. The horses are already at the gate for the one thirty race,' Patel said, looking through his top-of-the-range binoculars.

'Got a decent amount on, have you?' Morley enquired, rubbing his hands together as he took a seat next to the man who needed his help.

'You could say that. Mumbai One is mine. He's the favourite, you know,' the host announced proudly. Then he asked, as he followed the runners around the course, 'Think you can get rid of that chappie Nicolaou?'

'Thought you told me you'd got back everything he took from you,' the inspector said, his suspicions suddenly alerted.

'Indeed I have,' Patel confirmed, anticipating that the sports bag of money would be with him shortly. Then he shouted, 'Well done,' as the jockey in red and green hoops was the first to cross the finishing line on a heavily panting Mumbai One. 'But you should know that man has done considerable harm to my reputation,' he murmured.

A smile then came to Patel's face as his three-year-old thoroughbred was led to the winners' enclosure and paraded to the press along with his jockey, Rory Keen, and his trainer from Newmarket, Harry Tansley.

Brian Morley looked across at him, bemused not only by the guy's winning streak, but also by the preposterous allegation that Raj Patel was somehow the innocent party in the criminal investigation into his company.

'What are you getting at?' Morley said.

'Quite simply that I wish our Mr Nicolaou to take the rap for the case that you people have brought against me.'

'But that's—' Morley began. Raj Patel butted in.

'What? Immoral? Is that what you were going to say? Inspector, may I remind you that I always managed to keep a low profile until you introduced me to that crook?

So I think it's only right that you have to bear some of the responsibility, don't you?' Without waiting for an answer, he went on.

'I've got it on good authority that Michael Nicolaou has – how shall I say? – provided you over the years with a lifestyle normally out of reach for a senior police inspector.'

'Are you trying to blackmail me?' the policeman gasped. His bulbous face had gone white and, despite the coolness of the afternoon, he was sweating profusely.

'My dear chap, I'm merely suggesting that, in my absence, while I was attending to my affairs in India, if anyone should take the blame, it should be him … since I had already delegated the running of the company to Nicolaou.'

'But Mr Patel, you know as well as I do that in this country, directors are jointly liable in criminal cases.'

'I'm quite aware of the law, Inspector Morley, but you are going to see to it that I'm in the clear. And if you succeed, which I hope for your sake that you do, there will be a nice bonus in it for you, which will dwarf the slim pickings you've received over the years from your accountant friend.'

'And the rest of the board?' Morley asked.

'Not your worry, old boy. I have their signed resignations. They just need to be dated. All *you* have to do is to say that Nicolaou was operating behind our backs and you can look forward to a peaceful retirement.'

Brian Morley was speechless. He got up and drifted despondently away, feeling that he had been well and truly screwed, and knowing that he was unable to do anything about it.

The smartly dressed woman put her overnight case on the carousel and strode confidently through the metal detector. It triggered off a loud beeping sound.

A chubby young girl from security immediately appeared.

'Got anything in your pockets like keys or coins?' she asked, beginning a thorough frisking of the passenger.

'No, nothing. Maybe it's my belt, though,' Suzanne replied innocently.

'Take it off for us, love, and go back through again,' said an older woman, who was manning the metal detector.

Suzanne did as she was told, and passed through without a problem. She collected her belt and went over to get her case, when to her surprise she noticed that it had been separated from the rest.

This time a male member of airport staff appeared.

'Just a routine check, madam. Would you mind opening your case for me?'

'No problem at all,' she replied, wondering why she had been singled out.

'Where are you travelling to?' he asked.

'Estepona. Lovely place, it is. Have you ever been there?' Suzanne said in a chatty tone.

Rummaging through her personal items, the man found ten packets of pristine fifty-pound notes stuffed in the side pockets.

'That's a lot of money just for the weekend,' he said suspiciously.

Suzanne shrugged.

'My boyfriend doesn't like me to go short.'

'Can I see your passport, please?'

Suzanne opened her handbag and passed it over.

'Just wait here a minute.' The security adviser went over to his supervisor.

A few minutes later a burly police officer appeared, holding a clipboard containing crude photographs of women in various disguises. They showed an uncanny likeness to the woman in a white Panama hat and sunglasses in front of them.

'Angela Brookes alias Vanessa Graham, you're wanted for questioning in connection with an organised crime ring on the Costa del Sol.'

'What on earth are you going on about? My name's Suzanne Greenberg. Look at my passport. You've got me muddled up with someone else,' Suzanne said. She looked as if she was about to start mouthing off.

At that point, the officer was joined by a young policewoman.

'Best not to make a fuss, ma'am,' she said calmly. 'Just accompany us and if, as you say, there's been a misunderstanding, you'll soon be on your way.'

A small crowd of passengers, en route to the departure hall, had gathered with their personal items to view the spectacle.

The red-headed woman, not unhappy to find herself the centre of attention, was escorted smiling and posing, then was bundled into the back of a police car and driven off to Paddington Green police station.

There the suspect, flanked by the two officers, was led up the steps of the characterless 1960s building. Just as she was being taken to the interview room, the familiar figure of Chief Inspector Morley brushed past her.

'Hello, Brian, love,' the suspect called out. 'Didn't expect to see you today.'

'Suzanne? What the hell?'

The two other policemen looked at each other in amazement.

'You know the detective inspector?' the well-built one said.

'Of course we do, don't we, precious? Michael and him do ever so much business together. Bet your Catherine is looking forward to that holiday of hers at our place in Spain.'

Brian Morley knew then that his days were numbered. As he walked back to his office, the only thing he had to console himself with was that if he was going down, he would make damn sure that he took that slimebag Michael Nicolaou and that fat fuck Raj Patel with him.

An hour later, embarrassed that they had apprehended the wrong person, the officers arranged for Suzanne to be driven back to Heathrow Airport to await the next flight to Malaga...her ticket paid for courtesy of the Metropolitan Police.

35

Greenberg switched on the television and settled down to a supper of fish and chips, feeling happier than he had in a long time. Georges's suggestion that he work for him in his restaurant business had come out of the blue and as a welcome surprise. The two of them had actually planned to open their own place after they left school, but by the time his friend had received his catering qualification from the École hôtelière in Lausanne, Greenberg had got fed up waiting and had instead taken his creative talents into the theatre.

Greenberg was just about to pour out the rest of his can of Carlsberg lager when there was a ring at the door of his apartment. He wasn't expecting anyone. He opened it – and in stepped Issy Williams, his former assistant, with the evening paper under her arm. She was looking far less settled than when they had last seen each other.

'Issy, what on earth are *you* doing here?' Greenberg spluttered, completely stunned. 'I mean, how did you know where to find me?'

'I followed you home that afternoon when you came to collect your things.'

'Why? I don't understand,' Greenberg replied, still baffled.

Issy looked him in the face and said determinedly, 'It had been preying on my mind, the way that they took your business away from you because you were late with the rent. It just wasn't fair.' She looked away, mumbling, 'I felt so guilty.'

'But there was no way *you* were to blame for that,' Greenberg said to reassure her, wondering how she could possibly have known the reason for his problems. 'What is it? Are you trying to tell me there's more to it than that?'

Suddenly, the young woman burst into tears.

'I know I shouldn't have done what I did,' she sobbed, 'but I needed that job. Since my father got made redundant from HMRC, my family depends on my salary. He and my mum can't manage, as I have two younger brothers who are still at school.'

'Come and sit down and let me get you something to drink,' Greenberg offered kindly.

'No. I'm fine, really.' Issy gulped, and slowly regained her cool. 'So, do you forgive me for informing Ken Brookman's office about the Duke's?' She pulled out some tissues and blew her nose.

'Yes, of course,' Greenberg replied. 'You only did what anyone else would have done in your position.' But as he spoke, he was already asking himself who had given her the instruction.

'Thank you, thank you,' she said, throwing her arms around her old boss.

Thinking that was all there was to it, Greenberg needed no further persuasion to sit back down and return to his supper before it got too cold and greasy. Issy hadn't finished, however.

'I thought you might want to have a look at this,' she said, pointing to a headline in the paper. It read:

DI Brian Morley, Head of Criminal Investigation into

Explosion at House of Multiple Occupation in East London, Charged with Corruption.

'There was something about it on the news,' Greenberg said, showing little interest and adding more ketchup to his chips.

'But it says that the Duke's is involved.'

'Don't tell me they're planning on making a show about it. I can see it now,' Greenberg said, rolling his eyes:

'*Inspector Clouseau Gets His Fingers Burnt.*'

He snorted with laughter, and coughed up a small fragment of fish that had got stuck in his throat.

'*No*,' Issy said urgently. 'What I'm trying to say is that the people who caused all that trouble in the paper are apparently the same as the ones who own the Duke's. Ken Brookman is furious about what all the bad publicity will do to his business.'

'I'm sure he is. But why are you telling me all this?' Was there some other reason for her visit? Greenberg wondered.

'It's just that Mr Brookman won't be taking me with him when he leaves. So I thought I might be able to come back and work for you.'

'It's a bit too late for that, I'm afraid. You see, I've moved on to other things. Sorry I can't be of help.' Greenberg took another gulp of his lager.

There was a momentary lull as it became clear to the visitor that she had wasted her journey.

'I understand. Well, I won't trouble you any further,' she said, leaving Greenberg to finish what was left of his dinner.

Shortly afterwards, he heard the sound of the street door being shut firmly behind her. Out of curiosity, Greenberg picked up the newspaper she had discarded and found himself following the story that had made the headlines. It gave extensive coverage to Detective Inspector Brian Morley who, after admitting to taking bribes linked to the tragedy in Newham, East London, had been forced to resign from the force that he had served loyally for thirty years. The report then went on to say:

In a series of dawn raids across Central London, arrests were made at the homes of several senior executives of Longton Enterprises, the concern headed up by multimillionaire businessman Raj Patel.

Longton Enterprises, the proprietor of the famous Duke's Theatre in St Martin's Lane, is facing criminal charges as a result of the fatal explosion of a gas boiler six weeks ago at one of its properties. The company is also being investigated for money laundering activities involving an extensive network of offshore bank accounts, thought to have been masterminded by an unnamed individual with connections to high-ranking police officers.

Shaking his head, Greenberg put the paper down, cleared away the remnants of his dinner and went to bed.

A few days later, foregoing his normal morning routine for a reason that he couldn't explain, Greenberg had the desire to go up to town. He took the Tube to Leicester Square and, as he headed for St Martin's Lane, he felt a welcome rush of adrenalin, something that had been absent for a very long time.

As he approached his former theatre he saw to his surprise that it had gone dark. The place had been abandoned and no one answered when he knocked loudly on the door. Strangely, the empty feeling that had stayed with him after he had been evicted from the Duke's swiftly dissipated and was immediately replaced by a feeling of enormous optimism.

Greenberg's mind began working overtime as he walked back towards the Tube. Then, discovering that he didn't want to go home yet, he took himself instead to Covent Garden and to the office that had for many weeks fallen into disuse.

Would I really be able to get hold of the Duke's? he kept asking himself. The money was still in his account. Thank goodness he hadn't acted precipitously and transferred it back to Jacques.

The thought that he might no longer have to kowtow to those other snotty West End theatres only increased his determination to put his show on at his old venue. If it *had* closed down, surely there must be someone who could tell him who to talk to.

Greenberg decided to call in on Richard Jacobs, the sole practitioner accountant who had an office across the hall, who he had become quite friendly with.

'Hello, Olga. Is Richard available for a quick word?' he asked the receptionist.

'His four o'clock appointment hasn't arrived yet, so I'm sure he'll give you a few minutes,' she said pleasantly. 'Haven't seen you around for a while, Mr Greenberg,' she commented, picking up the phone to her boss.

Greenberg just smiled.

'It's fine,' she told him, replacing the phone. 'Richard says you can go straight in.'

The accountant greeted him and came over to shake hands with his neighbour.

'Hi, Peter, what's up?' In Greenberg's mind, the young

guy looked barely old enough to have qualified.

'Richard, how do I find out who to talk to about a theatre that's closed down?' he asked, wasting no time.

'Is it owned by an individual or a company?' Richard Jacobs said briskly.

'I think it's a company called Longton Enterprises,' Greenberg answered, remembering the name from the papers.

'Wait a minute. They're the ones all over the news!' the young accountant exclaimed.

'Is that good or bad?' Greenberg wanted to know.

'I'd wager, with the type of fine they're going to be facing – running into millions – they'll probably be wound up by the court, if they haven't been already.'

'Can you help me?' Greenberg enquired.

'Indeed I can. It just so happens that my friend Henry Redstone is the insolvency partner at KTRW, one of the biggest accountancy practices in the country. With a high-profile case like this, if he hasn't got the job, he'll have a jolly good idea who has. Let me make a few phone calls and I'll get back to you. I have your mobile number and email address.'

'That would be great, thank you,' Greenberg responded, glad that he had decided to pop in on the off-chance.

'A pleasure. And you know where to come if you want me to act for you. There are still some of us left who do things according to the book.'

'Sorry, what do you mean?' Greenberg asked.

'It's just come up on Reuters. The mystery man who was the mastermind behind the company you just mentioned is an accountant named Michael Nicolaou. Apparently he was arrested a few hours ago, going through Spanish customs.'

Greenberg nodded. He managed to mutter a polite goodbye to Richard, and then Olga, before stumbling into his own office, barely able to absorb what he had just heard. He went straight to his computer and typed in 'BBC News' to see whether there was anything on the story. Maybe it was just a coincidence that the person had the same name.

It was no mistake. There, right in front of his eyes, was the man who had taken such pleasure in his downfall. However, it was impossible to detect by his relaxed expression that the former West End auditor had suffered anything more than an inconvenience. What Greenberg hadn't fathomed was that Mikey's theft of Greenberg's wife, his beautiful home and his very *raison d'être*, his career, had not been enough. Mikey's greed extended much further than that. The fellow was involved in criminal activity on a much more ambitious scale.

Greenberg's thoughts turned to Suzanne. He wondered if his ex-wife was aware of the type of man she had become mixed up with. He searched through the narrative again for any mention of her name, but there was none.

She has my number, Greenberg told himself. If she was in trouble, she could contact him. He sincerely hoped she had nothing to do with any of this.

PART FOUR

The Boy at the Window

36

Dominic disembarked from the Alitalia flight that had just arrived at Heathrow Airport from Venice. Here he said an emotional farewell to Alejandro, who was catching a connecting flight home to New York, and made his way out into the cold December morning. This impromptu stopover in London was, as far as his partner knew, purely to do with business. Dominic hadn't told Alejandro the true reason for his visit: that he had to confront his mother Clare about his past.

Dominic had kept his promise to Arlene and had read the script after their meeting in Central Park. Even though the names had been changed and the story had been skilfully adapted for commercial theatre, the discovery that it purported to be about his birth mother had seemed completely absurd. After all, didn't his birth certificate quite clearly state Clare Langley as his mother? Nevertheless, it succeeded in sowing a seed of doubt in his mind that left him feeling unsettled. Several intense sessions ensued with Sandra Cohen, his therapist, with the aim of helping him to try and come to terms with its contents.

If it hadn't been for the episode at the nursery window that was described with such clarity, he would have been inclined to dismiss the tale as a work of fiction. But now it all began to make sense. The little boy in his dream was *him*. And the person he was craning to see from the window was his real mother, Nadine Bertrand, crying up to him until she gave up and walked away. And the fact that his parents had withheld this knowledge from him – had withheld his *mother* from him – persuading him to believe instead that it was a figment of an overactive imagination, did accurately portray his experience.

However, the allegation that for two years his parents had colluded to deviously prise him away from his birth mother – and when they succeeded, had systematically erased all trace of her, even forging his birth certificate – seemed preposterous. He agonised over the whole episode.

What if it was true? And what if their actions had caused the woman to take her own life? As his therapist had said, he needed verification so that he could dismiss what might simply be a pernicious attempt to discredit him and his family.

In either case, the thought that the story might be performed on the stage and go public sent him into a severe panic.

Dominic got out of the black cab at Onslow Square and proceeded with his luggage up the steps to the house. As he put the key in the lock, a grey-haired woman in a dressing gown appeared at the door. By the blank look in her eyes, it was clear that she hadn't exaggerated her medical condition.

'Hello, Mother,' he said, entering the once impeccable home, which from the outside, at least, had been allowed to fall into disrepair. 'It's Dominic. I've come to London to see you.'

The old lady put a vein-covered hand up against her mouth as if she had just seen a ghost.

Dominic's obsession for the truth was all of a sudden replaced with heart-wrenching pity. Struggling to control himself, he led his mother gently by the arm along the hall into the drawing room that had seemed so grand when he was a child. Now, with its shabby furnishings and stale aroma, it looked more like a headmaster's study in a seedy public school.

'I have a son named Dominic,' Clare Langley said, suddenly coming to life, 'but he lives in America. He's a famous director. I can show you some photographs, if you like.' She went over to an old mahogany bookcase and pulled out a dusty green album.

Dominic sat quietly, wondering whether the family photos would jog her memory. For the next half hour she rambled on, occasionally shaking her head gleefully when she recognised a particular image from the past. It seemed strange that whenever there was a picture of his father, her expression changed and she went swiftly on to the next page. What was also evident was that there were no pictures of a baby.

'I wanted a child so much,' Clare Langley said sadly, as if she were party to his thoughts. 'Do you have children?' she asked, turning to Dominic.

'Mother, you know that I'm not married.'

'I have a son. His name is Dominic. He's probably the same age as you.'

'That's *me*,' Dominic stressed. 'Can't you see that I'm the same person in the photographs?'

'So you decided to come back home?' Clare Langley remarked, her alertness temporarily restored.

'You wrote to me three months ago in New York, saying that you weren't well and that there was something you wanted to tell me,' Dominic reminded his mother, certain that in her present condition, even with a great deal of assistance, she wouldn't be up to writing a letter.

'I don't remember you replying,' she said, a note of disappointment in her voice.

'No, you're quite right. I thought that I would surprise you by coming to London instead,' he lied, feeling ashamed that he had left it so long.

'I've had Nanny make your room ready for you,' she said, reverting to her former state.

'Mother, Aileen's been gone for at least thirty years,' Dominic began.

There was a knock at the door and in came a woman in a pink uniform, holding a glass of water and two tablets, saying, 'It's time for your medication, Mrs Langley.'

'Maggie, this is my son Dominic,' she announced proudly, swallowing the pills without a fuss.

'Very pleased to meet you. She talks about you all the time,' the carer said.

'Aileen, Dominic is back from school for the holidays. Make sure his room is ready for him, will you?' his mother went on, once again slipping back into the past.

Dominic glanced at the helper.

'I'm sorry,' he said quietly.

'That's all right. She's no trouble,' Maggie replied. She bent down to her employer. 'Now I will bring your lunch.' She turned to Dominic. 'Would you like something?'

'No, I'm fine, thank you. Shall I feed her?' Dominic asked feebly.

'Your mother can do it herself,' she said.

Dominic got up and followed the carer out of the room to the kitchen.

'Maggie, how long has she been like this?' he asked.

'Madam got worse after she received the news about Mr Charles,' the doll-like woman said, while preparing the tray for his mother.

'What news was that?'

The carer looked taken aback. Did this man really not know about his father's demise? She cleared her throat, then said, 'Mr Charles, he died – nearly six months ago now. I'm very sorry, sir.'

It was a shock.

'I didn't know,' Dominic said. That was obviously the reason why his mother had written, asking him to come to London, so she could break the news about his father to him in person. Sadly, he couldn't feel any sense of loss for the man who had been such a disruptive influence. Dominic despised his father, it was as simple as that, and he didn't need anybody telling him who was responsible for his mother's wretched mental state. Growing up, he had had plenty of first-hand experience of his father's callousness.

'And so who looks after my mother's affairs and pays your wages?' Dominic asked, returning to more practical matters.

'You do not have to worry. Mr Lothbury takes care of everything,' Maggie said, referring to the aged solicitor who, to the best of Dominic's knowledge, had looked after the family's interests for the last forty years.

Dominic returned to the drawing room and sat with his mother while she slowly ate her broth. The deterioration brought about by the demise of the man she had obviously loved so deeply, seemed terribly unfair. Sandra Cohen's assessment of the effects of a one-sided relationship had been entirely accurate.

Dominic had seen enough.

Without the confirmation of his past that he had been so desperate to obtain, he collected his bags, walked to the edge of Sloane Avenue and hailed a taxi to take him to the Capital Hotel in Knightsbridge. The visit to his mother had drained him emotionally. That, together with the news of the death of his father, had left him bereft of the answers he so badly needed.

At that moment, he wished that Alejandro was waiting for him instead of being halfway back to New York. Nevertheless, he had given Maggie his private number and address in New York and had told her to contact him if she needed anything.

Dominic spent the evening drinking heavily in the hotel bar, still feeling unsure about his true identity. With no one else he could turn to, he would have no choice but to live the rest of his life with that uncertainty.

What he could do, however, was call Brad in New York and ask him for Peter Greenberg's number. He had done his homework on the producer. With nothing but a string of recent failures to his name, it was clear that Greenberg was resorting to any means at his disposal to restore his reputation. No way was Dominic going to allow that to happen at his expense. Before he went home, he was going to make damn sure that Greenberg's show would never, *ever* see the light of day.

The next morning, by the time Greenberg arrived at the office, there was a message on his phone from Richard Jacobs to confirm that KTRW had been appointed receivers to Longton Enterprises and would be handling the disposal of the Duke's Theatre on behalf of the court. Richard advised him to sit tight and await details of the auction.

Finding it hard to believe anyone else would be interested in the place, Greenberg was pleased that he was at last able to update Jacques with some progress. The same afternoon, he telephoned Georges to tell him that he wouldn't be taking up his offer of a job, after all.

He could never give up the theatre.

37

Greenberg remained in his seat, unable to fully comprehend what he'd done, long after the packed West London venue had emptied. Never having attended an auction before, his nerves had begun to get the better of him and, despite the cold winter's afternoon, damp patches had formed under his arms. Fortunately, the Duke's consisted of two lots: the freehold of the building and the far less desirable medium-term lease for the theatre, which had belonged to an associate company of Longton Enterprises. Finding that he was the only interested party with regard to the lease, his bid was accepted. He supplied his details to the auctioneer and was given thirty days to have the lease assigned to his company, Peter Greenberg Productions.

Waiting for him in the reception area when he returned to the office was a man who looked familiar, somehow. He wore a leather bomber jacket, and his collar was pulled up tight around his neck. There was a tense expression on his face.

'Peter Greenberg? I don't know if you remember me,' Dominic Langley said, keeping his distance. 'We met briefly a few months ago in New York.'

'Yes. Yes, of course,' Greenberg replied, completely baffled by the director's presence. 'How did you manage to find me?'

'Brad de Winter, Arlene Davidson…*that* wasn't a problem,' Dominic said impatiently, inferring that there was something of far greater importance on his mind.

'Can I get you some coffee? It's really cold out there today,' Greenberg offered.

'No, thank you. Look, there's something we need to straighten out,' Dominic said tersely.

'I take it that you're referring to the script,' Greenberg replied, assuming this was the reason for the man's hostile demeanour.

'Damn right I am,' Dominic said, raising his voice.

'Look, I'm sure we can sort this out calmly,' Greenberg responded, conscious that the disturbance had already aroused the attention of others within earshot. But it made no difference. Unable to restrain himself, Dominic Langley was determined to unleash his anger on the person whose delving into his past had caused him so much anguish.

'Let me make myself absolutely clear,' he said heatedly. 'I don't know what possessed you to come up with that story, but I'm warning you that if it hits the stage – or anywhere else, for that matter – you'll find yourself at the wrong end of a very expensive lawsuit, which according to my sources you are in no financial position to defend.'

Greenberg was too numb to offer a response. All he knew was that, having just committed himself to the Duke's, he was facing a potential catastrophe. He could see now that it had been a huge mistake, not telling Dominic from the beginning how the idea for the show had come about. Making him aware for the first time through the script about the tragic circumstances of his birth mother was, on reflection, the height of folly. It was obvious that it had come as a major shock to the younger man, and that explained his current behaviour.

Greenberg knew that if he allowed Dominic to walk out now, he was finished. He had to think of something quickly. There was a pause while he considered his response, then he decided on a change of tack.

'Dominic, I can see now that I should never have agreed to take on the project,' he said, attempting to appease the younger man.

'What do you mean? I thought it was your idea,' Dominic snapped back.

'My dear fellow, there's a lot you don't know. However, you've made your position absolutely plain and the last thing I want to do is upset you any further, so you'll have to excuse me,' Greenberg said, moving away. 'I have rather a lot of work to do on a theatre I've just purchased.'

Dominic's face dropped. He had been caught off balance. Although it was a high-risk strategy, Greenberg knew he had no choice.

'So, you'll agree not to go ahead with the script?' Dominic said meekly. His aggression had dispersed and he had become more conciliatory.

'Of course. It's completely up to you. But if I were in your position, before I made that decision, I would want to know everything I could about my past.'

'My father's dead and my mother's ill. Who else is there?'

'You could start with me,' Greenberg said gently.

Dominic thought for a moment then nodded his agreement. He accompanied the producer back to his office. Neither of them knew what they were going to be able to accomplish. There was just a tentative thread keeping them together.

It was already dark outside. Greenberg pulled up a solitary chair for his visitor. He was well aware that there was a long way to go to convince the man, whose acquaintance he had been seeking for almost a year, that he wasn't the opportunist that Dominic had imagined.

Now, sitting a few feet away, under strained circumstances, admittedly, he was suddenly at a loss to know where to begin.

Dominic was the first to speak.

'You intimated that you knew my mother, didn't you?'

Greenberg sighed.

'Yes, or so I thought at the time.'

'It seems you must have known her pretty well, to have come up with all that stuff about her,' Dominic said bitterly. 'Unless, of course, the whole thing was fabricated.'

'No, it's all true.' Greenberg kept his words purposely brief, assessing that it would be a better tactic for Dominic to carry on asking the questions. Then he added, 'It was only after she died that I got to know the true Nadine.'

Hearing confirmation of his mother's name for the first time produced a strange expression on Dominic's face.

'In case you're wondering about the other characters, their names were changed, for legal purposes. But I and a certain other interested party wanted to call the show *Nadine*.'

'So do I take it that you weren't working entirely on your own?'

'Dominic, as I said, your mother was a complex woman, one who I happened to love very much, but there were

291

aspects to her short life that I only discovered later on.'

'I would very much like to learn everything you know about her,' Dominic said, caught up in the saga of his lost family.

'Look, it's getting late and there's still a great deal to talk about. Perhaps it would be better to carry on tomorrow.' Greenberg yawned as he got up from his desk. It had been a long day and, since there was so much at stake, he wanted to be in a clearer frame of mind.

'That's going to be difficult,' Dominic replied, making no attempt to leave. 'I've got a flight back to the States at midday tomorrow, so if you don't mind, I'd like to continue. Maybe we could get together for a drink later on.'

'All right,' Greenberg agreed. 'Where are you staying?'

Dominic reached into his pocket for his phone and read off the address of his hotel.

'Eight o'clock in the Capital Bar?'

'I'll be there,' Greenberg promised and saw his visitor out.

Ready to drop from the strain of the last few hours, he treated himself to a taxi home to Camden, feeling like a boxer taking a brief respite before going into the ring for the next round. Being so totally absorbed in the encounter with Dominic, securing the Duke's had gone straight out of his mind, as had calling on Richard Jacobs, without whose help it wouldn't have happened. Not having Richard's private number, he would make it his first priority in the morning.

Conscious that he hadn't eaten a thing all day, Greenberg made himself a double-decker cheese and pickle sandwich and a mug of hot tea before showering and changing his clothes. He tried to assess his mood.

If someone had told him the day before that in a period of less than twenty-four hours he would get his theatre back and that Dominic Langley would track him down, he wouldn't have believed them. The reality now, however, was that he was purely focused on winning Nadine's son over in the few hours available to him so that Dominic would delay his trip back to New York.

After entering the exclusive five-star hotel, Greenberg found his way to the bar. He spotted Dominic, dressed in a sweatshirt and blue denim jeans, reclining in a wooden-framed armchair, looking completely unrecognisable from the fraught individual of just two or three hours ago. On the table in front of him was an opened bottle of eighteen-year-old Macallan malt whisky.

Dominic greeted the arrival of his guest with a wave of his arm. Feeling overdressed in a suit and tie, Greenberg went across to the man who had completely monopolised his thoughts.

'What would you like?' Dominic said.

'Malt's fine,' Greenberg responded, eyeing up the fine whisky.

'Do you have any photographs of her?' Dominic asked, gesturing to a cool-looking young waiter to bring over another glass.

'Of Nadine? Yes, I've got her albums. She was always particular about keeping them updated.'

'No, I meant with you this evening.'

Greenberg apologised, inwardly berating himself.

'They're in the office, I'm afraid. It was most remiss of me.' He'd let slip a perfect opportunity to secure his credentials. He wondered whether that would cost him dearly.

'From when she was a dancer?' Dominic continued, undeterred.

'Yes. Nadine appeared for me on tour and I managed to get her some other parts for West End shows,' Greenberg explained.

'So, in the story, you were the other man in the background.'

'In more than one sense, but my relationship with her was not of crucial importance.' Greenberg took a large gulp of whisky. A look of bliss appeared on his face as the fiery liquid hit the back of his throat.

'But it is to me. You see, Peter, as I said, I want to know *everything* about the woman *you claim* was my mother,' Dominic said resolutely.

Seeing that he still hadn't obtained the other man's trust, Greenberg thought carefully about his next move.

'How long have you got?' he asked.

'I've cancelled my flight and now have an open ticket back to the States, if that answers your question,' Dominic told him. Lifting the bottle, he poured them each another drink.

It was past two in the morning by the time Greenberg finished recounting his experiences of Nadine from the very first time she had captivated him on the West End stage.

Apart from seeking the occasional clarification, Dominic listened attentively while various aspects of his mother's life were unfolded to him.

'Of course, there's not that much about her childhood, when she was growing up in Paris,' Dominic commented finally, 'and there is no real evidence that she was actually my birth mother.'

Greenberg had anticipated that Dominic would raise the issue of his birth and had at least prepared for this eventuality. He reflected on the last time he had seen Jacques and the episode in his private study when Jacques had supplied him with the combination to his safe, in order to hand him the proof that he was now being asked to produce.

Greenberg reached into the inside pocket of his suit jacket and took out a folded document, which he passed to Dominic.

Dominic looked at his birth certificate, dated 15 June 1975, and gasped. For there in black in white was the mother's name: *Nadine Bertrand*. Somehow or other, Clare Langley's name must have been entered on a subsequent document. She was not, as he had always been led to believe, his real mother.

'I'm sorry. This must come as quite a shock,' Greenberg said kindly, genuinely concerned about the state of the young man sitting opposite him.

'This changes everything,' Dominic muttered, so softly that he could barely be heard. 'Peter, I'm sorry to have doubted you. Please will you forgive me?'

'Yes, yes, of course. You weren't to know,' Greenberg said sympathetically.

'But how did you manage to get hold of this?' Dominic poured them both another generous measure of the malt whisky. His hand was shaking and the look in his eyes was that of a little boy who had just discovered a terrible secret.

'It was part of the due diligence we undertook before

we started on the script,' Greenberg revealed. Some instinct warned him that it was premature to talk about the role Jacques had played in the project. Although it now appeared that Dominic was convinced that the script was authentic, he still hadn't agreed for it to be performed.

Greenberg then excused himself and, unsteady on his feet from the whisky, he staggered to the lavatory. He must have been in there longer than he had imagined because when he returned, there was no sign of Dominic and their table had been taken up by a young couple.

Surprised that Dominic had gone off without saying anything, Greenberg put it down to the possibility that he too was suffering from too much to drink and had wandered off to bed.

The next morning, after he arrived at the office, Greenberg filled Richard Jacobs in with the results of the auction. He added that he remained unaware of the identity of his new landlord. He then telephoned Dominic's hotel, only to be told that their guest had checked out without leaving any messages.

Greenberg immediately assumed that Dominic needed time alone to come to terms with everything he had discovered about his mother. It was, indeed, a lot for the young man to take in.

38

Dominic examined himself in his bedroom mirror. He'd put back on most of the weight he'd lost. He thought back on those last eight weeks. The worst fears about his identity had been realised, and the two encounters, first with his mother and then with Greenberg, had left him completely devastated and unable to function.

After fleeing back to New York as quickly as he could, hoping the nightmare would go away, he had taken to his bed. A deep depression engulfed his whole being. He was oblivious even to the affections of Alejandro who, frightened by the change that had come over him since returning from London, had moved out and returned to his West Side studio.

Now he had proof of his mother, Nadine, his dreams had taken on a greater intensity. Even though he still hadn't seen a picture of her, he imagined them looking similar to one another. In one particularly distressing scene they were playing in a park, when suddenly he was snatched out of her arms and led away by his father, while another woman, who he didn't recognise, remained in the background.

'But I want my other mummy,' he cried out.

'She's dead. That's why you are coming to live with us,' his father said angrily, grabbing him painfully by the arm.

Only when he awoke did he comprehend that the other

woman in his dream must have been Clare Langley who, until just a few weeks ago, he had always thought of as his real mother. But why had she just stood there silently, doing nothing to help him?

At other times he dreamt that he was underwater, being dragged further and further down, not putting up a struggle, as the last breath was slowly drawn out of him. Subconsciously, he was trying to replicate the scenes from Greenberg's script of his mother's life, with him taking the main part.

He wasn't aware of it but he had become a recluse, only sneaking out late at night when no one would recognise him. Everything had lost its meaning, and worse, he lacked the will to change anything.

At the beginning of the third week, and at his lowest point, Brad de Winter, concerned that he hadn't been able to get through on the phone, turned up without warning at Dominic's apartment. Visibly shocked by the dishevelled appearance of his friend and the sight of the half-eaten plates of food and empty bottles strewn over the floor, Brad realised that medical supervision was urgently needed and somehow managed to drag out of Dominic the name of his therapist.

Admitted as an emergency patient to the Mount Sinai Hospital in East Harlem, he was placed under the care of Sandra Cohen, who was the consultant psychiatrist there. Like his mother Nadine before him, Dominic was diagnosed with clinical depression and put on a course of serotonin medication to stabilise him. Initially, the drug made him even more languid and disorientated. The doctors increased his private sessions with Sandra

Cohen, supplemented by group psychotherapy classes, and prescribed a strict exercise regime. Gradually, his condition improved.

Now, daily workouts with his personal trainer were giving him a new sense of well-being. The fact that he would be on medication for the rest of his life was a price worth paying if it prevented a recurrence of the illness that had nearly killed him. Never again, he vowed, would he allow himself to sink to the same levels of desperation. Weirdly, the prospect of living alone, hitherto an unthinkable proposition, didn't bother him. As a result of his treatment he had learnt to like himself for the first time.

Dominic stripped off and entered the walk-in shower. The ice-cold water on his newly toned body felt invigorating, but there was something missing in his life. He was bored. He needed the challenge of a new show to feel truly alive again.

He put on his towelling bathrobe and walked down the spiral staircase to the kitchen, where he took a jug of freshly made carrot juice out of the fridge and settled down to a healthy breakfast of muesli and low-fat yoghurt.

The day's post was confined to a single letter that carried a UK stamp. Inside, accompanying the official-looking document, was a short note from Maggie, his mother's carer, saying that she had forgotten to give it to him when he was in London.

Dominic looked again at the lawyer's correspondence, dated three months previously, naming him sole beneficiary in the estate of a Jacques Bertrand from Paris. For a moment he was certain that there must have been some mistake. But then he recalled hearing the same name before, only he couldn't place where.

Suddenly it came to him. Jumping up, he hurried over to his suede shoulder bag, which had remained untouched on his coat stand since he had returned from London. With trembling hands, he removed his folded birth certificate, naming Nadine Bertrand as his birth mother. It took him only a moment to realise that Jacques Bertrand was his maternal grandfather.

Now everything fell into place. This was what his mother had meant when she wrote that she had something important to disclose to him. And the reason why she was so desperate for him to come to London was that, now she was in receipt of the will of Jacques Bertrand, she felt she had no alternative but to tell him the whole truth about her son's past. But unfortunately, because of her illness, Clare had been in no fit state to do anything about it by the time he'd got to see her.

Dominic spent the remainder of the morning looking through the extensive list of assets that he had inherited. Of the estate, valued at over twenty million euros, the main items were an apartment in Paris and a house in Cannes in the south of France, as well as a sizeable portfolio of stocks and shares and a large amount of cash. The one thing that caught his attention, however, was a commercial building in Central London that housed a theatre.

Ignoring a number of minor legacies that completed the will, Dominic knew that he would have to make another trip to Europe. First to Paris, where he'd been requested to visit the offices of the lawyer Maître Marcel Dreyfus, and then again to London. This time, however, he was mentally strong enough to face whatever the past might throw at him.

The stormy conditions of the first months of 2014 gave way to an early spring. Greenberg stood at the back of the auditorium peering down at the stage. A smart new sign saying *Peter Greenberg Productions* had been put up outside, and after a quick tarting up of the front of house with the help of a few arts management students from Birkbeck College, who he had enlisted on work experience over the holiday period, the Duke's was open for business.

The plan was that the theatre would initially operate as a receiving house to producers with a sufficient following to fill the place. So long as their rent covered his running costs, he was happy to give them the majority of the box office receipts.

The Duke's reputation had to be rebuilt, this time on sound foundations. Already in receipt of half a dozen inquiries, Greenberg was feeling cautiously optimistic.

The notification just before Christmas that Jacques had died had upset him terribly. That he had been unable to fulfil the man's final wish of attending the premiere of *Nadine*, the show's working title, made it all the harder to bear. He had tried his best, but Dominic had not been back in contact since leaving London so abruptly. Sadly, the young man would now never know his grandfather – a man who had only wanted to make amends. It was a loss to them both.

Greenberg plodded upstairs to his office, which looked as shabby as when he had left it – no surprise, since Ken Brookman never laid out a penny unless he had to. Giving a month's notice on the office premises in Covent Garden, a few minicab rides were all it had taken to clear out the place and settle himself back at the Duke's.

After wandering into the next-door office, Greenberg, for no particular reason, casually opened the middle drawer of his former PA's desk. Apart from a few personal belongings – a hairbrush, a packet of Anadin painkillers – there was nothing much of interest. However, just as he was about to close it, he noticed that a dusty-looking cheque had been placed carefully under the old company seal.

Not expecting anything untoward, Greenberg picked it up. Then he saw that it had been made out to his former landlords, RP Investments. It only took him a minute to realise that it was the missing rent payment that had kick-started the loss of his business. So *that* was what Issy Williams had really been alluding to when she came to his home, but she was clearly unable to bring herself to admit the true extent of her guilt.

Greenberg didn't blame the young woman. It was obvious that someone had got to her, saying it would be in her best interests not to send off the all-important rent money. And there was only one person he could think of who was capable of such deceit.

Michael Nicolaou.

Greenberg stood trembling, clenching his fists in anger. He now had all the proof he needed. That man had deliberately set out to ruin him, and he was going to exact his revenge.

Snatching up his coat, Greenberg hurried down the stairs and out of the theatre, heading in no particular direction. All he could think of was finding the conniving bastard and tearing him apart with his bare hands. After a few minutes, breathing hard, he accepted that his pursuit was futile and calmed down.

Passing a news stand, he helped himself to a copy of the free evening paper and walked slowly back to the theatre. His attention was immediately attracted to the trial that had started of the individuals involved in Longton Enterprises. If found guilty, the report stated, the seven accused, including Michael Nicolaou, were facing sentences of up to fifteen years in prison.

As soon as Greenberg returned to the Duke's, he tore the cheque up into small pieces and threw it away in the wastepaper bin.

Michael Nicolaou had finally got what was coming to him. Greenberg didn't have to do anything. It was time to move on.

39

A fortnight passed. Slowly. Finding the right show for the opening had proved anything but straightforward. None of the scripts presented to Greenberg inspired him with much confidence. He was used to a much higher quality. The problem was that he had to generate some income, even if it meant compromising his standards.

One day, he was just about to pack up and go home when there was a knock at his office door.

Probably the last of the students, he said to himself. But, to his complete astonishment, in walked Dominic Langley.

'We meet again,' Dominic said, offering his hand to the man he had run out on two and a half months previously.

'I didn't expect—' Greenberg stuttered, completely taken aback.

'What, that you'd ever see me again?' Dominic replied light-heartedly. 'I suppose I do owe you an explanation for my disappearing act.'

'There's really no need,' Greenberg said, more interested in what had brought about the complete transformation in the younger man. The strain that had been caused by the revelations of his past had been replaced with buoyancy, which Greenberg found thoroughly disconcerting.

The image flashed through his mind of Nadine when she had just finished onstage, with the adrenalin still pumping through her veins. He remembered feeling similarly unsettled, knowing how, just a few hours before, she had been engulfed in a dark mood. The parallel between mother and son seemed uncanny.

'No, please hear me out. There's a lot I have to say.'

'Fine. Pull up a chair,' Greenberg gestured, intrigued.

'You see, I was unwell for many weeks. I've only recently got myself together again.'

'You mean you couldn't deal with what you found out?' Greenberg interjected.

'So much of it didn't make sense. I started imagining all sorts of things. Really, I just couldn't cope and ended up in hospital.'

'Dominic, I'm so sorry. If I'd known—' Greenberg felt horribly guilty.

'There was nothing that you could have done. I had to come to terms with it all myself. And it took a long time. It was rather like learning to ride a motorbike again after suffering a serious accident. My confidence was shot to pieces.'

'Did you receive help?'

'Yes. And now I'm fine.'

'That's great,' Greenberg said with genuine feeling. 'So … you want to take up where we left off?'

'Not exactly,' Dominic replied cagily.

'Sorry, I'm not with you,' Greenberg said, again in the dark.

'A few days after I left hospital something happened that enabled me to uncover further aspects of my past, ones that I never knew existed.'

Greenberg was confused. Was there a missing element in this saga that he was unaware of?

'And you think I can be of help in some way,' he guessed.

'Most definitely. You are obviously not aware who owns this place,' Dominic said, casting his eyes around the room.

'What are you getting at? I believe that I own it,' Greenberg retorted, becoming rattled.

Is this some kind of payback for the trauma the guy has suffered? he thought.

'I wasn't referring to the theatre,' Dominic continued, retaining his placid attitude.

'You're talking about the building, then?'

Dominic nodded.

'I don't think I understand,' Greenberg said gruffly. Then it dawned on him that maybe he was sitting opposite his landlord. But how was that possible?

'It was left to me with a mass of other stuff in my grandfather's will,' Dominic disclosed.

'Jacques,' Greenberg heard himself call out. As he struggled to absorb this astonishing revelation his mind turned to the auction. He'd been so focused on obtaining the new lease of the theatre that he had completely ignored the bidders for the freehold. But how did the old man know about it in the first place? Even more disturbing was the thought that Jacques had gone behind his back.

It seemed that since Jacques hadn't heard from him for months, he must have assumed that Greenberg had been unable to get hold of Dominic and, determined to go ahead with his plan, he had therefore resorted to a different, ingenious route.

To guarantee his grandson's involvement, the old man must have given an instruction to whoever he had appointed to represent his interests, to get hold of the building at any cost. That he had managed to track Dominic down should have come as no surprise. Hadn't Greenberg himself also been the subject of the wily Frenchman's ingenuity, when the idea of the show about his daughter was first mooted?

'I can see it's come as quite a shock,' Dominic commented after the long pause.

'I really don't know what to say, except that if you have other plans for the building – and there's still a substantial amount of the money Jacques left – I mean, putting on the show *was* his idea…'

Greenberg couldn't stop babbling. Wringing his hands, he was unusually flustered and had become flushed in the face.

'There's no need to be so hasty,' Dominic said, taking over the mantle of calm in an ironic reversal of roles. He thought for a moment then added, 'It seems to me we're very much in the same position, what with Grandfather – or should I call him *Grandpère* – apparently providing you with the funds to produce the show and me ending up owning the place. It's rather like he's thrown us together, don't you think?' He chuckled, finding the whole scenario amusing.

Greenberg, sensing that perhaps all might not be lost, forced a wary smile.

Dominic went on.

'I must admit that when all this came to light, my initial reaction was that none of it had anything to do with me. But then I decided that if my French grandfather had wanted me to become involved in the place, he must have had a very good reason. It would be wrong to disregard his wishes, don't you think?'

'What changed your mind?' Greenberg wanted to know.

'How long have you got?' Dominic said, and beamed.

'Something tells me we've been here before,' Greenberg said dryly, having recovered from his earlier floundering.

Dominic laughed.

'I don't suppose you have a coffee here, by any chance? I haven't had a thing since this morning.'

'I think that can be arranged.' Greenberg immediately dialled downstairs and asked the student manning the front desk to go out to the local Pret à Manger coffee shop and buy two coffees and a selection of sandwiches.

There was still so much to talk about. After a while, Greenberg asked, 'Dominic, do you intend being in London for long?'

'If I tell you I have an open ticket back to the States, you probably won't believe me, especially after last time,' Dominic said.

'There's no need to go back—' Greenberg started to say.

Dominic interrupted him.

'I thought a lot about you while I was recovering in hospital.'

'In what way?' Greenberg looked puzzled.

'I know you said that the show was my grandfather's idea in the first place, but I'm curious about what really motivated you to agree to do it when it obviously brought back so many painful memories.'

'I've asked myself the same question a thousand times,' Greenberg responded, scratching his head. 'You see, I didn't realise, even after all these years, how deeply my love still runs for Nadine.'

'You mean you needed closure,' Dominic said perceptively.

'Yes, and Jacques provided me with the financial means to try and obtain it.'

'That's when you came looking for me?'

'I needed your approval.'

'And if I hadn't wanted you to produce it, would you have gone ahead, irrespectively?'

'What, and end up getting sued?' Greenberg quipped.

Both men laughed.

'Anyway, Dominic, you still haven't given me any indication that you will agree,' Greenberg said, rising to the challenge.

Just then, an unshaven young man in a tatty jeans jacket knocked and came into the office with a Pret carrier bag containing the coffees and sandwiches. He handed it to his boss before nodding politely at both men and leaving.

'What you don't know,' Dominic continued, after taking a mouthful or two of the coffee, 'is that while I was in Paris to see my grandfather's lawyers I came across a lady called Sophie Moret. Apparently she knew Nadine, and for many years had remained in close contact with Jacques. It was natural that he should want to see her taken care of in his will. What happened was that the lawyer informed me that Sophie wanted to meet me. He gave me her address.'

Dominic's expression had suddenly become more intense.

Greenberg, meanwhile, was recalling his own encounter with the same woman after Nadine had died and remembering the guilt she had felt for betraying her friend.

'We talked for hours,' Dominic continued. 'She had moved from Switzerland to a small apartment in Montmartre. That lady had been my father Charles's mistress for years. It was an opportunity to get to know her at long last.'

'It must have been somewhat awkward,' Greenberg guessed, biting off a large piece of his egg and tomato roll.

'Not really. She was actually a very nice person. Far too good for my shit of a father.'

'I only met her the once,' Greenberg said. 'It was shortly after Nadine died, and she attended the opening performance of my production, which your mother was to have appeared in.'

'Sophie mentioned that she knew you.'

'I'm surprised she remembered. It was nearly forty years ago.'

'She told me you were the kindest man she had ever met and that you absolutely adored my mother,' Dominic divulged, sipping his coffee. 'Also, she gave me this.' He reached into his jacket and produced a photograph of the twenty-two-year-old Nadine.

Greenberg looked at it and felt a wave of emotion as he recalled the effect the enchanting dancer had had upon him.

'That's absolutely true,' he said huskily, trying to control himself. He was, however, beginning to wonder where all this was leading. Did all the bonhomie have a sting in its tail?

'Which brings me to the main reason why I wanted to see you again.'

At this, Greenberg sat up, fearing the worst.

'Apparently, Nadine wrote a diary, so Sophie informed me.'

'Yes, she did. There were quite a number of them,

actually,' Greenberg confirmed.

'I don't suppose you know whether they are still in existence, do you?' Dominic asked hopefully.

'Yes, I have kept them with me always,' Greenberg said in a low voice.

'Do you think that I might have a look at them? I believe they are extremely detailed.'

Greenberg got up and went over to his old bookcase that leant unsteadily against the back wall of the office and took out a box containing several small black diaries. He handed them reverently to the visitor.

'You'll find that they have been labelled in date order, and they should still be in good condition. The earlier ones in French have been translated into English. They now belong to you, my boy. I was merely their custodian.'

'A bit more than that, from what I've been told,' Dominic said.

'Sorry. You've lost me.'

'Haven't you ever wondered how they ended up in your possession?'

'There was no next of kin, and—' Greenberg began to explain.

'Precisely.'

Greenberg thought for a moment. He had always assumed that he had inherited the diaries by chance. But now it suddenly made sense. Nadine must have realised that he was the only one she could rely on to take care of her affairs after she died. That he would make things right with her son one day.

'Do you mind if I take them away with me?'

'No, of course not,' Greenberg said, recovering his equilibrium. It was time to let go of them, for her son to take them into his care. He then asked, 'Are you staying at the same place as last time?'

'No. I'm staying in my mother's house in Chelsea.'

Greenberg frowned.

'It's fine. I've made my peace with her. She had intended to tell me about my past when she received notification from my grandfather's lawyers,' Dominic said tersely, but did not elaborate any further. In reality, he was aware that Clare's intentions had been very far from honourable.

'I bear her no ill feeling. In any case,' he added, 'she's the only family I have left.'

'I understand,' Greenberg said, feeling great admiration for the younger man. Knowing that Clare Langley had been party to stealing him away from Nadine, he didn't think that he himself would have been so forgiving.

After agreeing to see each other soon the two of them said goodbye.

Greenberg didn't have to wait long. The very next day, Dominic – looking haggard and deprived of sleep – was waiting for him when he arrived at the theatre. The younger man was clutching the diaries protectively against his chest as if they were artefacts of priceless value.

'Greenberg,' he said, adopting the way Nadine always addressed him, 'you'll never guess what I've just discovered.' He had the look on his face of a small boy who had just found an extra present in his Christmas stocking.

'I'm Jewish,' he announced excitedly. 'I'm just like you. Well, except perhaps for one or two extra bits.'

'Well, in that case, come right on in,' Greenberg said, not sure what all the fuss was about.

40

Summer, 2015

Greenberg sat back on his comfortable new chair, equally comfortable with his new trim physique. He gazed around the air-conditioned room, which bore little resemblance to the grubby space that he had leased eighteen months earlier. The worn-out carpet had been replaced with light oak wooden flooring and the dreary pieces of second-hand furniture had all gone. They had been replaced with a range of fitted white lacquer units.

Since Dominic had insisted on a complete refurbishment of the theatre and the offices above, with everything undertaken entirely at his cost, who was he to refuse?

Greenberg should have been feeling happy. Owner of the hottest property in town, his reputation as a top West End producer restored, everything was as it should have been. And yet... He reflected on all that had happened over the last year, and about the events that had helped him reach his decision.

Nadine's diaries had affected Dominic deeply but had cemented an enduring relationship between the two of them. To Greenberg's great relief, Dominic was desperate to be involved with a show about his mother. However, it wasn't all plain sailing.

Dominic considered the script as it stood to be too thin. It needed, in his words, to be 'far more edgy' and to include all the aspects of Nadine's private life that were missing.

It had been Greenberg's decision to be deliberately uncontroversial. There was so much about Nadine he wanted to keep secret, to preserve a perfect image of her. But she was no longer his, to do with as he wished. Her only child had claimed his right to her. Now Dominic would be the one to bring her back to life and to the attention of the public.

There was no question of anyone other than Dominic directing the piece. This was *his* show, and he had become completely possessive about it. The only point of dissension between them was when he decided that the script should be rewritten as a modern opera. As far as Greenberg was concerned, that was a step too far. But Dominic was so taken with the idea of putting on a spectacular about his mother's life that he wouldn't back down and eventually got his way.

To his credit, he threw himself headlong into the project, first ensuring that the script was right, down to the minutest detail, then arranging for the score to be written and rewritten, often overruling his musical director in the process. When the first one threatened to resign, he was immediately replaced with another. Dominic had got through three by the time he was happy with the melodies.

When it came to work Dominic displayed a ruthless streak, which accounted for his formidable reputation.

Often working eighteen-hour days, he expected the same commitment from everyone involved in the production.

For the first time in his career he, Peter Greenberg, had been relegated to the status of a bystander. Yes, in theory, it was still his production, but Dominic wanted total control and had the financial means to ensure he could create the show he wanted. Yet Greenberg didn't feel at all aggrieved. This was how it was meant to be. Of course, Dominic sought his counsel when he needed confirmation of some of the more troubling episodes of his mother's life, which, since he hadn't witnessed them himself, seemed too far-fetched.

Dominic took to visiting the cemetery where his mother was buried. Greenberg went with him the first time, remaining in the background while Dominic, his head bowed, placed a handful of pebbles on her grave according to the ancient Jewish custom. Dominic said that he found it a cathartic experience, the start of a journey in tracing his roots.

Perhaps, like Dominic, there was a part missing in Greenberg's own life that he now would have the time to explore. His father Raymond had always been proud of his Jewish heritage. It felt like the right moment to discover it for himself.

The change in Dominic was as dramatic as the opera he had committed himself to. For him, it had become a process of self-discovery — a process, as he said, that was more revealing than all the years of therapy he had already undergone. By the time the show was ready, he was completely transformed, a man who had been forced to confront his past through most unusual means.

Greenberg himself had not been completely idle. After all, it was his contact with Miles Goulding of TLM International, the PR and marketing agency, that had stoked the public's fervour in connection with Dominic Langley's return to the West End. Of course, the masterstroke was to suggest a new name for the theatre. To their mind, the Duke's, especially with the recent adverse publicity, had a negative connotation. It was unanimously decided, therefore, to rename it the Bertrand Theatre after the man responsible for its revival.

Dominic had a hard time trying to find the right actress to play Nadine. All the main casting agencies were invited to come up with a suitable candidate. Hours of auditions, without producing anything worthwhile, left him feeling frustrated.

Both he and Greenberg were aware it would take someone extraordinary to do justice to the part, but whereas Greenberg had been sufficiently impressed with a couple of the girls, Dominic disagreed, saying he'd rather the show be cancelled than have to settle for second best.

Nothing worked until Dominic had a brainwave and went over to Paris to the Conservatoire, which his mother had attended in 1970. There, given access to the latest batch of students about to qualify, he identified a waiflike nineteen-year-old dancer named Francine Vardie, who 'blew him away'. As he told Greenberg on the phone from Paris:

'The energy that flows out of her is supernatural. I've never witnessed anything like it before. Just wait till you see her in action.' The enthusiasm in his voice waned a little when he added, 'The only problem is that her voice isn't powerful enough, especially as she'll have to cope with being onstage for two and a half hours.'

'I'm sure we can help her with that,' Greenberg answered reasonably. 'The Conservatoire can arrange to increase her private lessons, and we can send someone over as well.' He didn't doubt for one second that Dom had found the right young woman to play the part.

With each week that flew by, the prospect of being unprepared for the opening seemed increasingly likely. What disturbed Greenberg most was the colossal amounts of money that were being expended on the production: building the stage, paying the musicians and actors, the cost of their costumes… The list was endless. Three quarters of a million pounds of the money Jacques had given him had gone before they had even opened. Dominic had insisted on the best of everything. On top of that, Greenberg was still honouring his lease and paying rent.

But he needn't have worried.

Nadine premiered at the Bertrand Theatre on 30 November 2014, a year to the day after it had originally been scheduled. It was an evening Greenberg would never forget.

The French dancer's debut on the London West End stage took place in the opening scene, while in the background stood the handsome man she would fall in love with and whose child she would bear, only for him to later manipulate her for his own selfish ends.

From the first note, the hushed audience was completely mesmerised.

Then, in the last act, the curtains opened to reveal that the stage had been dramatically transformed into a bridge spanning the River Thames. Gasps of horror came from those watching when Nadine, having lost everything, stood balancing precariously *en pointe* on the ledge while a lone violin played the haunting theme tune. She let out a cry, and as the orchestra reached its crescendo, drowning out the violinist in a discordant crash, she fell. The last image in the absolute silence before the lights went down was of a red silk scarf floating up towards the star-filled night sky.

The eleven curtain calls and rapturous applause for the cast still rang in his ears. It had been a magical evening – for all but the scores of disappointed people traipsing the streets on the lookout for spare tickets, which were changing hands at five times their face value.

The press was equally enthusiastic. Only Peter Greenberg could have pulled off such a high-risk venture, was how *The Times* described it. And of Dominic Langley: *A Welcome Return to the West End by One of England's Most Sought-after Directors* headlined in the *Telegraph*. Special praise was handed out to the young lead playing Nadine. 'A star in the making' was how most tabloids described her. A long run was predicted. And a world tour to follow, they said, couldn't be ruled out.

Word got around – from where Greenberg had no idea – that the show was based on real life. That week alone, he had phone calls from MGM and Sony Pictures enquiring about the film rights. *Nadine* the musical had grown into a legend, and everyone wanted a part of her.

Greenberg had been so desperate to prove the West End wrong, to demonstrate that he still had what it took to make a success, yet with full houses every night, future sales guaranteed for the next two years and money flowing in at a faster rate than he could keep up with, strangely it never meant a great deal.

He had become accustomed to the modest lifestyle that had been forced upon him: the one-bedroom flat in Camden, which he had managed to buy at a good price, using public transport because he no longer had the desire to drive an expensive car, and Drummond the black Scottie dog providing him with exercise and the entrance qualification to join the exclusive set of dog walkers in Regent's Park's Inner Circle. He had everything he needed.

Most importantly, he had got back his self-respect. Above all, he had fulfilled his obligation, albeit forty years later, to Nadine. Finally reunited with her child, she had achieved in death what had eluded her during her lifetime. He hoped she would have approved. For Peter Greenberg, the spark remained. He knew now that nothing would ever extinguish it.

Greenberg gave a cursory look through the documents pertaining to the surrender of his lease and added his signature. Dominic had tried to talk him out of it. Now he had moved to London, the younger man wanted them to work together on some new projects that he had in mind. It was flattering to be asked. But, at the age of sixty-five, the truth was that Greenberg had outlived his usefulness. It was agreed they would part company once the show transferred to Broadway.

'I'm off,' he called out to his PA in the next-door office. 'The papers are ready. Make sure they go out before you leave tonight.'

'What, are you going home already? *Another* half-day?' Marcia Davis grumbled deliberately loudly to herself.

Grinning to himself, Greenberg put on his jacket and walked slowly out of the office. It was good to have his familiar PA back. Marcia had worked by his side all through the good years, until a marital crisis, now resolved, had caused her to leave.

In the meantime, young Issy Williams, thinking that her skills were better suited elsewhere, had been accepted on a police graduate scheme. Naturally he agreed to her request for a favourable reference, neither of them mentioning the landlord's payment that hadn't been sent. As far as Greenberg was concerned, it was best forgotten. He had other issues on his mind, like how he was going to spend his retirement.

Maybe he would take Suzanne up on her offer. She had phoned him several times, asking him to come and join her in Spain. She was working as a waitress at a karaoke bar in Torremolinos and seemed to be getting by, but with Mikey serving a reduced sentence after pleading guilty to corruption, she said she didn't relish the thought of spending the next seven years on her own.

Taking the bus home, he thought how ironic it would be if they got back together – two lonely people needing companionship, Suddenly, the prospect of a month in the sun sounded quite appealing.

A Saturday Evening in a Snowstorm...

New York, 2016

The huge crowd, oblivious of the weather, gathered outside the Lyceum Theatre on West 45th Street, waiting patiently for the cast to appear.

Then a roar went up, accompanied by the flash of press photographers' cameras as Francine Vardie, the young woman who for the last year had made the part of Nadine her own, hurried out of the stage door and into a waiting limousine. She was soon followed by the dapper English actor, Robin Courtfield, who played Charles Langley, together with the rest of the cast and finally a relieved Brad de Winter, the show's assistant director. Forced to step in at the last moment, an eventuality he'd prepared for but never expected, he needn't have worried. Dominic had been stranded at JFK Airport with Alejandro, who had been staying with him in London, so the pair had missed the start. However, unbeknownst to Brad, Dominic was watching from the wings.

At the end of the performance, the renowned director leapt on to the stage and was the first to lead the applause for his protégé, who had acquitted himself faultlessly.

Greenberg left his seat in the front row, from where he'd

watched the performance. However many times he saw the show, he always shed tears in the final moments.

Once outside in the street, he put up his coat collar, shivering as he quickened his pace. Tonight he was feeling his age. He'd declined the invitation to the opening party, choosing instead to walk back to the Library, the same hotel where he had stayed two and a half years ago. Now he was no longer involved, the only reason he had attended at all was because Dominic had insisted he attend the first night. He said that he couldn't bear the thought of his 'mentor', as he referred to Greenberg, extricating himself entirely from the show that he, more than anyone else, had made happen. That was the reason why, at Dominic's insistence, they met for lunch at least once a week, when the younger man would seek his advice on the most personal aspects of his life.

Greenberg recalled the occasion when he offered Dominic the diamond ring that had accompanied the proposal of marriage to his mother. Dominic declined, saying that having just discovered 'the father he wished he had had', it was only right that it should stay with him.

It was at these times that Greenberg looked back on his life and regretted that he had never had a family of his own.

Just as he passed into Madison Avenue, a small car drew up beside him and the driver wound down the window and peered out. Through the thickly falling snow, Greenberg vaguely noted that the woman had bare arms and was in a black evening dress – and that despite the freezing temperature her face glowed.

'Can I offer you a ride?' Arlene Davidson called out.

*

'What are the chances of bumping into you? It's an amazing coincidence,' Greenberg said, climbing into the car and settling into the warmth of the seat next to her.

'You tell me,' Arlene replied, giving the person she'd been tracking a flirtatious look. He had lost weight, she noticed, and was looking good.

'Really, I had no idea,' Greenberg said truthfully. He spotted a theatre programme from *Nadine* poking out from her handbag on the ledge between their seats. She must have come to see it, and noticed that he was involved in the production. Had she come looking for him? His heart leapt.

'I don't suppose there's any chance you'd be interested in joining me for a late snack?' he asked impulsively.

'Let me guess. You haven't had a thing to eat all day and hunger's suddenly got the better of you?' Arlene teased.

Greenberg smiled at her.

'Something like that.'

'I know just the place,' Arlene promised. Driving carefully in the snowstorm, she was lucky to find a parking space outside a lively restaurant in Little Italy.

'It's a bit like retracing our steps, isn't it?' Greenberg said, remembering it was the same establishment they'd frequented two and half years ago, and that it served the best veal *paillard* he'd ever tasted.

'Another coincidence,' Arlene quipped as they entered together, hurrying through the snow, and were shown to a discreet table.

'How did you know they'd have a free table?' Greenberg wondered.

'Let's just say … I have a standard reservation for late-night clients from out of town.'

'I'm not sure I like the sound of that,' Greenberg said, playing along.

'Take it as a compliment.' Arlene gave him one of the looks he remembered so vividly.

'Well, in that case, I'm flattered that it's my turn,' he responded.

'You know that's not what I meant.'

Greenberg smiled behind the menu he was pretending to read. Although he was enjoying the repartee immensely, the evening so far felt more like a sparring contest than a potential rekindling of a romantic relationship.

Three hours passed effortlessly as they ordered and ate their way through a series of Italian dishes, accompanied by two fine bottles of wine.

Then came the question they were both waiting for.

'So, how long do you intend on being in New York?' Arlene enquired finally, taking a sip of her *grappa*.

'I'm supposed to be on the midday BA flight tomorrow,' Greenberg hedged.

'So, I've a few hours left to try to change your mind?' And before Greenberg had a chance to reply, Arlene got up from the table and without any explanation, snatched her coat from the maître d' and resolutely left the restaurant.

Greenberg was dumbfounded. If he'd said something to offend her, he was at loss to know what it might have been. She'd shown the same erratic reaction that time in her apartment after they had just made love. Perhaps he just didn't understand what went on in women's heads. Should he pay the bill and leave? No, he'd order a pot of coffee to give himself more time, just in case she did come back.

Then, just as abruptly, Arlene reappeared, shivering,

with a morning copy of the *New York Times* tucked under her arm, marked damply by the falling snow.

'Thought this might help you decide,' she said, directing Greenberg's attention to a photo of the rapturous crowd scenes captured outside the theatre hours earlier and the headline that read:

Peter Greenberg's Nadine *Triumphs on Broadway*

'It was Dominic's show. I really had nothing to do with it,' Greenberg stressed. He was just relieved to see her again.

'Obviously, someone must have thought otherwise,' Arlene said, doing her best to keep a straight face as she passed her coat to the waiter and retook her seat at the table.

'And I suppose you wouldn't know who that someone was, by any chance?' Greenberg queried suspiciously.

'From what I heard, you never fully received the recognition you deserved. This seemed the perfect opportunity to put it right, wouldn't you agree?'

'I'm not sure what you mean. The reviews in London were extremely favourable,' Greenberg countered.

'And Dominic being Dominic, he probably took more than his share of the accolades,' Arlene said perceptively.

'That's not fair. It was his show. Anyway, I didn't think you were that interested in what was occurring on the other side of the pond,' Greenberg probed, wondering where all this was all leading.

'Let's just say it was mainly Dom's idea to get your name mentioned,' Arlene said, choosing her words carefully

'And you had absolutely no part in it?'

Arlene's silence was sufficient confirmation as far as Greenberg was concerned. Hand in glove with Dominic, this extraordinary woman, who he'd been foolish enough to let slip through his fingers, had cared enough to make sure he was present at the first night on Broadway, so she could meet up with him again – and try to persuade him to stay.

'You still haven't given me *your* answer,' she said quietly.

Greenberg reached across and took Arlene's hand.

'Since I appear to be the toast of the town, I'd better stick around to enjoy it, don't you think?' he responded, his voice full of his usual warmth.

As they sat in the back of their cab, having left the little car behind, Greenberg breathed in Arlene's perfume, a scent that reminded him of their first try at love. His heart swelled with hope.

Maybe it wasn't too late, after all.

Acknowledgements

I would like to thank my family for their unwavering support and for being prepared to share in my journey.

My thanks also go to everyone at 2QT for agreeing to publish this book and especially to my editor Joan Deitch for her continued guidance and help in making *Nadine* a reality.

Lightning Source UK Ltd.
Milton Keynes UK
UKHW022022180319
339367UK00003B/13/P